DIRTY GAME

Also by Shannon Holmes

B-more Careful

Bad Girlz

Never Go Home Again

DIRTY GAME

Shannon Holmes

St. Martin's Griffin
New York

This is a work of fiction. All of the characters, organizations, and events portrayed in this novel are either products of the author's imagination are used fictitiously.

www.stmartins.com

Library of Congress Cataloging-in-Publication Data are available upon request.

ISBN-13: 978-0-312-35901-0
ISBN-10: 0-312-35901-2

First Edition: May 2007

10 9 8 7 6 5 4 3 2 1

In memory of

My grandfather Aaron Holmes. Rest in peace. Without you there is no me.

Cousin Terry Moore. If there is such a thing as dying with dignity, then you did it. You lived your life and died on your own terms. I'm glad our paths crossed again and I really got a chance to know you. Love always, Ya Li'l Cuz.

Makeba Lowry. Even though I never got a chance to meet you, if I could tell you anything it would be: your mother loved you dearly.

Linda Hightower, Aunt Ruth Stevens, Joey Padro, and Zaida Fonseca.

Rest in peace to all the other family members we've lost over the past year or so.

And dedicated to

The beautiful babies my family and I have been blessed with: Malaikia "Lakey" Holmes (Sorry It Took Daddy So Long), Amiyah Martin, Brianna Smalls, Elijah Sylvester Montrel, and Avery Adams.

Flatter and I may not believe you.
Criticize me and I may not like you.
Ignore me and I may not forgive you.
Encourage me and I promise you, I will not forget you!

DIRTY GAME

CHAPTER 1

As the ten-car, graffiti-covered, northbound Number Two train, commonly referred to as the iron horse, sped down the elevated train tracks toward the 176th Street subway station, it brought with it an unmistakable sound. A deafening, ear splitting, thunderous noise, it echoed off the various closed storefronts, car lots, parking garages, and buildings that lined Jerome Avenue. The train came to a sudden halt, making its designated stop at the station and depositing its minority residents back to their desolate urban neighborhood, back to their dismal reality.

This section of New York City was known as the South Bronx. First it was hit hard by a rash of tenement building fires started by greedy, unscrupulous landlords seeking a big insurance settlement from properties they deemed worthless, rundown, or beyond repair. They figured that torching their buildings was more profitable than spending the money to rehabilitate them for low-income residents to reside in. They'd rather rid themselves of these undesirable properties and turn a profit in the process. Their decisions were strictly from a business standpoint, motivated by pure greed, nothing more and nothing less.

What they never took into account was the effect that this crime would have on the buildings' residents or the Borough of the Bronx. Soon a rash of copycat criminals began repeating this crime, over and over again. Irreplaceable personal items went up in smoke along with these tenement buildings. Countless lives were ruined or altered. Many families were forced to relocate from their place of birth to even worse living conditions like the city shelters or the tough city housing projects.

Like a bad case of the chicken pox, this insurance fraud scam quickly spread across the South Bronx, making it resemble a ghost town in some war-torn foreign country. Where buildings once stood and life once flourished, there were now vacant lots with mounds of rubble. The concrete structures were replaced by shattered dreams and lost souls.

The abandoned and charred skeletal remains of these buildings were evident as far as the eye could see. Later, the crack-cocaine epidemic came along and finished off the job that the arsonists had started. It killed off any remaining hopes, dreams, or chances that the neighborhood had of recovery or revival, further crippling the Bronx for decades to come. This section of New York City was amongst the poorest in the nation. The boogie-down Bronx, the home of hip-hop, became known as the burnt-down Bronx.

On a chilly fall evening in the South Bronx, a trap was being set that would bring about some deadly consequences. Parked in a car underneath the train station was Kenny Greene, also known as Ken-Ken. He was a tall, dark-skinned, well-built ladies' man whose specialty was strong-arm robbery. He was also one half of a duo, husband-and-wife con team.

Ken-Ken's wife, Maria, was a gorgeous Puerto Rican woman with long straight red hair that flowed down to the small of her back. She had a light trace of hair just above her juicy lips and a beautiful black mole that sat atop them. It was the kind that women always artificially added with a black eyeliner pencil, in an effort to enhance their facial features. Maria was also naturally blessed with a body that could stop traffic. She had a pair of firm breasts that stood at attention, a butt big and wide enough to sit a drink on, a flawless caramel complexion, and long sexy legs.

Dressed in a red-hot miniskirt with a matching leather jacket and six-inch stiletto pumps, she looked every bit like the hooker she was desperately trying to portray. Unbeknownst to everybody except family and friends, Maria was seven months pregnant with the couple's first child.

But looking at her, one wouldn't be able to tell. Her pregnancy agreed with her. And besides that, the men, paying customers, tricks or Johns, were too busy lusting off her bodacious body to closely examine her stomach. Even if they had noticed, it probably wouldn't have mattered.

The mission that the couple was currently on had been Maria's idea. With a baby on the way she wanted to stack all the money she could, while she still could. Pretty soon she'd be way too big, too far along in her pregnancy, to even think about doing things like this. She came from a family where breaking the law was a way of life. It was accepted and maybe even expected of her. Both of her brothers and father were currently serving time in various prisons in upstate New York for their parts in various crimes. For the Torres family, lawlessness was in their blood.

Maria was taught the art of pickpocketing, or jostling, as it is known in New York City, by her brothers. She in turn passed her knowledge along, teaching her then boyfriend, Ken-Ken, how to pickpocket successfully.

Now Ken-Ken and Maria were the picture-perfect couple.

Growing up as kids, they lived in the same building and couldn't stand each other. Maria and Ken-Ken constantly argued, staying at each other's throat. As they grew older the arguments became more heated, and several times they almost came to blows. Maria's brothers even contemplated doing severe bodily harm to Ken-Ken. They issued threats to him on several occasions, warning him what they would do to him if he laid a hand on their sister.

A long time ago older people in the building predicted that one day they would be a couple since they always fought like one. Sure enough, as they headed into puberty their hormones took over. Suddenly they stopped fighting and became strongly attracted to each another. After a few years of fooling around, dating, the breakups, and the make-ups it was decided by Maria's mother that they should get married. The couple agreed and they got hitched downtown in a small ceremony at City Hall.

It was a small, simple ceremony with only a select few friends and family members in attendance. Though the couple married young, they still managed to maintain martial bliss. Never second-guessing their decision, Ken-Ken and Maria never thought about what they gave up, only what they had gained—everlasting love.

Ken-Ken was old-fashioned in certain ways. He thought that the man should always provide for the woman. He took pride in being the family provider and hated the idea of having his woman in on a criminal caper, in harm's way. He knew that on the street nothing was certain and anything was possible. But he had no choice. Maria insisted that she be included. They were a family that did everything together, literally. They were a team criminally, codefendants to the end.

Besides that, Maria was critical to the success of the trap. She was the bait. While Ken-Ken waited in a car nearby Maria lured the tricks to a secluded side block under the pretense of prostituting.

Then Ken-Ken would arrive just before she was to perform some lewd sexual act, preferably while they were discussing a price, and knock out the trick. If things went according to plan, the two would then relieve him of all his valuables, cash, and credit cards and flee the scene.

As the minority commuters began to trickle down the train station steps, singly, in pairs, or in groups, they quickly dispersed and went their separate ways, heading home. Amongst the last few remaining groups was a livid, young, black couple. From all the noise they were making and their body language, they appeared to be engaging in a heated argument. This scene captured Ken-Ken's full attention.

"Muthfucka, you ain't hardly slick!" the young woman yelled. "I seen ya black azz starin' at dat bitch on da train. Ya black azz thought I didn't see dat? Well, think again, nigga!"

The young man replied innocently, "Whut girl? You buggin'! I don't know whut da fuck you talkin' 'bout! I wuzn't payin dat bitch no mind. If anything she wuz lookin' at me! She wuz sweatin' me. I can't help dat."

"Nigga, don't play dumb! Ya azz ain't az stupid az you look! But since you got amnesia, you can forget 'bout hittin' dis tanite! Go get some pussy from da bitch, you lil-dick muthafucka! You can't fuck anyway!" The young woman picked up the pace of her walk in an effort to distance herself from him.

Unable to control his anger any longer, the young man resorted to violence, figuring it was the only recourse that he had. Since she had publicly insulted him, attacking his manhood, without warning he struck. Running up on the young lady from behind, he kicked her straight in the butt.

"Fuck you, hoe!" he shouted at the top his lungs. "Ya pussy iz trash anyway! You bum bitch!"

The woman stumbled, almost tripping over her own feet, from the unexpected force of the blow. After a few missteps she regained her balance. Instinctively she bent down in the gutter, picked up a half-empty glass soda bottle, and with all her might she launched it at his head.

Luckily he ducked just in time, displaying a catlike reflex to avoid the projectile. The bottle went whistling by his head before shattering harmlessly on the ground. It broke into thousands of pieces, littering the sidewalk with tiny shards of glass.

The young man suddenly began thinking to himself just how funny this situation was. He burst out in uncontrollable laughter. Running off into the opposite direction, he continued to laugh nonstop while taunting the girl.

He didn't care about the girl, anyway. She wasn't his girlfriend. She was just somebody he was trying to lay up with for the night. He only came around her when he wanted some sex.

"You bitch azz nigga! I'ma get my brotha ta fuck ya punk azz up! Watch!" she cried out at the fleeing figure. "You gone get yourz! We see whut'z so funny when my brotha beats ya azz down! Nigga, laugh now and cry later! You gonna get yourz!"

"Whuteva, bitch! Fuck you and ya soft azz brotha!" he yelled back over his shoulder, not the least bit worried about her threat. As far as he was concerned, he had too much backup around the way to let anything happen to him. If her brother or her people came to his block looking for him, there would be problems for them.

From the comfort of his car, Ken-Ken watched the entire incident from start to finish. He was very much amused by the ghetto dispute.

As minor as the distraction was, it temporarily caused Ken-Ken to take his hawklike eyes off Maria, diverting his attention from the task at hand. This momentary lapse of judgment would prove to be critical. He would live to regret this moment. It was an instant frozen in time, one of those life-altering events that in retrospect, if he could have done it all over again, he would have been more observant. He would have concentrated harder, thus eliminating any distractions.

A few feet up the block, Maria had flagged down a potential vic. He was a thin white man dressed in a blue pinstriped three-piece suit, driving a burgundy 300E Mercedes Benz with New Jersey license plates. This particular strip of Jerome Avenue was frequented by white men from across the Hudson River, who came over to the Bronx in search of black and Hispanic female crack whores.

"Hey, good looking! What ya got cookin?" the trick calmly asked, repeating some corny line from some seventies TV show.

Maria replied, "Name ya pleasure. I got cable out here. HBO, head, booty, and other things. I'll take you around da world and back again."

To Maria, this white trick looked and smelled like new money. He was probably some big businessman from corporate America. She just knew he'd be loaded with cash and credit cards. Maria would bet her life his wallet was filled with Visas and MasterCards with an unlimited lines of credit. After this heist they were gonna be straight for a while, she figured. Maria was going to do a lot of shopping for the baby at the expense of this trick.

But what Maria didn't know was that this man was a demented regular customer out for revenge. He had caught gonorrhea from some Hispanic crack whore a few weeks ago. This set off a chain of devastating events in his life. After contracting the disease, he in turn took it home and gave it to his wife of twenty-some years. When she got diagnosed with a sexually transmitted disease during a routine check-up, she then promptly filed for divorce.

Currently she was in the process of taking all his assets in court including the house, the three European luxury sedans, and his six-figure bank account. Everything she could get her hands on. And it was all because he had to satisfy his insatiable craving for minority crack hookers. In his sick mind the hookers were to blame, not him.

This homicidal maniac swore he'd find and kill the whore who burned him and ruined his life. It didn't matter to him that he might spill innocent blood in the process. So be it. It didn't matter that Maria wasn't the one who burned him, she'd do. In his mind somebody was gonna pay. Motivated by revenge, the man couldn't think clearly. It led him to strike out at the first Puerto Rican hooker he saw that night. And as fate would have it, that person was Maria.

Nervously the trick glanced around for any signs of the cops. He didn't want anything to interfere with his murderous intentions. He had an appetite for destruction that he had to satisfy, right now.

"Get in the car, sweetie, I'm trying to go around the world." He grinned slyly. "You think you can take me there? Huh?"

"Hell fuckin yeah!" Maria snapped. "I sure can! Quick, fast, and in a hurry!" From past experience, Maria knew she had to engage her tricks in this type of flirtatious conversation in order not to alert them to her larcenous intentions. She had to exercise a little patience in order to make the mark feel at ease, just long enough to rob him.

"You gotta pay to play, Daddy! No romance witout finance, as they say. Know whatimean, good lookin?" Maria seductively said while licking her lips. "Now first things first, let's see dat cash, honey. Money makes da world go 'round, Daddy. And money makes me freaky, ifyaknowwhutImean? Show me sumthin. Get my pussy wet!"

The trick quickly complied, removing a large wad of money from his jacket pocket. He hoped that the sight of the money would entice her enough to get into his car. He would then take her to some seedy motel to rape and sodomize her before killing her.

By now Maria was bent over slightly inside the passenger's window. From this vantage point, she could see clearly that he was holding nothing but hundreds, fiftys, and twenty-dollar bills in his hand. She flashed a bright smile at the trick as she began scratching her head. This was a signal to Ken-Ken that everything was good to go, that they had hit a lick. They had finally found a mark. Unfortunately for Maria, Ken-Ken never saw her signal. His attention was fixed firmly on the young couple carrying on in the middle of the street.

Suddenly a strange premonition came over Maria. She saw her life flash right before her eyes. For a moment she locked eyes with her would-be killer. Staring into his cold blue eyes she saw no signs of life, just pure evil. They betrayed the sly smile that spread across his lips. In an instant Maria quickly examined the contents of the car. The dim streetlight caught the glimmer of chrome from a gun, covered by a newspaper, lying in the passenger seat. Even that didn't frighten or deter her. Maria decided to try her hand anyway, believing that the trick didn't have the heart to shoot her. Acting instinctively, she quickly reached into the car and snatched the money out of his hand. Turning her back, she ran as fast as her high-heeled shoes could carry her. She ran directly toward Ken-Ken, her protector.

At that very moment Ken-Ken happened to glance up and see

his wife running full speed in his direction. His gut feeling told him something was very wrong, as if the sight of her sprinting in high heels weren't enough. Though Maria may have thought she was running very fast, she couldn't outrun a bullet.

Calmly the trick raised his 357 Magnum and took aim, lining her up in the gun's sight. Then, with the precision of an assassin, he squeezed the trigger. The large chrome cannon roared twice and the muzzle flashed, simultaneously discharging two rounds.

The gun was loaded with the dumdum bullets. This was ammunition legally made to do the most damage to its victim. The bullets found their intended target. Two slugs slammed into Maria's back, momentarily lifting her up off her feet before sending her crashing to the concrete.

For a brief moment Ken-Ken froze up, paralyzed by the deafening gun shots. In horror he watched the deadly scene play itself out, knowing that he was powerless to stop it. The sound of tires screeching snapped him back into reality. He had a crucial decision to make. He could either chase the gunman or try to save his wife. Ken-Ken opted for the latter. With regret he looked on in disgust as the killer made his escape. He could only pray that their paths would cross again.

Exiting his car, Ken-Ken ran at top speed to the spot where Maria lay sprawled out, gravely injured and nearly motionless on the ground. Once he reached her he could hear the weak moans she emitted. He saw no evidence of entry wounds on her body until he rolled her over, placing her head in his lap. Then he finally saw the damage that the weapon had done. The gaping exit wounds in her chest that the bullets caused frightened Ken-Ken. He was shocked at how badly she was hurt.

"Maria! Maria!" he cried, while staring into her tear-filled eyes. "Hold on, baby, it's gonna be aiight."

"Kenny... Kenny," she whimpered in her thick Spanish accent, still clutching the blood-soaked money. "It burns! Kenny, it burns!"

"*Mami*, hang in there, ya gonna be aiight. I'ma get ya ta da hospital and they'll fix you right up as good as new," Ken-Ken said.

Even Ken-Ken didn't believe those words of comfort. He had said them only to keep hopes of survival high. Over and over again he desperately tried to reassure Maria that she would make it. As he did so, her heart was pumping out an incredible stream of blood at a fast rate, flowing out of her body and running into the gutter.

"Help! Help! Help!" Ken-Ken screamed frantically, trying to attract someone's attention on the deserted block. "Somebody help me! Somebody plueezzze! My wife has been shot. Help!"

Fortunately, God heard his cries for help. An alert transit cop, who just happened to be patrolling the nearby subway station, heard all the commotion and radioed for the police and an ambulance.

"Ken-Ken, I'm gettin' sleepy . . . ," Maria said, fighting to keep her eyes open. "I can't keep em open . . . they keep closin'."

"Don't go ta sleep, Maria! Fight it! Fight it!" Ken-Ken commanded, as if she could control it.

Try as she might, there was nothing Maria could do to stay conscious. The two bullets had started her on an irreversible trip into the hereafter.

Seeing that Maria could barely keep her eyes open, Ken-Ken resorted to desperate measures. Gently he began smacking her across the face in an effort to revive her. The act had little success. Maria kept drifting further and further from the land of the living.

Ken-Ken resisted the overwhelming urge to break down and cry, but he had to be strong for the both of them. *This is all my fault*, he told himself over and over again. If only he had been on his job. If? The question echoed in his brain.

Suddenly, way off in the distance, he heard the loud wail from the sirens of the ambulance and the police cars. Ken-Ken began to get optimistic. By the grace of God, maybe, just maybe, they might be able to save Maria's life. Ken-Ken clung to that flimsy hope, because hope is all he had.

The police and ambulance arrived almost at the same time, and the emergency medical technicians rushed into action. They placed Maria's limp body on the stretcher and wheeled it toward the back of the ambulance. They immediately noticed that she was pregnant. Even though she had a weak pulse, they knew she wouldn't make it. Their main concern was to try and save the unborn child. The mother's life was virtually over.

"Who shot her?" the policemen inconsiderately asked Ken-Ken.

"Did you get a good look at the shooter?" "What in the world was she doing down here?" "Do you know what she got shot with?" "Does your wife have a history of prostitution?" The officers continued to barrage him with questions.

Ken-Ken shook his head no over and over again. He was going into a state of shock and didn't even have the presence of mind to respond verbally.

The ambulance took off like a rocket with Ken-Ken and Maria inside. Having radioed ahead, a trauma team was on standby once they reached their destination. Feverishly the EMT worker, placed an oxygen mask over Maria's nose and mouth and ran an IV into her arm. But secretly he knew, even before he started this procedure, that she was a goner. He had seen so many trauma patients over the years that he could just about predict who was going to live and who was going to die. She'd lost too much blood. He was just going through the motions, fighting a battle that only God could win.

"Maria, don't die on me!" Ken-Ken begged her while holding her limp hand.

Unbeknownst to Ken-Ken, Maria was already gone and nothing could bring her back. The Grim Reaper had silently separated her soul from her body. "I luv you, Maria! You hear me? I luv you."

The ambulance raced through the streets of New York, summoning all the horsepower the engine could muster, and in a few minutes it reached the hospital. The emergency room doors flew open, where about a half dozen doctors and nurses were waiting to assess the damage to the patient. They began speaking medical lingo that Ken-Ken couldn't quite understand. But he obediently followed as they rushed her down the long hospital corridors and into the operating room.

"Sir, you can't go in there. That's a restricted area," an obese white nurse said. "Medical personal only! No civilians beyond that point. Sorry, sir."

"But dat's my wife!" Ken-Ken said, not fully comprehending what was said. His only thought was to be by his wife's side. He wanted to be there for Maria in her darkest hour, when she needed him the most.

"I understand that, sir," the nurse said, "but the operating room is off limits to everybody except medical personnel. In there you would just be doing her more harm than good. Don't worry, she's in good hands."

Her vote of confidence did nothing for Ken-Ken's nerves. He managed to stop himself from entering the operating room against his better judgment and came to the conclusion there was nothing left for him to do but pray. This horrific experience suddenly renewed his belief in God. He walked slowly to the waiting area and kneeled down and prayed, desperately trying to recall all those special Christian prayers he had learned as a child.

Meanwhile, inside the operating room, the trauma team and doctors performed emergency surgery on Maria. During the complicated surgery she suddenly flatlined. All the monitors and machines of life support began to make a strange beeping noise, which signaled loss of life to the surgeons. Several attempts were made to resuscitate her. But nothing worked. Quickly they realized she was dead and there was no bringing her back. So the decision was made to save the life of the unborn fetus.

The doctors delivered a premature baby girl by Cesarean section. Under these strenuous conditions the baby appeared to be healthy, but any long-term birth defects had yet to be determined. After the successful delivery, a doctor went to give the grieving husband a mixed blessing, the good and bad news.

Still on his knees, Ken-Ken never heard the physician approach.

"Excuse me, sir. Forgive me if I'm wrong, but weren't you accompanying the Hispanic young lady that we bought in here about three hours ago?" the doctor gently asked.

"Yeah!" Ken-Ken said as he lifted his head up out of the chair. "How is she, Doc? Is she gonna be aiight?"

This was the part of the job that the doctor absolutely detested, the part medical school could never prepare him for. How was he supposed to explain to grief-stricken family members that their loved one had perished? How was he supposed to explain that they couldn't save their life?

Emotions tend to run high under these adverse circumstances.

They overcame all rational thinking. Families wanted answers now. How and why did their love one die? And sometimes no matter how much diplomacy he used, it just wasn't enough to satisfy their inquiry. They thought that everybody who came through those emergency doors was supposed to make it. But he knew better. Modern medicine couldn't save everyone. He knew that only God knows why some shall live but others shall die. This was an enigma that stumped even the most skilled physicians. Situations like this only reaffirmed his faith in God. The doctor decided to give Ken-Ken the good news first, in an attempt to soften the blow. He took pity on him.

"Well, sir..." His voice began to trail off. "You are now the proud father of a beautiful baby girl."

His statement wasn't enough to make Ken-Ken forget about the love of his life. There was nothing that the doctor could say could that would make him forget about his Maria.

"But... but whut about my wife?" Ken-Ken asked, dreading the answer. "How iz she?"

The doctor swallowed hard as he struggled to find the words that would help him explain the tragedy.

"Unfortunately, we couldn't save her. She lost a lot of blood. The bullets severed some major arteries, causing extensive internal bleeding," the doctor solemnly explained, giving Ken-Ken the best definition he could of the extent of her injuries in layman's terms.

Immediately, heartbreak and anguish registered on Ken-Ken's face. Tears filled his eyes. He broke down and cried. There was nothing else he could do in his time of despair.

"No! No! Maria's not dead!" Ken-Ken wept. "She can't be. She can't be." He never realized he could lose so much and gain so much in a blink of an eye. But the game was funny like that. One day it will be your best friend and the next day it will turn on you like a jilted lover, stabbing you in the back.

Showing compassion to his fellow man, the doctor came over and tried to comfort him by rubbing his shoulders.

"It will be alright, sir. Everything is going to be alright. Things happen for a reason," the doctor softly repeated. "It's in God's hands. He knows best."

"Where's my daughter?" Ken-Ken asked suddenly. "I want ta see my daughter."

"Come on. Get up and follow me," the doctor said. "I'll take you to her."

He then reached down and extended his hand to Ken-Ken, helping him up off the floor. Quickly he placed an arm around his shoulder, and together they walked toward the ICU ward.

This genuine show of raw emotion was humanity and compassion in its truest form. Tragic events like death had a way of breaking down all racial barriers, bringing out the best in most people. And the physician was no exception. He embraced his fellow human being, and for a brief moment Ken-Ken's pain was his pain, too.

At the ICU ward Ken-Ken pressed in face against the clean thick glass, struggling to get a glimpse of his past and his future. A wave of relief washed over him. Finally, he laid eyes on his daughter. She looked frail in comparison to the other infants in the ward. Still, she was the precious fruit of his blessed but short union with his lovely wife, Maria. From the other side of the glass, Ken-Ken stood watch over his sleeping daughter, praying and thinking. From that moment on, he promised himself, he'd dedicate the rest of his life to his daughter. Like in a game of chess, she was the queen and he was the pawn. He would make any sacrifice to protect his queen, even if that meant losing his own life. So be it. He made a vow to himself to move heaven and earth before he would let any harm come her way.

God help anyone or anything that got in the way of Ken-Ken raising his child.

CHAPTER 2

It was a blistery cold day in December, one of the coldest days ever on record. The falling temperatures made headlines throughout the tristate area. The news and weather authorities had issued severe warnings. On days like this people only came outside because they had to. Most preferred to retreat from Mother Nature to the warm comforts of their own home. But for Ken-Ken it was the day he took his daughter, Destiny, home from the hospital. The first few months of her young life had been spent there and now she was healthy enough to go home.

"Ummm, excuse me, nurse," Ken-Ken began. "I'm here to pick up my daughter. The doctors have released her from da hospital today. Could you please tell me where do I pick her up at?"

Ken-Ken stood before a long counter at the nurse's command post in the pediatric section of the hospital. He looked down at the small, frail white nurse, whose skin appeared pale and leathery. She had not aged gracefully.

The elderly white registered nurse who ran the post never even bothered to make eye contact with Ken-Ken and instead kept her eyes glued to the huge mound of paperwork on her desk. She felt she was overworked and underpaid. And all she wanted to do was receive her paycheck, benefits, pension, and go home. To her he was just another problem, waiting to be solved. She sought to get rid of him as soon as possible.

"What's the child's name, sir?" she asked robotically.

"Excuse me?" Ken replied, caught off guard.

"The patient's name, please," she repeated, clearly aggravated. "What is your daughter's name sir? You do know that, correct?"

"Oh! Oh, my fault," he said. "Her name is Destiny Greene."

Just saying his daughter's name sounded strange to Ken-Ken. For weeks after her birth, Destiny had gone nameless. The medical staff had resorted to calling her Baby X. During the first weeks of Destiny's life Ken-Ken had been under so much grief and stress that naming his child hadn't seemed very important, only her survival. Then one day, while holding her in his arms, Ken-Ken decided that because she had been born under such extraordinary circumstances, he wanted her name to have meaning. He didn't just want it to sound cute or exotic. After thinking long and hard, he came up with Destiny. He felt it was destiny that she lived through all the drama.

"Thank you," she said. "Gimme a minute while I look her up in the computer."

Through her thick horn-rimmed bifocal glasses she quickly scanned the computer screen. She ran her eyes up and down the long list of patients until she found the name of the patient in question.

"Destiny Greene. She's right here. According to these charts she's being discharged today."

Ken-Ken stared at the nurse in disbelief. The blank expression on his face said it all, *Tell me something I don't know, dummy.*

"I just told you dat, ma'am," he snapped. "Could you please tell me where to pick her up at? I'm kinda inna rush. Dis is unbelievable."

"Listen, mister, you don't have to get smart with me. I'm just doing my job," she told him. "I swear everyone's inna hurry these days. Haven't y'all ever heard the old saying, 'Good things come to those who wait'? Or 'Patience is a virtue'? My God! You people kill me!"

Now Ken-Ken was pissed off. He didn't like the idea of some elderly white woman scolding him. In the streets she wouldn't even dare look his way, but in this hospital setting she was suddenly tough. If there was one thing he hated, it was seeing someone in authority abusing their power. He thought that was such a cowardly act. A real self-respecting person would never stoop so low.

"If you can hold ya horses long enough, I'll have one of the nurses bring your daughter right here to you," she said. "You know Rome wuzn't built in a day."

"Thanks," Ken-Ken replied flatly, not meaning a word of it.

Instead of taking a seat and waiting patiently, Ken-Ken began pacing the floor like madman. In response, the nurse shot a few evil stares his way. But Ken-Ken paid her no mind. To him this whole day was almost unreal. It was as if he were dreaming. Ken-Ken wanted to hurry up and take his daughter home before something or someone spoiled his dream, before the doctors came up with another reason to keep her. Ken-Ken subscribed to Murphy's Law—anything that could go wrong, would go wrong.

After spending the first two months of her life in an incubator at the intensive care unit of Bronx Lebanon Hospital, being closely monitored by doctors and nurses, the child was finally medically cleared to go home. And there wasn't anyone happier than Ken-Ken, her father.

Like any concerned parent, he had stood vigil at his child's incubator while she fought valiantly for her life, Ken-Ken's blind faith had been rewarded with the precious gift of life. His daughter had pulled through where so many other premature infants had perished. Destiny was a survivor.

As a single parent, Ken-Ken faced some tough obstacles ahead. He was left with the dual task of being both mother and father, a stern disciplinarian, a provider, and a gentle comforter. He had no choice; his wife was dead and gone. This was the challenge life had presented to him. Still, he promised himself long ago he would never do things like beat his child. He would discipline her verbally. Ken-Ken wanted his daughter to respect him but never to fear him. He wanted her to be able to come to him with any problem she had. Because he was all she had.

"Mr. Greene?" a nurse called out. "Mr. Greene?"

Ken-Ken was momentarily caught off guard, lost in his thoughts. "Yeah, dat's me!" he replied. "I'm right here."

"Sorry ta keep you waitin' so long, but I had to change her diaper. She made stink-stink," the nurse explained. "I couldn't have my lil snoogums runnin' 'round here stinkin'. Not after all we have been through."

The young nurse carefully handed the baby over to her father. Ken-Ken gently cradled the small child in his arms. He moved the blankets ever so gently away from her face so he could take a sneak peak at his child. It was amazing to him how even at this tender age Destiny had adultlike facial features. To Ken-Ken it was eerie just how much his daughter looked exactly like a tiny version of Maria.

"Thanks Miss . . . ?" he said. "I didn't catch ya name."

"Patterson," she replied. "It's Ms. Patterson."

"Thanks, Ms. Patterson! Thank you fa everything! Thanks fa lookin' out fa my daughter like she wuz yourz. Alotta da things you did for her you didn't have to."

"No need ta thank me!" she said. "Everything I did for your child, I did from the bottom of my heart. I don't seek the praises of man. But thanks just the same. I get my blessings from God. You know, I really grew attached to that daughter of yours, Mr. Greene. I'm gonna miss her! I'm gonna miss her like crazy. She was the highlight of my day."

"Yeah, and she's gonna miss you too," Ken-Ken told her. "But don't worry, I'll bring her by from time ta time, ta see you."

"Don't say that. I'ma hold you to dat too! Don't make me no promise you can't keep," she replied.

"Nah, Ms. Patterson. I ain't gonna play you like dat. I mean whut I say and I say whut I mean. I'ma do dat fa real. Word up!"

"I'll be lookin' forward to that too!" she told him with a smile. "Now listen, remember Destiny's a chest child. She likes to be rocked to sleep on ya chest. And she spits up quite often. I think you should change her milk to a lactose-free formula. And always remember when you changing her diaper wipe from front to back. We don't want her lil coochie ta get a nasty rash."

Ken-Ken listened intently as he received last-minute care instructions from the nurse. He nodded every so often while soaking up every morsel of information. He was determined to give his daughter the best care he possibly could. Just in case things got too hard for him to bear, he had a strong support group in place with Maria's mother and his own, but the day-to-day care would rest solely on him.

Once again, he thanked the nurse for everything and then Ken-Ken turned and walked toward the elevator. He was finally headed home.

"Hey, there, lil Destiny," he said gently. "Just in case ya probably wonderin' who da hell dis crazy nigger talkin' to you iz. It's me, poppa-dukes. Get use ta dis voice. You'll be hearin' it alot! Listen, baby girl, we gonna be tighter than Batman and Robin. Ain't nuttin' in dis world gonna ever come between us. Matter fact, it's me and you one on one against the world! And guess what, they ain't got no wins either."

Armed with blankets, Pampers, and a baby bag, Ken-Ken made sure the infant was wrapped up tight and exited the hospital. He stepped out of the warm hospital into the arctic air and hailed a cab.

This was the beginning of the first day of his new life. Now he was a family man; no more life of crime. That life had ended the minute Destiny was born. His days of running the streets were a thing of the past. When Destiny got old enough he promised to tell her all about it, though. He wouldn't hide a thing from her. At the drop of a dime, if need be, he'd sacrifice his life for hers. That's how he looked at it. This was how dedicated he planned on being to his daughter.

Ken-Ken arrived at his graffiti-laden tenement building on Davidson Avenue. Normally the lobby was crowded with dealers and crack heads alike. But today the brutal weather had chased everyone indoors. Drug deals and drug usage were now taking place behind closed doors, away from the public eye.

As Ken-Ken entered the building he was glad to find it empty. He didn't feel like navigating his way through this concrete jungle with his child. Ken-Ken was feeling so overprotective that if someone even accidentally bumped into him while he had his daughter in his arms, he might have killed them.

Because the elevator was broken again, he was forced to hike up five flights of stairs with baby in his arms. As Ken-Ken climbed the steps, time and time again he stepped in piss. Ken-Ken wrinkled his nose trying to avoid the foul odor of piss. He held his breath and quickened his pace.

"Nasty fuckin' niggas!" he cursed. "I wish I would catch a nigga pissin' in da fuckin' stairs. I'll break my foot off in his ass! Word up! Triflin' muthafuckas! Dis don't make no goddamn sense. I swear it don't!"

Ken-Ken arrived at his battered, brown, paint-chipped door, slightly out of breath. The hike up the steps had taken more out of him than he thought. He made a mental note to himself to stop smoking those Newport 100s. Ken-Ken knew he couldn't afford to be in poor physical condition. This was the last time he'd ever feel like this, he promised himself. He walked into the apartment and the door made a loud squeaky sound as Ken-Ken slammed it shut.

After entering his modest apartment, he turned and began to instinctively fasten his numerous locks. As he did so an old saying his mother used to say came to mind. "If the world were peachy keen, then we wouldn't have locks on doors. It's better to be safe than sorry."

The harsh reality was that they lived in a high-crime, low-income neighborhood, which spawned a dog-eat-dog mentality amongst its residents. No one seemed to want to see the next person get ahead. In this South Bronx neighborhood, if someone flashed a nickel over lunch money, they'd more than likely be robbed. Times were hard but life in the South Bronx was even harder. The crack cocaine epidemic was running rampant and the world outside their door was a war zone. And no one wanted to be a casualty of this war. No one wanted to become a statistic.

Inside the apartment was a different story. It was nicely decorated. One could tell that a woman had a hand in decorating it. Maria had tackled the entire task by herself. Her pride and joy was the baby's room. It was truly a shame that she didn't live to see the day their baby would sleep in this room.

Previously, he and Maria had lived in a cramped one-bedroom apartment over in the Grand Concourse section of the Bronx. With the money they made from their crime sprees, they had taken it and put down a few months' rent and a security deposit on a bigger place on Davidson Avenue.

Maria had shared a room with her three brothers, Carlos, Harry, and Juan. Her parents were too poor to afford a bigger apartment and the only time she had some privacy was when she went to the bathroom. Maria swore her child would never share the same fate. She would give up her own privacy before that happened.

Maria had planned to spoil Destiny rotten. Everything she never had, she was determined to give to her daughter, by hook or crook.

The door to Destiny's room was closed and had a bright red ribbon decorating it. Ken-Ken broke the seal, as if it were the grand opening of a new business, watching it gently fall to the floor. Then he grabbed the doorknob and opened the door.

"Taaadaah! You like or whut?" he asked Destiny. "I hope so! A great woman, ya mother put dis together fa you. Dis great big ole room iz all yourz room. Welcome home Ma. It ain't much but it's all we got."

Inside the room were miscellaneous baby things, everything from a stroller, a crib, and cases of Similac and boxes of diapers. Ken-Ken had every product imaginable to take care of his child, courtesy of a makeshift baby shower that his family had thrown. He had everything he needed but a female to help him raise his seed.

Removing the blanket from her face, he held her up high, slowly giving Destiny a bird's-eye view of her room. It was painted in a soft pink. A giant hand-painted picture of a cartoon character, a baby blue Smurfette, adorned one wall. On the other Ken-Ken had commissioned some local graffiti artist to hand-paint a giant life-size portrait of his deceased wife. The likeness was incredible. This was done so Destiny would always know who her mother was and so he'd never forget the love of his life. As if looking at his daughter wasn't reminder enough.

"See dat lady right there? Dat's Maria, ya momz! She's not wit us anymore," he said. "At least not in the physical form anyway. But her spirit will always be here, watchin' over you, watchin' over us. Makin' sure you do right and protectin' us."

Suddenly a tear began to trickle down his cheek and Ken-Ken was overcome by sorrow. Quickly he wiped away the teardrop and regained his composure. Though he was heartbroken and depressed, Ken-Ken realized this was not time to be soft or emotional. He had to be strong for Destiny's sake. There would be many more rainy days ahead, a lot more storms for them to weather together.

In his mind Ken-Ken would never forgive himself for slipping. It had cost him dearly. Because of that tragedy he was destined forever to think about Maria. Now, the new burning question that gnawed at him was, how would Maria want him to raise their child? It was a question he couldn't possibly answer. Yet it worried him. He would spend the rest of his life torturing himself. Ken-Ken would never fully be able to avoid the issue, what if?

CHAPTER 3

As the years went by, Destiny seemed to go from adolescent to woman in a blink of an eye. She now stood five foot seven inches, with a delicious caramel brown complexion and shoulder-length, straight, jet-black hair and a wicked hourglass shape that most grown women envied.

"Ma, Illga! Look at me I wuz a funny lookin' baby. You sure I wasn't adopted?" Destiny said to her mother while looking at her baby pictures. She shook her head in disbelief. "Ga'head and laugh, Mommy. I know you want to."

Almost from the time she was old enough to hold a conversation, Destiny began talking to her deceased mother. In her mind as well as aloud she pretended to be talking to her mom. Whenever she was lonely, depressed, scared, sad, or just in need of womanly advice, it got her through the tough times.

Currently, she held a large plaque in her hand. It contained a pair of bronzed baby shoes and a large framed photograph. Her round doe-like eyes captured her childhood innocence. What she wouldn't give to return to the days of being shielded from the world in her father's strong protective arms. To return to the safety of her mother's womb. To hug her mother, to have her yell at her, to have her mother alive.

As it stood, though, all the wishful thinking in the world couldn't bring her mother back from the grave. There was nothing she could do to change fate. It just wasn't to be.

All of a sudden the phone rang.

For Destiny it couldn't come at a better time. Thoughts of her deceased mother almost always brought her to tears. Sometimes she would get mad at God, thinking that He had robbed her of the opportunity of knowing and being raised by her mother. Destiny had to admit though that her dad did a hell of a good job on his own. Yet as good as he was with her, she still missed the tender, loving care of a woman. She was rough around the edges and had some tomboyish ways.

"Hello?" she said when she picked up the phone.

"Happy birthday ta you! Happy birthday ta you!" her father sang softly.

"Daddy?" she said. "You so crazy!"

He continued, "How old are you now? How old are you now?"

"Aiightt, Daddy you killin' me!" Destiny joked. "Let somebody who can actually sing do dat!"

"Hey, you gotta give ya old man an E for effort," he shot back.

"How 'bout a D for nice try!" Destiny retorted.

"They say they only appreciate you when you dead and you gone. . . ." The minute he made the statement Ken-Ken realized his mistake and mentally kicked himself for even mentioning death. Especially on a day like this.

Today was not only his daughter's birthday and the anniversary of her mother's death, but it marked the very first time she was going to visit Maria's gravesite.

"How old are you now?" he asked, quickly turning attention away from the sadness. "Huh?"

"Daddy, you don't know how old I am?" she asked, genuinely hurt.

"C'mon now!" he fired back. "Of course I know. I just wanted to hear you say it. It sounds better."

"I don't believe you," she said. "Why would you even play like dat? You tell me how old I am."

"Seventeen!" he coolly replied. "Baby, don't ever doubt ya daddy."

Silently, Destined blew out a sigh of relief. She would have been very disappointed in her father had he answered incorrectly. After all, she was his only child. He should know her like the back of his hand. And he did.

"Are you still goin' ova . . . ta see ya mother?"

"Yeah," she answered confidently. "My plans ain't changed. I'm goin ta do whut I said I would do."

"Baby, I would feel alot more comfortable if you waited fa me ta come home ta go wit you," he said. "I don't like da idea of you travelin' way out ta Jersey by yaself."

"Daddy, there you go. Ya bein' overprotective again. We already talked about dis last nite. I already told you, dis iz sumthin' I gotta do alone," she insisted. "All by my lonely."

"Des, why don't you just take Makeba along wit you? Could you do that fa me?"

"No Daddy. Makeba iz my girl and everything, but dis iz personal. Dis iz a moment I don't care to share wit nobody. Not even you. No disrespect, Daddy. But dat'z just how I feel. Point blank. End of story. I really don't wanna talk about it no more. I wish you just respect my decision."

Destiny had an independent spirit and try as he might it was hard for Ken-Ken to sever the umbilical cord. He hated facing the fact that his baby girl was growing up and that there were things in the world he couldn't protect her from. Most of the time it was his daughter's struggle for independence that scared him the most. Ken-Ken just wasn't ready to let go. He knew life, much like the streets, was unforgiving. One slipup or mistake and your life could be lost or ruined forever. He was living proof of that.

But Ken-Ken knew it was senseless to try and talk Destiny into doing what he wanted her to do. They were too much alike—extremely stubborn. Though her decision didn't sit well with him, he decided to let it go, before the discussion led to a heated argument. And he didn't want to upset his daughter, at least not on this day.

"We still on fa tonite, right?" he asked. "Dinner on me? Right?"

"No doubt, Daddy," Destiny said. "I wanna go ta Sammy's on City Island. I gotta taste fa sum seafood."

"Aiiight, talk ta ya later," he said, sounding a bit disappointed. "Call me as soon as you get back. Aiight?"

"You got dat. Luv you."

"Luv you too," he told her. "Be safe."

"Bye," they seemed to say in unison.

After placing the telephone back on the receiver, Destiny sat down on the edge of her bed and stared blankly off into space. Too many thoughts began to race through her head, each jockeying for position. Despite her brave statement, she was stalling for time. She was looking for excuses not to go to the cemetery and right about now any reason would do.

Her thoughts shifted to the block. In particular, an older, handsome thug named Jerome Wells, a.k.a. "Rome." Just the mere thought of him sent chills down her spine. Rome was six feet tall, dark skinned with a rock-hard physique. On his two front teeth Rome had a pair of shiny gold caps. They seemed to enhance his good looks. Destiny had had a crush on him ever since she was little, even though she knew he was always in and out of prison. He had had his eye on her for quite some time now, and one day he had stepped to her.

"A yo, shorty. You wit da slim waist and pretty face! Hold up fa a minute," Rome ordered.

Destiny froze in her tracks when she heard that voice. His smooth voice broke her out in goosebumps. She knew exactly who that voice belonged to. Her future man.

On the city sidewalk Destiny paused and turned, watching as the man of her dreams approached with each step Rome took toward her, Destiny's heart began to beat faster. She was so nervous she almost dropped the groceries she was carrying.

Cooly Rome took his time reaching her as he admired her beauty. There was no way he was going to run over to Destiny. He could never let her know how bad he wanted her.

"I seen you strugglin' wit dat bag. And me bein' da gentlemen dat I am I wuz wonderin' if you needed some help. You know these niggers out here ain't got no manners. They don't know a lady when they see one."

Destiny merely smiled at the comment and handed over her grocery bag. She watched as his biceps constricted into a hard, tight muscle. Immediately a romantic thought came to mind and she wished she was wrapped up in his arms.

Though this was their first encounter, the very first time the two had so much as said hi, they were well aware of each other's existence. But Destiny was younger than Rome and in his eyes she was jailbait. Besides, he had too much respect for Ken-Ken to ever violate him in this manner. Rome knew the code of the streets. He knew very well what happens when one violates a street dude's family. So Rome had no choice but to desire Destiny from afar. He knew that Destiny would one day be a winner. Way back he promised himself that she would be his. Today the opportunity presented itself, and Rome, ever the opportunist, used it to put his bid in.

Rome continued, "Oh, by da way my name iz—"

"Rome," Destiny stated. "I already know who you are."

A sly smile creased Rome's lips and he puffed up his chest a little, feeling himself. He was proud that he had indeed achieved a certain level of street fame, even if it didn't extend outside of his neighborhood.

The couple walked and talked as they made their way down the block toward Destiny's building. They shared light conversation, but for Rome it was more than that. He was trying to see exactly where the young girl's head was at, so he could form his plan of attack.

What Rome didn't know was that Destiny was more than willing to have a romantic relationship with him. She was feeling him. She liked everything about him. He didn't really have to kick any game to her; she just naturally embraced him.

From that day on, Rome and Destiny would see more and more of each other.

Destiny had gladly given him conversation and her phone number. When her father wasn't around or when he was fast asleep, these two would talk for hours sharing secret conversations. Destiny wished it was Rome and not her father taking her to dinner tonight. But that thought alone sent her on a guilt trip.

Suddenly there was a quick succession of loud knocks on the front door. Destiny snapped out of her trance and walked briskly through the apartment to answer the door. She looked through the peephole and saw her best friend Makeba.

She flung the door wide open and let her friend in.

Makeba was the exact opposite of Destiny in every way, most

notably physically. She was short, standing all of five feet two inches high. She was light skinned, with short, nappy hair that she kept done in long extension braids to help it grow, a flat chest, and no behind to speak of. Her physical appearance caused her to lack self-confidence and boys easily took advantage of her.

When Makeba was younger her cousins would tease her till she cried. They said she had a face only her mother could love. One even added, "You look like you got beat with an ugly stick."

The fact that her own family picked on her hurt Makeba deeply. She would hear their taunts in her head forever. Later it caused her to act out sexually. She became promiscuous at twelve years old. She gave it up to the first boy who showed the least bit of interest in her.

What her friend lacked in the self-confidence department, Destiny more than made up for with a swagger that bordered on conceit. Now, Makeba was book smart. The girl could outperform just about any kid in school. Her specialty was math. When it came to numbers and figures Makeba could precisely calculate them in her head. Destiny's strength lay in her street smarts. She could match wits with the best of them. While Destiny was in the midst of a hustle, Makeba was quietly on the sidelines anazyling the whole situation. Makeba shunned the spotlight and preferred to move in silence. At times she pretended to be dumber than she really was to gain the advantage. But as everyone in the streets knew, it was the quiet ones that you had to look out for. Real bad boys or girls move in silence. Destiny was the leader and Makeba was the follower. But above all else they were friends.

That alone was a major accomplishment for Destiny since she didn't make friends easily. Being an only child, she learned to do everything alone. She was distrustful of people, especially other females. Her father had always told her, "The less people that knew your business the better. And everyone that you call your friend doesn't necessarily mean you well." She thought they gossiped too much and kept too much drama stirred up. Destiny didn't like all the he-say-she-say stuff that usually accompanied female relationships.

Makeba brought none of the traditional female baggage or hangups with her. Like Destiny, she was an only child. So she understood perfectly when to talk and when to be silent, when Destiny wanted company and when she needed to be alone.

In turn, Destiny was protective of Makeba, like a big sister. She knew Makeba wasn't a fighter, but a thinker. If you messed with Makeba, then you had Destiny to deal with.

"Whut'z good, Makeba? Whut you doin' up so early?" Destiny asked, walking back to her bedroom. "You know you ain't no mornin' person."

She went over to the mirror and started fixing her hair.

Makeba sat on her bed and watched her.

"You ain't lyin' bout dat," Makeba said. "Da phone woke me up. Somebody kept crank callin' my house and hangin' up. So since I wuz up, I just came by ta see whut'z up wit you. Whut you 'bout ta get into?"

"I'm goin' out ta visit my momz gravesite out in Jersey, member? I told you about it last night." Destiny continued to mess with her hair, agitated.

"Oh, yeah, dat's right you did say somethin' 'bout dat," Makeba said, nodding. "Need me ta roll wit you out there? I ain't doin' nuttin'."

"Nah, I'm good!" she snapped, glaring at her in the mirror. "I need ta do dis alone. Solo."

Destiny was pissed. She thought that her best friend had forgotten all about her birthday. She had been in her house for five minutes now and hadn't said a damn thing. How could she? Destiny fumed. She'd never once forgotten Makeba's birthday.

After a final inspection of herself in the mirror, she turned and faced Makeba.

"Yo, here, Destiny," she said, smiling. "Happy birthday!"

From behind her back Makeba had produced a small gold-wrapped box with a red bow neatly attached. She extended her hand and passed the birthday present to her friend.

"My bad!" Destiny said as she took the gift.

"Whut?" Makeba asked. "Whut you talkin' 'bout?"

"Bitch, I wuz cursin' ya azz in my mind!" Destiny told her, smiling. "I thought you forgot all 'bout me."

Makeba laughed. "Never dat! You know it not even dat type of party."

Eagerly Destiny ripped into the box. From the size and shape of it, she knew immediately that it was jewelry.

"Damn! Thanks, Makeba," Destiny said. "I always wanted one of these!"

It was a ten-carat gold name chain, with Destiny's name written in cursive. Even though the gift was slum jewelry, there was no way Destiny could have afforded to give her friend this kind of gift for her birthday. Makeba could afford it because she came from a two-parent, two-income household. She didn't have to work. All she had to do was get good grades and she got a nice allowance.

Destiny didn't get everything she wanted but she had everything she needed. Times were hard in the Greene household with Ken-Ken being the sole breadwinner of the family. He barely got by with his meager earnings as a gypsy cab driver.

In the game of life, clearly Destiny was a have-not, but she was happy with her position in life primarily because she didn't know any better. So Destiny appreciated the gift more than her friend would ever know. It was the first piece of jewelry she had ever owned.

Destiny remembered when she and Makeba met for the first time. It hadn't gone so good. Destiny had mistakenly taken Makeba's turn jumping rope. Though Makeba hadn't shown any signs of hostility, she had disliked Destiny from that point on. That was until she lost a pair of expensive eyeglasses that her parents had bought her. Makeba had been scared to death that she would get an ass whipping if her parents discovered the glasses were gone. Destiny happened to find them in the building and had returned them to her. Ever since then they had been thick as thieves.

Destiny examined the necklace, turning it from side to side.

"C'mere, let me put it 'round ya neck." Makeba told her.

Destiny was taller than her friend, so she bent over, pulling her hair away from her neck. Makeba fastened the chain around her neck.

When that was done, Destiny stepped back in front of the mirror. She liked the way that the gold chain glimmered around her neck. She could get used to things like this. The chain made her feel prettier and more important. It was as if suddenly she was somebody.

Striking different poses with the chain on, Destiny styled and profiled in the mirror. She broke out into an ear-to-ear grin.

With a quick glance at the clock, Destiny suddenly realized she had better get a move on. She was taking the New Jersey Path train and it might run late.

"Yo, I gotta go," she said. "I'll holler atcha when I get back, aiight?' "

"Aiight," Makeba replied. "I'll see ya later."

CHAPTER 4

Ten years ago

It was an unseasonably warm fall day in September, and big, bright yellow school buses were everywhere. It was the first day of school in New York City.

"Oh, Daddy, look at all da big buses," Destiny said. "Daddy, I wanna ride on da bus ta school too. Why can't I get a ride?"

"Destiny, how many times I gotta tell you we live too close to ya school fa them to send a bus to pick you up?" her father explained. "Most of those kids live far away."

"Aw, shoot Daddy, dat'z not fair!" she said sadly. "What about the other kids? Some of them live close by too. I seen them before."

Like every other kid, Destiny was immaculately dressed in a cute designer denim jean suit with a crisp new pair of Nike sneakers her father had bought her. Her hair was neatly done in thick cornrows, courtesy of her dad, who had learned how to braid hair by trial and error.

Holding hands with her father, they navigated the mean streets of the South Bronx. Even at this time of morning these blocks were alive with activity. The working class was going to or coming from work, depending on what shift they worked. While only hours ago, some of these same city blocks had been alive with another kind of activity. Drug traffic. Drug paraphernalia littered the sidewalks and gutters. Even though she had stepped on a few, all Destiny could think of was the first day of school.

The closer they got to the vicinity of the school, the more Destiny noticed other parents bringing their kids to school also. The only difference between her and them was, they were accompanied by their mothers and she by her father. It was like a light switch had gone off in her head.

"Daddy?" she said looking up at him. "Where's my mommy? How come she won't walk me to school like all the rest of the kids' mommies?"

Ken-Ken stopped in the middle of the block and looked down at his daughter, caught completely off guard by the question.

Then he said, "Destiny, listen.... Mommy's ...," he stuttered. "Mommy's ... gone!"

Destiny looked up at her father's distraught face, puzzled by his brief explanation.

"What's dat mean? I don't understand why she can't walk me ta school like da other kids' mommies. Why don't she come see me? Doesn't she love me?" she asked. "I want my mommy!"

Ken-Ken looked away from her for a long time, overcome by guilt. He never felt so helpless in his life. After awhile he seemed to regain his composure.

"Mommy's gone," he said gently. "She can't come take you to school and she can't come see you. Not now. Not ever."

"Why?" Destiny demanded to know. "I want her to take me to school just like da other kids."

Ken-Ken reached down and scooped up his daughter in his arms, bringing her closer to him, closer to his heart.

"Mommy's gone," he repeated softly in her ear. "It's just me and you, baby. I'm fa you. And I'll always be here fa you. I'ma take good care of you too. Don't you ever worry."

That night Destiny prayed, "God take care of me and Daddy! Protect us from all da bad people in da world. And please don't let me be dead like Mommy. I don't wanna be dead! OK?"

From that day on Destiny likened death to loss. Or lack of material things. Because her mother had died she lacked lots of things. And never was this more apparent till she spent a night over Makeba's house.

Destiny was a homebody. One day Makeba's mother invited her to a sleepover she was having and her father readily accepted the invitation. Ken-Ken wanted his daughter to socialize with kids her own age. Besides that, he knew that Makeba's parents were good people, honest, and hardworking.

Against her will Destiny found herself smack dab in the middle of a group of talkative females. Amongst these girls she chose to be more of an observer, even a reluctant participant.

During the course of the evening, and well into the night, the girls busied themselves with a variety of activities. First they baked chocolate chip cookies from scratch. Then they took turns painting each other's nails. After that they watched a few movies. Around bedtime idle talk soon turned to boys and who liked who.

"If Gerard ever asked me out I would go out with him," one girl admitted. "He's a cutie."

"Word!" another girl added. "Dat nigger is fine as a muthafucka! Mad chicks be sweatin him, though."

"Fuck Gerard!" Makeba stated. "Dat nigger iz not all dat!"

Up until this point Destiny had had no idea how raunchy Makeba was. But all that was about to change. She was about to get her first taste of the real Makeba, not the one she knew in passing.

"Stop hatin'!" someone yelled. "You mad cauze he don't want you."

"Plueeazze! I had dat nigger already. He old news," Makeba said. "We fucked last year."

If Destiny was surprised by Makeba's candidness, she didn't show it. She sat in the circle with a nonchalant look on her face. To the rest of the group this admission wasn't a real surprise. They knew that Makeba was a real big slut. They weren't her friends at all. They were just over there to eat up her food and talk about her like a dog behind her back.

The majority of this group was sexually active, except Destiny but from the disgusted looks on their faces even they were appalled by this.

"God damn, Makeba, who haven't you fucked?" someone spat.

A sly smile spread across Makeba's face, as if she had done something slick. She may have thought what she did with Gerard was cool but no one else seemed to think so. Destiny was the only female in the room who could have cared less.

After that it seemed like the mood turned too sour to talk. One by one each girl began to pretend to be sleepy. Soon the lights were cut off in the living room and the girls called it a night.

While the rest of the girls went to sleep bitter, Destiny went to sleep envious of Makeba. Just before she drifted off, she remembered the day's events, in particular Makeba's lovely interaction with her mother.

Makeba's mom had catered to her every whim. When Makeba said the girls wanted pizza her mother ran outside into the pouring rain and bought back a pizza pie. Destiny marveled at how spoiled Makeba was. How she had her mother wrapped around her pinky. She yearned to have a mother in her own life. So watching Makeba abuse this privilege disturbed her. Destiny thought, *She don't know how good she got it.*

Another harsh fact that the sleepover highlighted was just how poor Destiny really was. She saw firsthand how the "Joneses" lived. Because Makeba was an only child from a two-parent home, she lived in the ghetto lap of luxury. On display in their home was every new appliance available. It wasn't just the appliances, the DVD player, and the 62-inch projection screen TV that made Destiny feel inferior. It was the little things like clothing. She wore cut-off jean shorts and a tank top while the other girls wore fashion pajama sets.

"Tickets please, ma'am," the conductor repeated loudly for the third time. His frustration had grown each time he had had to repeat himself. The white man's face turned beet red from anger. If there was one thing he hated, it was to be ignored. Immediately he assumed it was deliberate. Since he was standing right in front of Destiny, he wonder how in heaven's name could she not see him, let alone hear him. He thought maybe the woman was a fare beater. If that was the case, then he would enjoy nothing more than to have the police escort her off the train at the next stop.

"Oh, sorry, sir. My fault!" Destiny apologized. "I wuzn't payin' attention. I wuz daydreamin'."

"Must have been some dream," he remarked sarcastically. "You didn't hear a word I said."

Reaching inside her purse, she retrieved her train ticket. Destiny handed it over to the man and watched as he punched a few holes in it, hung the ticket above her seat, then moved on down the aisle to the next passenger, repeating the procedure.

"Ticket, sir." His voice began to fade into the distance.

It didn't take long for Destiny to get right back into that deep train of thought. While the train raced at high speed through New Jersey, she stared aimlessly again out the window, looking at nothing in particular. She willingly revisited her childhood, her life-altering experiences with her father. She still saw these events vividly, as if they happened yesterday. Some stood out more than others.

Ten years ago

"Des?" her father called through the crack in the door. "Destiny, you dressed yet?"

Destiny heard every word her father said, yet she wouldn't fix her mouth to reply. Inside her bedroom, she sat in silence on her bed, fully clothed, fuming.

Destiny was upset because her father was making her go out on a date with him and his new lady friend, Sharon, to the Bronx Zoo. She wanted no part of it either. Like a wild animal she was territorial, overprotective, and extremely jealous of her father dealing with any other female. It had been just her and her father for the past ten years. They shared a special bond. So why couldn't it stay that way? Destiny looked upon any and every female as a threat to their relationship. She couldn't let anyone break their bond.

She wanted her father all to herself. All her life it had been all about her. Destiny figured it was too late in the game to even consider letting some other female fill her mother's shoes.

To her no woman was good enough for her dad. No women except her dear departed mother.

"Destiny!" Ken-Ken raised his voice. "Are you dressed or whut? I know you hear me. Answer me."

Destiny huffed and puffed to herself before she replied. "Yeah, I'm dressed," she stated flatly.

"Well, let's get ready ta go," he said. "Sharon's waitin' fa us at her house. C'mon, now. We gonna be late!"

After running almost every stoplight in the South Bronx, Ken-Ken managed to make it over to Sharon's place on time.

"Hi, sweetie!" came the overexaggerated greeting. "Hey little one! Ooohhh, you such a doll baby. Cute as a button. Kenny, you ain't tell me ya kid was this beautiful. Girl, one day boys are gonna be fighting over you. Watch what I tell you."

"Over my dead body!" Ken-Ken snapped. "Don't be fillin' her head up wit dat nonsense."

"Oh, Kenny, hush!" she replied. "I'm only telling you the truth. Whether you like it or not."

Destiny stared at Sharon, giving her the evil eye. She didn't need Sharon to tell her she was pretty.

Tell me sumthin' I don't know, she thought to herself.

Though Sharon was beautiful, well dressed, and well mannered, Destiny wasn't the least bit impressed by her.

Her take-charge swagger rubbed Destiny the wrong way.

"Whut exhibit we gonna see first?" Ken-Ken wondered aloud as they stood at the Bronx Zoo's entrance.

"Kenny, I wish you would speak proper English. And leave that Ebonics stuff alone. You're setting a bad example for your daughter," Sharon said.

Ken-Ken ignored her. "Let's go to da Reptile House," he said.

"Sounds like a plan to me," Sharon said. "I always liked snakes growing up as a child. How about you, Destiny? What's your favorite animal?"

Destiny remained silent, choosing to go with the flow. Physically she was there but mentally she was miles away.

The trio paid the cost of admission, and then they embarked on a fun-filled day at the zoo. It was one of Destiny's favorite places to go, even though she wasn't feeling real social today. She developed a love of animals by spending countless hours watching animal shows with her dad on TV.

Once inside the zoo, they visited every major tourist attraction, including the children's zoo, which was a personal favorite of Destiny's. This day belonged to her, and they did whatever it was she wanted to do. They were merely appeasing her before they dropped the bomb on her that Sharon was moving in.

All the walking and sightseeing had made Ken-Ken thirsty. Several times he stopped at the concession stands and guzzled down a few twenty-four-ounce sodas. Then nature called.

"Excuse me, ya'll," he said, "I gotta go to da bathroom. Be right back!"

Destiny patiently watched until her father disappeared inside the bathroom. Then she turned to her father's lady friend.

"So, Ms. Sharon, how do you feel 'bout my father?" she asked. "Because I think you should know dat my Dad ain't a one-woman man. He told me himself he'll neva settle down wit just one woman. Afta while they get on his nerves. Just thought I should let you know. I'd hate to see you get yaself all hurt and everythang."

Sharon looked dumbfounded.

"Oh, yeah?" Sharon asked. "What makes you say dat?"

"I know my father. He's a dog!" Destiny said reasonably. "I should know, I only been 'round him all my life. I seen him run woman in and outta his bedroom. Like da soul train line. One after another. He thinks he's a playa."

"Oh, really?" Sharon said. "Is dat a fact?"

"Hope you don't think I'm makin' all dis up either?" she asked. "But my father said women can get only one thang fa him and dat's—"

"Shut your mouth!" Sharon snapped. "You better not finish that sentence. I had enough of this shit. I ain't tryin' ta hear anymore. This is utterly ridiculous."

But Destiny could tell by the worried look on Sharon's face that she had hit the woman in the heart. Her lies tapped directly into Sharon's fears, giving them an air of validity. She knew Sharon was probably looking for a husband she could have babies with. She thought Ken-Ken was the one.

Well, not if Destiny had anything to say about it.

But before she could play with Sharon's head again, the woman got up, turned on her heels, and stomped off. Without so much as a good-bye.

"See you when I see you!" Destiny said aloud. "Mommy, dat one wuz fa you!"

Shortly after, Ken-Ken reappeared, eager to pick up where they had left off.

"Yo, where's Sharon at?" he asked, casting a suspicious eye on her.

"I don't know where she went," Destiny said innocently. "I thought she wuz wit you."

"How you think dat when I left her out here wit you?"

"Afta you went to da bathroom, I went too. When I came back she wuz gone," she said.

Destiny was finding it increasingly hard to keep a straight face. She should have gotten an Academy Award nomination for her acting.

Needless to say, after that day Ken-Ken never brought another woman around his daughter again.

Suddenly the train conductor appeared and announced that they would be temporarily delayed due to track work up ahead. Destiny continued to stare out the window while the other passengers moaned with displeasure.

At the tender age of twelve, Destiny committed her first crime. She was with Makeba, going home on the Number Four train from a relative's house in Harlem.

There had been barely enough room for her and Makeba to stand up. They were forced to stand by the door. Destiny scanned the mean mugs of the subway riders as the train rumbled noisily through the pitch black tunnels toward the Bronx. Makeba and Destiny made small talk as the train made its designated stops. Suddenly the train unexpectedly made a sudden stop, causing Makeba to unintentionally bump into another young strap hanger.

"Bitch, watch where da fuck you goin'!" the young African American girl cursed. "Bumpin' into me like dat! Stupid muthafucka!"

"Sorry. My fault," Makeba said softly.

Immediately Destiny stepped up.

"Sorry fa whut? Man, fuck her!" Destiny barked. "You bumped into her by accident. It wuzn't ya fault!"

"Whateva!" came the hostile reply. "You don't like it? Then do sumthin' bout it." With the heated words being exchanged, the threat of a fight hung in the air. The other subway passengers began moving away, distancing themselves from any physical altercation.

Destiny was ready to fight the girl. She didn't like the way she came out with her mouth. She was just trying to be a bully, and Destiny hated bullies. The only thing that stopped her from fighting the girl was a promise she had made to her father to chill out. She had been in a rash of fights lately, mostly with boys, around her block. If she came home with so much as a scratch on her face, then Ken-Ken would forbid her from riding the subway by herself again. With that in mind, she didn't press the issue. Her freedom was something she didn't want restricted.

But the other girl wouldn't let the issue die so easily. She stared hard at Destiny, rolling her eyes and sucking her teeth. But to her credit Destiny didn't take the bait. As long as the girl didn't call Destiny out of her name or put her hands on her, she was completely under control.

As they stared each other down, the glimmer of a gold chain with a matching gold crucifix caught Destiny's eye. The sight of the chain got Destiny's mind going. She turned to Makeba and whispered in her ear, "Yo, I'm about ta snatch dis dumb bitch's chain! So just go along wit da program, aiight?"

Makeba shot her an expression that let Destiny know that she wasn't down with that. Still, Destiny being Destiny, she ignored the look, thus forcing Makeba to play along.

"Look, our stop iz comin' up next." she told Makeba. "Get off da train witout me. I'm act like I'm stayin' on. Aiight!"

Makeba shook her head but said, "Okay."

The train zoomed through the tunnel and pulled up to a well lit train station at 149th Street and the Grand Concourse. Destiny and Makeba had to get off the Number Four train in order to catch the Number Two train, which would drop them off in their neighborhood. The train doors opened and a wave of people exited and entered the other train. Makeba was swept up in the mass movement. In a matter of seconds Destiny lost sight of her.

"Yo, I'll see you later!" Destiny called out. "I'll call you when I get home. Bye!" With the threat of being jumped gone, the girl dropped her guard and took one of the last remaining empty seats, which happened to be near the door, right by Destiny.

The subway car doors were about to close at any moment as the train was only allotted a precious few minutes to make its designated station stops. Knowing this, Destiny struck. Quickly she ripped the chain off her neck with such a force that it briefly pulled the girl's neck along with it, till finally it popped. Then without a moment to spare, she slid between the closing subway car doors, just in the nick of time.

Instinctively, the other girl lunged at Destiny's fleeing figure, but it was too late. The train had already begun to depart, and there was no stopping it. She stood looking teary-eyed through the window, shouting insults at Destiny, who merely replied by laughing and giving the girl the finger.

The success of her first crime gave her a strange high, a rush she had never experienced before. Since there was no way in the world she could explain its sudden appearance to her father she and Makeba headed to the local dope boys to pawn the chain.

Present Day

Finally Destiny reached her stop. She hopped into a cab and headed to the cemetery. Before she knew it, Destiny was standing solemnly before her mother's gravesite.

Out of respect, she first bowed her head before quickly making the sign of the cross with her right hand. Then she kneeled down and gently placed the bouquet of flowers on her mother's grave.

"Maria Torres. Sunrise, May 12, 1966. Sunset, Oct 14, 1987," she read to herself.

Destiny stared angrily at the plain rock, which masqueraded as a tombstone. She promised herself to one day replace it with a beautiful massive marble one. Her mom deserved better. It was plain and simple to Destiny. It cost to live and to die.

"Hey, Mom whut'z goin' on?" she began. "Me, I'm aiight. I can't complain.... I finally made it out here. After all these years, right? Well, I ain't gonna sit here and lie ta you, I'm doin' OK in school. Can't front I could do betta though ... but.... you know how dat go. I promise I'll do betta next marking period."

Destiny continued to make small talk, but the closer she got to matters of the heart, Destiny began to struggle to find the right words. "Ma ... I miss you so much, you don't even know da half. Daddy been good ta me. Real good. You picked a good man, I hope you know dat. He really knows how ta hold it down. He's a man amongst men. Trust me niggas like him don't come a dime a dozen. Good dude. He told all about how he used to get money back in da day. And how when I was born he deaded all dat street stuff for me. Ma, I know I might sound a lil bit ungrateful but we struggling. Every time I open the mailbox there's more bills. I wanna do sumthin, step up and help him ... but Daddy ain't havin' it.... He too proud ... Ma, I know I could help too. We not even livin', we just exsistin'. One day, watch, I'ma put us on easy street. We deserve it after everything dis family been through. But ... I don't know how ta say dis, but I'll say it anyway.... Every girl needs a mother. Can't no man teach a girl how ta be a woman. Nuttin' against Daddy but it's da truth," she said. "I feel like I wuz robbed. God robbed me of da chance of knowin' you. . . . You know sumtimez. . . . Sumtimez I wish I wuz neva born. . . ."

Destiny got all choked up. It was like a dam had broken and tears began streaming down her face and her body was racked with sobs.

Unable to talk anymore, Destiny just stood before her mother's grave and let a lifetime of pain, anger, and regret, pour out of her body. She never envisioned her trip would turn out like this. She thought she was strong enough to handle it, after all these years. But she wasn't. It hurt just as bad as the first time she realized her mother was gone.

Being weak had never been Destiny's style, so after a few minutes of feeling sorry for herself, she summoned up the courage to leave.

Destiny wiped her face, gathered her composure, and straightened her clothes.

"Mommy, I miss you. And I'll love you always," Destiny said. "I'll be back one day soon ta see you."

Every birthday that followed Destiny celebrated it by visiting her mother's gravesite.

CHAPTER 5

A gentle kiss on the forehead was all it took to rouse Destiny from a good night's sleep. She opened one eye.

"Mornin', Daddy," she mumbled into her pillow.

"Yeah, good mornin' ta you. Get up, girl!" her father said. "You gone be late fa school."

Though Destiny was older now and had an alarm clock, he father still woke her up before he left for work every morning.

"Daddy, chill. I been up!" she shot back. "I wuz jus layin' here."

Ken-Ken shot his daughter a smirk that seemed to say, "You expect me to believe that?" He stood over her refusing to move a muscle till she got out of her bed.

Looking up at her father from a comfortable position in bed, Destiny had to admit he was still a physically imposing figure. If he wasn't her dad she might be intimidated by him. Ken-Ken's chest was broad and his arms were thick as tree stumps. He was still capable of inflicting severe damage on someone.

Ken-Ken was a man's man. His presence alone demanded respect. So when he told his daughter the war stories about his and her mother's exploits in the streets, she believed him. At times it was hard for Destiny to picture her father as a thug, a cold heartless predator, when he was so gentle and kind around her.

"Des, c'mon now, get up!" he said. "I can only hope you're dis slow when it's time ta go Christmas shoppin'. You'll save me a whole lotta money."

"Aiight!" she said, rolling out of bed. "I'm getting' up now."

Satisfied, Ken-Ken turned to leave her room and head off to work.

"Dad, wait a minute. I need a couple dollars fa lunch. I'm broke," she said.

Without giving it a second thought, Ken-Ken reached into his pocket and gave his daughter his last. A twenty-dollar bill.

"Thanks, Dad!" Destiny said smiling. "You da man. I luv you."

He smiled. "I luv you too. Now hurry up and get dressed before you be late fa school."

Over the years, the two had made it a habit to tell each other that they loved each other on a regular basis. It made their day to hear the other say it. And Ken-Ken knew that in his line of work, driving cabs, anything could happen. Driving cabs was a hustle, no matter how you looked at it. When one is hustling, a real hustler knows there's a chance, however great or small, that they won't make it back home.

Ken-Ken found out that raising a child was difficult in more ways than one. Aside from the single parenting issues he was forced to deal with, the financial responsibilities proved to be equally as taxing. Daily the bills seemed to mount. And the older Destiny got the more expensive everything seemed to become.

Later, as Ken-Ken drove, scouring the city streets for potential fares, he thought back on something his mother was fond of saying, "To live is to make bills." He never realized how true that statement was until now. Every night when he came home from work and checked his mailbox, he found a new bill waiting to be paid. Soon he fell behind. If it wasn't one thing it was another.

Ken-Ken felt like he was robbing Peter to pay Paul. A few times Ken-Ken had to revert back to the "stick up game" to feed his family. He was thankful that those times were few and far between. Of course each and every time he committed a robbery he felt terrible, knowing he had just risked his daughter's future. He was no good to her dead or in jail. But God knew his intentions, he reasoned. By hook or by crook he was going to provide for his child.

He had always told his daughter to "exhaust all legal means first, before you do anything illegal. The streets will always be there. But that job may not."

An hour later, Ken-Ken had his first ride. On Burnside Avenue, he picked up an elderly African American woman. Her destination was North Central Hospital, near Moshula Parkway. He got there in a heartbeat. Everything and everybody in New York City was in a rush, and cab drivers and their fares were no different.

"Have a nice day, ma'am," he said, helping the elderly woman out of his cab.

"Oh, you too, baby," she replied. "You're such a gentleman."

"Thank you, ma'am. I try. It don't take nuttin' ta be nice."

"Sho' you right baby!" she said. "Keep doin' what you doin."

After catching the first fare, Ken-Ken was on a roll. Fares seemed to come back to back to back. Some customers even tried to flag him down when he already had a fare. He picked one young girl up on the way to school, dropped her off in front of Roosevelt High School, in the Bronx. From there he picked up two truants on their way to a hooky party.

"Ma, I been feelin' you fa a dumb long time," the young man whispered. "We been kickin' it ova da phone fa a hot minute now. So whut'z da deal? Yo, we goin' ta Dee's crib and you know Dee gonna be getting' hit off by Tonya. So I'm sayin' whut'z good wit us? Whut we gone be doin'?"

As a cab driver, Ken-Ken was privy to a lot of conversation, some personal, some immoral, and some even criminal. One time he was even forced at gunpoint to use his cab as a getaway car.

But good thing about driving a cab in New York City was, his customers kept him abreast to the happening in the streets. He knew all the latest fashion trends, what was in and what was out. Ken-Ken stayed current with the latest street lingo. So he knew his male passenger was just, "runnin' game." When he ran the streets in his younger years he was always told, "Game always recognized game."

He could only hope that the female had enough common sense to see through this charade.

As he drove, Ken-Ken watched them through his rearview mirror, just to see how receptive to the idea the girl really was. In his mind he kept saying to himself, *This could be my Destiny.*

As he shot the young man a few icy grill stares, the young man caught them too, but paid Ken-Ken no mind. He was too focused on getting in the girl's pants.

"Tayshaun," she began. "I'm sayin' I thought we wuz just gonna chill and watch a few movies. Whut happened ta dat? I really don't care whut da next chick and da next nigga iz doin'. Dat'z on them! If Tonya wanna play herself out then let her go right ahead."

"C'mon now, Ma, dis a hooky party. People get busy at hooky parties," he said. "You know muthafuckas be havin' sex. Whut you think be happenin' at 'em? You can't be serious."

From his rearview mirror Ken-Ken could see that the boy was growing more and more frustrated by the minute. At any moment he knew the kid was going to lose his cool. He could see the aggravation registering on his face.

"I ain't doin' nuttin'. I'm good," she stated firmly. "I ain't ready ta take it there wit you yet. Matter fact you can just take me right back ta school."

"Whut?" the boy exploded. "Fuck you, bitch! You a jump-off anyway! You ain't wifey material. I wuz jus gassin' you up."

"Ya mother!" the girl fired back. "You fuckin' ugly nigga!"

Before anyone knew what was happening, the boy jumped out of the cab at a red light. Ken-Ken didn't even try to stop the kid either. *Good riddance,* he thought to himself.

The girl began to panic, realizing she was alone in a gypsy cab, with a strange man, with no money.

"Mister. I don't have no money," she said nervously. "And I don't know how I'ma pay you."

"Don't worry about dat," Ken-Ken replied. "Dis one's on me."

Ken-Ken laughed to himself. He was tickled pink that the girl made the right decision. He made a U-turn and took her right back to school. This one was going to stay someone's little girl one more day.

Four years ago

Ken-Ken drove through the streets of the Bronx at breakneck speed, to his daughter's junior high school. On the way over he wondered what was so important that the school officials had to call him on his cell phone and ask him to get to the school immediately, to pick up Destiny.

I bet she's been in another fight, he thought. At least Ken-Ken knew Destiny could hold her own.

Destiny was a tomboy and from his apartment window, he had witnessed his daughter put it on more than a few boys who thought they were bad or tough.

"Kenneth Greene," he announced to a secretary in the principle's office. "I gotta call ta come pick up my daughter, Destiny Greene."

"Yes, sir, we've been expectin' you," she said. "Here's a pass. She's in the nurse's office."

"Da nurse's office? Whut'z da matter wit her?" he asked, beginning to panic. "Has she been in a fight or sumthin'?"

"No, sir, it's nothing of that nature," she said, refusing to elaborate further. "The nurse's office is down the hall, the last door on your right-hand side."

Ken-Ken grabbed the pass off the counter and in one motion shot out the door. When he arrived at the nurse's office, he found Destiny sitting on a bench. She appeared to be perfectly fine. Immediately he noticed the jacket wrapped tightly around her waist.

"Yo, Destiny whut'z da matter wit you?" he asked. "You aiight? Whut you doin' in here?"

"Daddy, calm down fa a second. It'z nuttin'. I'm fine. I just had my period today," she blurted out.

"Oh," Ken-Ken said, shocked. "How dat happen?"

Destiny gave her father a look. "You have ta ask Mother Nature. How am I suppose ta know?"

Ken-Ken stared at Destiny. It seemed like overnight, they had arrived at this moment. His baby girl was becoming a woman.

Ken-Ken swallowed hard. There was no way to avoid it now. He had to have that talk about the facts of life with Destiny.

"Go get ya things," he said. "We're goin' home."

Back at the apartment Ken-Ken sat her down and said. "Listen Destiny . . . ," he began. "Dis really ain't my cup of tea. . . . I really don't know how to say dis . . . but somebody gotta do it."

Ken-Ken felt ridiculously awkward. He paused for a moment, thinking long and hard. "Girl, you growin' up now. You gettin' older. . . . and—"

"And?" she interrupted. "And whut, Daddy? Whut you tryin' ta say?"

"And you gonna start likin' boys. And they gonna start likin' you," he said quickly. "You ain't ugly by a long shot."

"Daddy, I ain't thinkin' 'bout no boyz!" Destiny said, grimacing. "They all musky and stink."

"You might not like 'em now," Ken-Ken said firmly. "But in time all dat will change. . . . Anyway, today you officially became a woman. Dat blood you saw in ya panties wuz sumthin' called a menstrual discharge, a period. Every woman experiences dat once a month. Ta make a long story short, Destiny, now you can become pregnant! . . . When semen, which comes from a boy's penis, fertilizes da egg, which you carry . . . dat happens when a boy and girl have sex."

By now Ken-Ken was sweating bullets. It was embarrassing talking about sex to his daughter. But if he had his way, guys were going to have their work cut out dealing with his daughter. Ken-Ken was going to pull her coat to the ways of men. Bedding his daughter would not be an easy task.

In his heart Ken-Ken felt like he did the best he could, raising his daughter. Yet he couldn't help but wonder, *Is my best good enough*?

He began to feel a tinge of guilt, because he had personally turned out more than a fair share of these girls, sexually. He ran through these kinds of females like clothes, discarding them after he had had his way.

Karma is a motherfucker! he told himself.

Ken-Ken could only hope that no man would do the same to

his daughter. But in the end, whichever way it went down, Destiny's reputation was in her own hands.

Every man should have a daughter, he thought. There would be a lot less players, playboys, gigolos, and pimps in the world.

"Dad, I gotta tell you sumthin," Destiny said, interrupting his thoughts. "Nana already told me 'bout da birds and the bees."

"Whut?" Ken-Ken said, shocked. "She did? Why you ain't tell me?"

"Calm down, Daddy, it'z not dat serious," she told him. "Be easy!"

Ken-Ken couldn't stay too upset, since it was his mother who had supplied the information. Later that day, Destiny poked fun at her father's makeshift sex talk. Together they laughed over the whole thing.

This Monday turned out *to be not so bad, after all.* Ken-Ken made it through the day with little or no problems. On top of that he had made more than a few dollars. He was on his way home, driving down Walton Avenue, when he was flagged down by a group of teenage boys. His first impression of the group was they were harmless.

"A, yo cabbie! Cabbie!" someone yelled. "Yo!"

Ken-Kens first instinct was to ignore them and keep going. From previous experience he knew that groups of young kids almost always spelled trouble. They either attempted to rob cab drivers or jumped out the cab without paying their fare. Either way the cab driver took the loss.

Ken-Ken decided to give them the benefit of the doubt. He felt like if he didn't stop, he'd be no better than those racist cab drivers in midtown who didn't stop for minority youth.

Jamming on his brakes, Ken-Ken came to an abrupt stop. Through his rearview mirror he watched the group advance quickly toward the cab. They opened both passenger doors and entered.

"Where ya'll headed?" he asked, leaning into the passenger seat.

"Highbridge," one youth stated. "You know where dat's at, right?"

Ken-Ken already knew without being told what Highbridge was and where it was. He was born and raised in the Bronx. Highbridge was the name of some dangerous city housing projects. And traditionally housing projects spelled trouble, with a capital T, for anyone who wasn't a resident there, including the police. As a rule of thumb most cabbies tried to stay away from picking up fares or dropping off fares in the projects. One was bound to run into trouble sooner or later. It was just a matter of time.

At the moment Ken-Ken wasn't particularly concerned with the bad history of the projects. He was concerned with dropping off his last fare and going about his business.

"All those doors closed?" he questioned, surveying the three youth as they climbed into the back of the cab. "A light is blinking on my dashboard. Do me a favor, check the doors."

Complying with the request, the kids opened and closed the doors. Then they settled in for the ride.

"Yo, money up front," Ken-Ken suddenly demanded.

"Huh?" the Hispanic kid screamed. "It'z like dat? Whut you think, nigga's gonna rob you or sumthin? Bet if we wuz sum white muthafuckas, comin' from a Yankee game, you wouldn't ask us fa no money up front. You'd take them crackerz ta West Bubba Fuck fa next ta nuttin'!"

"Nigga, we got money!" another youth added. "Ain't nobody tryin' ta get ova on ya petty azz!"

"I swear you niggas kill me!" someone else said. "Worst than da fuckin' white man."

It was sad but true. The first kid was one hundred percent correct. Had he been a white person, no cab driver in the Bronx would have asked for money up front. That included Ken-Ken too. But the nature of the beast dictated that they do so to weed out the fare evaders from the true customers. That way no one's time was wasted and no money was lost. If someone didn't produce some cash quickly, then they weren't going anywhere. The cab drivers had a job to do and families to feed. They were like anyone else—they wanted to get paid for the service they provided. So this was their form of loss prevention.

The kids pretended to feel more offended by Ken-Ken's request than they really were. Even though they had heard that request dozens of times from other cab drivers, if they were looking for a reason to act up, they found it.

In disgust one youth balled up a ten-dollar bill and threw it up front. It took every ounce of self-restraint that Ken-Ken had to keep from jumping in the backseat and attacking the youth. Honestly, he didn't how much more of this kind of disrespectfulness he could take. But he also wasn't your average cab driver. Ken-Ken was a seasoned veteran of the streets. He had his own ways of making unruly fares respect him.

Before Ken-Ken was a hustler, thug, cab driver, or a father, he was a man first and foremost. As a man there's only so much disrespect one can tolerate before one demands respect. The youth didn't know it, but the situation could get ugly very quick. Although they had numbers, Ken-Ken had heart.

"Yo, homeboy, go up Ogden Avenue," one boy directed him. "We gotta drop somebody off."

"Yo money, my name ain't homeboy!" Ken-Ken spat.

The kid replied, "I don't know whut ya fuckin' name iz! Aiight? And personally I don't care."

Ken-Ken started to say something, but quickly thought better of it. He knew that would only add fuel to the fire. So like the wise man he was, Ken-Ken bit his tongue.

His second inclination was to put the kids out of his cab and call it a day. For some reason he didn't. Ken-Ken knew too well about the price of not playing one's vibe. It left the door open for something bad to happen.

Without saying a word, Ken-Ken did what he was told. He began to drive to his destination like a maniac. He couldn't get these disrespectful kids out of his cab fast enough. It was the end of a long day. He just wanted to make it home with no problems. Sounds of the city streets emitted through the cab as they drove in complete silence. An uneasy mood had swept though the cab, from the rowdy youth to Ken-Ken. It was a feeling he couldn't shake till he got them out of his cab.

Before long they arrived at the first destination. Ken-Ken pulled to the curb and remained silent.

"Yo, son, catch up wit you tamorrow. One!" the Hispanic kid said.

"Later, Dee," the African American kid said. "Yo, see ya azz tamorrow!" The cab door opened and closed without incident. Ken-Ken carefully pulled back into the flow of traffic. Now that there was one less occupant in the car, Ken-Ken felt more control of the situation, especially since the departed passenger seemed to be the rowdiest and the ringleader.

Ken-Ken proceeded to drive to the next destination, glancing in his rearview mirror every so often. He was just a few city blocks from dropping them off. Still, he didn't trust these kids as far as he could throw them.

Long ago he realized that his former status in the streets couldn't shield him from the young wolves. The new generation had a blatant disrespect for the older generation. They didn't care anything about who a person was. The streets have a short memory. They seemed to only recognize the work one was putting in now. So like any other cab driver he too was subject to the ill elements of the streets. Ken-Ken had come full circle, and the predator had now become the prey.

"Yo, pull ova right here!" the Hispanic kid demanded. "Right here!"

As Ken-Ken pulled to the curb, he was more focused on getting these kids out of his cab than anything else. He had a bad feeling about these two.

"You got change fa a twenty?" The Hispanic kid asked. "I hope you don't, cause dat's all we got. But if you don't . . . oh, well."

The Hispanic kid stuck a twenty-dollar bill in Ken-Ken's face. He grabbed it and proceeded to deduct the price of the fare from it.

"Here you go!" Ken-Ken quickly replied. "Ain't nuttin' in life free."

The transaction of currency had distracted Ken-Ken's attention. In one quick motion the stocky African American youth reached over the front seat and placed a pistol to his temple.

"Aiight, you know whut it iz! Don't turn dis into no homicide. Jus give up da paper and you good." The kid said.

By now the other Hispanic kid had hopped into the front set of the cab and began rifling through Ken-Ken's pocket. Inside his pants pockets he found close to three hundred dollars. Quickly he stuffed the cash in his pockets as Ken-Ken watched helplessly.

For reasons only known to him, Ken-Ken suddenly decided to put up some resistance. Maybe it was the fact that these robbers were robbing an ex-robber. Maybe his pride wouldn't allow it. Whatever the reason, Ken-Ken made his move, reaching for his assailant's gun. Quickly a brief struggle ensued. Each man tried desperately to gain control of the gun. It was a tussle only one would win. Each man fought with a desperation that came with knowing that if either of them lost the battle for the gun then surely the victor would shoot the loser. Possible kill him. The kid's friend quickly scrambled out of the front seat. He was too scared to help. Fearing he might be mistakenly shot, he scrambled out of the cab.

Boom! the weapon roared with a deadening fury.

The first shot missed its intended target, Ken-Ken's head, and shattered the windshield. Knowing he had just cheated death, Ken-Ken he held onto the barrel of the gun for dear life. But he realized that his grip was slipping the more they continued to struggle to gain control of the gun.

Meanwhile, the assailant's friend nervously watched the deadly scene unfold. His eyes darted from inside the cab to up and down the street, looking out for the police.

Suddenly the tide turned against Ken-Ken. The youth was able to snatch the gun away from him. Regaining his balance, he aimed the gun and squeezed the trigger. He let off a barrage of gunfire inside the cab. The kid was angry and scared now and he was trying to end Ken-Ken's life, because he knew if the tables had turned Ken-Ken would do the same.

Boom! Boom! the gun echoed loudly.

In a flash two shots ripped through the driver's seat. This time the bullets found their intended target and slammed into Ken-Ken's lower back. He felt that hot burning sensation as the bullets seared through his flesh. His limp body fell forward, landing on top of the steering wheel, causing the car horn to blare loudly.

The noise caused the two youth to panic. They fled the scene on foot, quickly disappearing into the projects. Fear propelled them to a safe getaway.

Destiny had just finished up her homework. She had been so engrossed in her algebra problems that she hadn't even realized what time it was. She glanced up at the digital clock on her dresser. It read 6:30 PM. Immediately her thoughts shifted to her father. He was unusually late.

Where da hell is Daddy at?

She called his cell phone repeatedly to see where he was and to ask him to pick her up something to eat on the way home. Destiny got no response.

Her gut told her something was very wrong. This was not like her father. During the week he usually was home to greet her when she came from school.

Hours later, the phone rang.

Destiny had just finished taking her shower. With the towel wrapped around her, she rushed toward her nightstand to answer it. She picked up the phone on its second ring.

"Daddy?" she anxiously spoke into the receiver.

"No, this Detective Daniel Snyder. New York City police department," a stern voice said. "Excuse me kid, is your mother at home?"

"My mother's deceased," she told him. "Why? Is sumthin' wrong? Where's my father?"

The detective went quiet on the other end of the line.

Finally he said, "Is there another adult relative around by chance that I can speak to?"

"No," she said. "There's only my grandma. And she don't live here. Why you wanna speak ta her anyway?"

Seeing that she wasn't going to get anywhere by questioning the detective, she relented and gave him the information.

"And whom am I asking to speak with?" the detective asked.

"Ms. Greene," she replied flatly.

Within minutes Destiny's worst fear was confirmed. Her grandmother called her and broke the devastating about her father's shooting. Quickly a nearby family member was dispatched to pick Destiny up and bring her to the hospital.

CHAPTER 6

Rome walked the streets of his South Bronx neighborhood as if he owned them. He was cock diesel after doing a short stint in prison for firearms possession. The justice system had become a revolving door for him. He was in and out of Riker's Island so much it was ridiculous. But it was cool with him. Prison, like the streets, made him feel like he was somebody. Now he was even bigger and badder and his swagger reflected his attitude. The first thing he did, even before going to see his mom, was hit the block to see what was popping.

It was summertime so Davidson Avenue was alive with activity, most of which was illegal. Once Rome stepped on the scene it was like all eyes were on him. For good reason too. A lot of hustlers on the block didn't trust Rome, even the ones who grew up with him. Rome was a mercenary. He would do anything to anybody, if the price was right. Rome was respected by few and feared by many. It was the only thing keeping him alive on the streets.

"A, yo, Rome!" someone called out. "Yo, right here!"

Rome turned around. Recognizing the familiar face, he walked toward the man.

"Oh, shit! Whut'z up, nigga? When you get out?" he asked. After a quick handshake the two men embraced.

Even a stranger could tell that there was love between the two. They went way back like a car seat. Juice and Rome were almost like brothers.

"Juice, whut'z good? Whut'z crackin' 'round here? Who gettin' it?"

Damn! Juice cursed to himself. *Dis nigga still on dat bullshit.*

Juice wasn't with that pickpocket, robbery, or whatever other crime Rome had in mind. There was no doubt that Rome was his man but enough was enough. Rome had been getting Juice in trouble since they were kids and he didn't want to go that route no more. The year that Rome had been away had made him realize this. He had other things to think about, like family. His girl was pregnant. There had to be more to life than the accumation of wealth or money, he thought. Now Juice even had a job as a security guard in an office building downtown. The only dilemma he now faced was explaining his new lifestyle to Rome.

"Yo, it ain't da type a party no more," Juice explained.

"Fuck dat 'pose ta mean, it ain't dat type a party?" Rome said.

"Yo, I'm sayin' since you been away shit changed," he began. "Fuckin' Giuliani and them niggas came up wit sumthin' called zero tolerance. They lockin' niggas up fa every lil thing. Niggas can't even hop da train no more. They givin' niggas bullpen therapy right in Central Bookings."

Rome barked, "Nigga, if you scared, say you scared. Ain't no fuckin' cracker gone stop me from eatin'. Word ta my mother! Nigga, I gotta have it."

Rome stared at his partner in disbelief. He couldn't believe Juice was getting soft on him. Though Juice was short, he had a heart as big as Texas. Previously, he would have been pumped up, down for whatever, whenever Rome came home. Rome was the mastermind behind their crimes, but Juice was usually right there with him. They had done a lot of dirt together, but Juice had never gone down for any of it. Whenever Rome got caught up in some botched caper, he took the rap and never snitched. So in his mind Juice owed him his undying loyalty.

"Yo, check dis out. Dem Jamaican niggas still got dat weed spot 'round da corner?" Rome asked.

"Yeah. Why?" Juice replied weakly.

"Good. We gone get them niggas tanite," he said.

"Yo, fam you gonna bag them niggas solo. I ain't wit it," Juice told him.

Anger raced through Rome's body. Rome began to breathe heavily and suddenly he was in Juice's face.

"Yo, look I ain't tryin' ta hear dat. You and *me* iz gonna run up in da spot tanite!" he said.

"I can't go," Juice said meekly. "A nigga gotta j-o-b now."

"Nigga, fuck dat job!" Rome barked. "We got moves ta make. Dat job shit iz dead."

Juice knew there was no point in arguing. Once Rome had his mind made up, it was do what he said or else. But Juice merely acted as if he was going along with the program. So he listened as Rome laid out the plan to rob the weed spot. They agreed to meet up at Rome's mother's house, where the guns were kept. From there they would proceed to rob the weed spot.

To Rome the success of the robbery hinged on Juice's participation for two reasons. First, Juice had a babyface and he was a regular weed smoker, which allowed him entrance to the apartment. The Jamaicans were very suspicious of strangers.

That night Juice was a no-show at the rendevous point. But Rome proceed with his plan anyway. Rome tried a kick-door-invasion on the drug spot, trying to force his way inside. But his poorly planned robbery attempt was met with gunfire. A brief shoot-out ensued and Rome barely escaped with his life.

Rome took Juice's absence as a sign of treason. And he sought to extract his revenge.

It was the wee hours of the morning when Juice returned home from work. Rome had been watching his coming and goings from a building across the street for a couple of days. Today Rome was hiding in the staircase leading to Juice's floor.

Juice climbed the stairs tiredly. All he could think about was getting inside his apartment and going to sleep. Maybe the lack of sleep caused him to slip but the sudden appearance of Rome startled him. Juice knew what was up the minute he spotted Rome, but he tried not to let his fear show.

"Whut'z up, you bitch ass nigga!" Rome greeted him. "Nigga, didn't I tell you ta meet me at da crib?"

"C'mon Rome, dat shit ain't 'bout nuttin," he pled. "I tried ta tell you I wuzn't wit dat no more."

"Nigga, you a fuckin' coward!" Rome told him. "I almost got killed tryin' ta bag those Jakes by myself. I don't know whut happened ta my man. But cowards like you don't deserve to live."

Rome pulled out a nine millimeter and shot Juice five times in the chest. Before Juice's body hit the floor, Rome had fled the scene.

Nobody told because they were too scared of him. The 'hood felt that if Rome could kill his friend then he could kill anybody.

Rome may have been a hustler, a thug, and a killer on the streets of New York, but when he was at home with his mother all of that got left behind. His mother was unaware of the true extent of her son's illegal activities.

Mrs.Wells was an old-fashioned woman who had had her son very late in life. Rome was her only child, so she tended to treat him like a baby. She tolerated all his trips to jail in hopes he would one day get himself together.

Mrs.Wells felt Rome's problems were all her fault. Rome came from a broken home. With no father figure or male role model he had fallen in with the wrong crowd early. He had been used by the older boys on the block to commit crimes. It had started with breaking into cars, then it quickly shifted to burglaries to drug dealing to armed robbery. Jerome Wells was truly a black boy lost.

"Jerome?" his mother gently whispered at his bedroom door.

On the other side of the door, Rome lay comfortably in bed with some freak he had met the night before. The girl gently nudged him in the ribs until he awoke. With her head, she motioned at the door.

"Jerome?" his mother whispered again.

"Yeah, ma," he said groggily.

"I'm about to leave for work," she replied. "You want something to eat before I go?"

"Naw, I'm good," he told her.

"Ok, I'm leaving then. I left you some money up on top of the TV in the living room. If you leave out this house make sure to lock up good."

"Aiight, ma," he said. "See you later."

Rome listened as her footsteps faded down the hall and the front door opened and then closed. Then and only then did Rome move a muscle. He didn't dare open his door while his mother was home. She would have had a heart attack if he knew Rome had a female up in his room. His mother was real funny when it came to that. Rome's room had always been his private sanctuary. She never violated his privacy, no matter how suspicious she was.

Since his release from jail, Rome hadn't done anything significant except for the killing. Unable to come up on some money, Rome did the next best thing. He began to relentlessly sow his wild oats with conquest after conquest of unsuspecting females. If he couldn't get any money out of a female, then he would only have sex with her once. He liked older women and young girls alike. The older women gave him money, while the younger ones he could manipulate.

"Put on ya clothes, bitch, you gotta go," Rome told the female laying next to him. "You gotta get da fuck up outta here before my momz come back."

The girl immediatedly caught an attitude, but she knew better than to complain. She jumped out of bed, gathered her clothes quickly, put them on, and headed out the door, giving it a loud slam for good measure.

Rome didn't give a damn how mad she was. Freaks like her came a dime a dozen. He should know, he had run through enough of them. Slowly Rome got out of bed and tended to his personal hygiene.

After getting himself together, Rome looked out of his bedroom window, scanning the block. It was still early. The the cast of characters hadn't assembled yet. Rome wondered what paper chase would he be on today? As he stood at the window lost in thought, suddenly a chick caught his eye. It was Destiny. Rome licked his lips. He had a thing for her. Watching her walk down the block gave Rome a hard-on.

He watched till she was out of sight. He had his mind set on locking down that young girl. Especially now that he had heard that her father had gotten shot and was now paralyzed. He seized that opportunity to be in her life on a regular basis. He routinely helped Ken-Ken and Destiny out. But now it was time to help himself.

CHAPTER 7

"C'mon, Daddy, one more!" Destiny pleaded. "You can do it! Don't give up. Yeah, there you go."

Six months had passed since Ken-Ken's senseless shooting and the police still hadn't found the two assailants. The doctors told Ken-Ken and his family how fortunate he was to have survived two bullets to his lower back. They were still lodged near his spine and couldn't be removed without causing further trauma.

The bad news was the bullets had damaged the vertebrae and nerves in his back. The doctor's diagnosis was he would be paralyzed for the rest of his life. Forever confined to his own personal hell, a wheelchair.

Even after the the lifesaving surgery Ken-Ken was constantly in and out of the hospital, battling life-threatening ailments like bed sores, despite Destiny's best efforts to care for him. Since they didn't have any insurance they had to make do the best way they knew how. Medicaid didn't provide a full-time home attendenant, so Destiny was left alone to tackle this task. Makeba came over to help as often as she could, which still wasn't enough. Her grandmother was too old to be of much use. And Destiny had too much pride to beg any of her relatives for assistance. It was now, in their time of need, that she learned the difference between good-time family members and true blood relatives. It hurt Destiny to her heart that she couldn't take care of the father who had taken such good care of her.

Destiny refused to believe that her father would be confined to a wheelchair for the rest of his life. On days when he wasn't motivated, she pushed Ken-Ken to do his rehabilitative exercises. She refused to let him get down on himself. She believed in her heart that he would walk again, but the real challenge was making him believe it.

But Ken-Ken often thought, *What comes around, goes around.* This was just God's way of repaying him for all the evil deeds he had committed in the streets.

Being stuck in a wheelchair had turned him bitter. He hated God, he hated the kids who had done this to him. He hated life. Above everything he hated to have to be so dependent upon Destiny. He had never wanted to be a burden on her.

"Aiight, Rome, let'z put him back in da chair," Destiny suggested. "Dat'z enough for the day."

Destiny had become so familiar with her father's threshold for pain, she could tell when he had reached his breaking point. Not wanting to break his spirit, she called it quits for the day.

"Ready when you are, Ma," Rome replied. "One . . . two . . . three . . . lift!"

Usually, Destiny had Makeba help her with her father's rehabilitation exercises, but lately Jerome had begun to show his face more frequently. Ken-Ken wondered what was up between him and Destiny, but he never said a word. His daughter was seventeen now. She had to learn how to handle her own affairs. He could no longer protect her from the opposite sex.

Placing his arms around their necks and taking hold of his

legs, Destiny and Rome lifted Ken-Ken up and gently placed him back into the wheelchair. Rome could have just as well performed the task by himself since Ken-Ken had lost so much weight. He was a shell of his former self.

"Thanks, Jerome," Ken-Ken told him. "Good lookin'."

"No problem, Mr. Greene. Anytime!" he replied. "You know how we do! I member when you use to look out fa me. Givin' me quarters back in da days."

Ken-Ken and Rome understood one another. He was an older boy who used to live in the building, who Ken-Ken watched grow up. Much like him, Jerome had taken to the streets at a young age, hustling, robbing, stealing, or doing whatever it takes to get ahead.

"Yo, I'll see yall later. I gotta bounce," Rome said. "Got sum BI I gotta handle."

"Aiight, Jerome, later," Destiny replied. "I'll call you."

If necessity was the mother of invention, then poverty was the catalyst for most crimes. It was the womb that birthed most criminals. Secretly, Destiny had been hustling with Rome for weeks in an effort to make ends meet. With her home situation the way it was, Destiny decided that the streets were her only course of action.

The only person other than Rome who knew about Destiny's street activities was Makeba, who promised not to breathe a word of it. When Destiny had confided in her friend what she was doing, the only thing Makeba told her was, "Be careful." Makeba was in no position to help her friend, but she sympathized with her.

Destiny knew her friend couldn't truly understand the method to her madness, but with that comment she showed Destiny that she supported her. And that meant a lot to Destiny.

Summertime in New York City was like no other place. Certain shopping districts attracted large amounts of people. In Manhattan, it was the Village, SoHo, Thirty-fourth Street, or One Hundred and Twenty-fifth Street. In Queens, it was Jamaica Avenue, and in Brooklyn it was Downtown Brooklyn. These spots were gold mines for the criminally minded.

For the residents of the Bronx, Fordham Road was one the major arteries of commerce. It boasted dozens upon dozens of legitimate businesses, everything from electronic stores to clothing to jewelry shops. This shopping district stretched for a little over a half a dozen blocks, from east to west. Directly outside of some these legitimate businesses were ghetto entrepreneurs, some pickpocketing, others robbing, and a few playing a game of chance called Three Card Molly.

The sidewalks were packed with vendors selling their goods and people going to and fro. Money was definitely out there for the taking. And Destiny was game.

"Watch da red! Red you win! Black you lose!" the dealer chanted. "Red, red you got ya bread! Black, black no money back!"

As usual, the game drew throngs of onlookers. Most of these people were eager to try their hand, test their luck at this ghetto game of chance. Everyone in the crowd speculated where the winning card was. And of course, they all thought they knew right where it was located.

"Word ta my mother, I know where da red card iz! If I had twenty dollars," someone said, "I'd get crazy paid. Word!"

If Destiny was nervous, she didn't show it. She performed before the large crowd like a seasoned veteran, cool as ice water on a hot summer's day. The cards were an extension of her hand. Her hands moved so fast that they seemed like a blur. One could never get a good long look at the card in question. It was a case of now you see it, now you don't.

Destiny was dressed in a revealing tube top that showed off her erect nipples and firm young breasts. Her skin-tight shorts left little to the imagination. Destiny was sexy and she knew it. And that was apart of her appeal. Usually gamblers were too busy trying to get a good look at her body to play close attention to the cards. It gave Destiny the edge and made her job that much easier.

Under Rome's tutelage Destiny was blossoming. She picked his brain for every ounce of information. The way of life that Rome had exposed her to was priceless, one she couldn't put a dollar sign on. If Rome didn't understand the wealth of the knowledge he possessed, Destiny did. She felt that if she successfully applied everything she was taught, then it would be a rare day when she was broke.

It was Destiny's cunning and pedigree that allowed her to succeed in the game. Along with Rome's thuggish reputation, that paved the way to her first real taste of success in the game.

With Rome by her side, Destiny fancied herself a Bonnie to his Clyde, a latter-day version of her parents. She relished the thought.

She continued to chant, "Watch da cards! Think you seen it? Put ya money down. Put up or shut up! Twenty gets ya forty. Forty gets ya eighty.... Ya'll know da deal! Money on da wood make da game go good! And money outta sight causes fights."

One overzealous onlooker eagerly jumped at the chance to win some easy money.

"I know right where dat shit at!" he bragged. "Ya'll mite az well pay me. Not now but right now! Separate minez from yourz!"

"You sure?" Destiny asked. "Are you one hundred percent positive? Cauze if you ain't don't touch dat card, sir!"

"Am I sure?" the man asked sarcastically. "Iz water wet? Iz an elephant heavy? Do a bear shit in da woods? You gotta be kiddin, right?"

"Aiight, since you put it dat way. Turn ova ya card," she suggested. "You ready, right?"

"Lil girl, I wuz born ready," he snapped. "I usta run da streets when you wuz wearin' diapers and wettin' da sheetz! Can't no new jack fool me."

Quickly the man reached for what he presumed was the winning card. As soon as he flipped the card over, his lips curled up in disgust. He couldn't believe his luck. He had picked a loser after talking all that mess. To save face, all the guy could do was walk away without saying a word.

He threw the card down and stomped off. The fact that he had been beaten out of his hard-earned cash didn't hurt him at all. But the fact that a girl did it made him mad as hell.

"Have a nice day!" Destiny called while scraping up her winnings. "Betta luck next time. Money talks, bullshit walks."

People like him didn't worry Destiny at all. She was comforted by the fact that Rome and his man Georgie, along with a host of lookouts, were nearby. They blended into the crowd, ready to pounce on any disgruntled gambler who didn't like the fact that the cards hadn't gone their way. So Destiny was able to do her thing comfortably. She knew that if anything jumped off they had her back.

In the streets you either ran game or got gamed. If you were on the receiving end of a scam, then you'd better know that there were no refunds in the streets, take it in blood. It was wise for you to take your losses and keep it moving, because it could always be worse. If one tried to go against the grain, then one could get hurt.

Destiny adapted quickly to the laws of the street and seemed to be a natural-born hustler. She took no mercy on any man, woman, or child who dared to play the game. Like death, it had no age limits or restrictions. The only thing that mattered was that the money was green. Once they placed their bets, they were all fair game.

Destiny was making a killing playing Three Card Molly. Yet she still couldn't flaunt her earnings. If she purchased expensive new things her father would only become suspicious. So she refrained because she didn't need that kind of drama in her life. She stashed most of it and tried to do a little at a time for her father.

But on Fordham Road, Destiny became a novelty act. The word had quickly spread about the pretty Three Card Molly girl with mad skills. Pretty soon, gangs of people came to see her do her thing. And that she did. She never disappointed. Destiny had her act down pat. Standing in the hot summer heat, many onlookers felt on any stage Destiny would be worth the price of admission, she was truly that entertaining. Her commentary was funny yet sarcastic and her hands moved faster than Ginsu knives.

As the day wore on, Destiny continued to attract throngs of onlookers and players as well, plus some she didn't care for like the police. They had better things to do, like arresting real hardcore criminals, so they only stopped by periodically to break up the games. As soon as they left, Destiny and company would be right back at it again. They'd just relocate a block away or sometimes come right back to the same spot.

"Watch da red! Red you win, black you lose! Red, red you got ya bread! Black, black no money back!" Destiny chanted. "Now, everybody got dat? Get it? Got it? Good! Place ya bets."

Once again she was working her magic, totally engrossed in the game. Destiny never noticed the parting of the crowd or that someone was making his way toward her.

By the time Rome detected the movement it was too late. He gritted his teeth in disgust for not spotting the problem sooner. There was nothing he could do now but watch the incident play out. He hoped for the best.

Since Ken-Ken still kept his ear to the street, he had gotten the word of a pretty, young Three Card Molly dealer. This mysterious Three Card Molly dealer sounded a lot like Destiny.

With the assistance of a close friend, he maneuvered his way toward the front of the crowd, then watched in amazement. There in the middle of the madness was his baby girl holding court. Ken-Ken's face flushed with disappointment. His worst possible dream had come true. His daughter had fallen victim to the game too.

The street life was something that Ken-Ken never wanted for his child. What kind of parent would? He wanted the world for his daughter. With him around, playing an active role in her life, he had truly believed there was nothing that Destiny couldn't be.

Ken-Ken knew that the game had too many pitfalls, too many ups and downs. It held no security for her at all. One day she would be on top of the world. The next she could be inside a jail cell or a morgue. Those were the only two assurances the game held—death or jail, pick your poison.

He wanted Destiny to graduate from high school, go to college, something that no one in his immediate family had done. He wanted to give her away, one day, when she got married. He wanted to be around when her babies had babies. Now it seemed like all his hopes and dreams were coming to a crashing end.

"Yo, c'mon man, let's go," he said to his friend. "I seen enough."

"You aiight, man?" his friend replied. "You want me to go up there and get her? Wanna say sumthin' ta her?"

"Nah, dat'z aiight," he answered. "I'll deal wit her later. I'll see her when she gets home."

Making a scene in public was never his style. Reversing in their tracks, they disappeared without even being seen by Destiny.

The front door squeaked as Destiny let herself into her apartment.

As she walked down the hallway through the silence of the apartment she thought she was alone. After being on her feet all day hustling, ducking and dodging the police, she wanted to sit down and relax. She went to the refrigerator and grabbed an ice cold soda. Then she went directly to the living room to relax and watch TV. It was Thursday evening, so *Martin* was about to come on. As she entered the living room, she was startled to find her father there.

"Dad!" she said, holding her chest. "You scared da mess out of me. Whut you doin' sittin' here all quiet and stuff?"

Immediately Destiny sensed that something was wrong with her father. She knew him too well. He never sat inside the house without some form of entertainment, the stereo or a television playing. She thought maybe he was battling another bout with depression. Ever since he got shot, Ken-Ken was never really the same, physically or mentally.

"I'm aiight," he lied. "Why, it look like somethin' wrong wit me?"

"Yeah," she replied frankly. "You look like you just lost ya best friend."

"Somethin' like dat," he said. "Grown folk bizness. I'ma grown-ass man, I'll get over it. Gotta put an "H" on my chest and handle it. Dat's life! You just gotta play da hand you wuz dealt. And hope you live long enough fa da man upstairs ta deal you a betta hand."

Seeing that her father was emotionally down in the dumps

depressed Destiny. She walked over and hugged him tightly, then gently kissed him on the forehead. To see him hurt, hurt her.

The show of emotion worked wonders on Ken-Ken's spirit. It was always good to know that the bond they shared was still intact. Still, it wasn't enough to avoid the issue.

Destiny walked over to the television and started to turn it on. But her father said, "Don't turn on dat TV yet. I wanna talk ta you."

Destiny turned to face him, looking concerned.

"Whut'z up, dad? Iz there a problem?" she asked. "Did I do sumthin wrong?"

"You can say dat," he said. "I've been feelin' a lil guilty lately. I haven't been able ta be da man dat I am, cauze of dese bullets dat are in my back."

Destiny sat on the couch. "Daddy, you ain't gotta explain nuttin' ta me. I know whut type of father and man you are. So don't go kickin' yaself or puttin' yaself down. Everything iz gonna be aiight!"

"I wish! Destiny, I wish! Look, I wuz up on Fordham Road taday... and I saw you. You wuz up on Fordham Road and Marion Avenue, playin' Three Card Molly."

"Dat—," she started to protest.

Her father raised his hand, cutting her off. Ken-Ken wasn't trying to hear it.

"Look, don't even try ta deny it," he replied. "I know whut I saw. My daughter up there playin' Three Card Molly."

Destiny's heart began to race. She had wanted to be the one to tell him, not hear about it on the streets. If she owed him anything, she owed him that.

"I know money ain't been right 'round here. Bills piling up left and right. Just because I'm in dis wheelchair, the bills ain't gonna stop comin'. Whut can you do? You gotta pay da bills. Ta live iz to make billz. See where I comin' from? Life iz just one vicious circle that all comes down ta money. Either you have it or you don't!" he said. "But all money ain't good. Dat's blood money out there in them streetz. Wit blood money there's a price ta pay. Sumtimez you pay for it now and sumtimez you pay later, but eventually you will pay." Ken-Ken shook his head.

"Destiny, dis is not da life I wanted fa you. I don't even have ta say dat, you already know how I feel. All I ever wanted fa you wuz ta have a betta life than mine. Yeah, I ran da streetz and did more than my fair share of dirt, but I did it partly outta ignorance and partly outta necessity. And now I know betta. I'm older and wiser now. If I knew then whut I know now, I probably would have done alotta thingz differently. You know me and ya mother, God bless her soul, we did our thing in da game in a whole different era. The game has changed, muthafuckas won't take their own weight no more. Everybody's tellin'. You dealin' wit a different breed of hustlers nowadays."

Ken-Ken paused for moment to collect himself. His emotions were starting to get the best of him.

"Somehow, some way you chose da game anyway. So it's my duty as a father to let you know just what you gettin' yaself into. And ta let you know if you choose to do dis, you do dis alone. There's no way in hell am I going to help you. I won't become ya rap partner or your codefendant. I'm still ya father, though, and I'll alwayz be here fa you. Regardless whut you choose or whut you become. My love iz unconditional. And you know dat. You alwayz be my daughter and I love you ta death. Ta da e-n-d! No matter whut! Dat I promise!"

Destiny listened intently to her father talk, unsure of where he was going with this speech. This was a side of him she had never seen. Out of love and respect, she listened carefully.

"Destiny, you doin' da wrong thing, fa all da right reasons.

I know you mean well, but they say, 'Da road ta hell is paved wit good intentions.' Know dat no amount of money can buy ya way in ta heaven and no amount of money can save ya azz from hell. Just like those suckers you trick out of money in Three Card Molly, in da game you win fa a little while, but eventually you gonna lose. And in da game when you lose, it either ya freedom or ya life, two of da most precious things you'll ever possess in dis world. See, I'ma keep it real wit you. Dat nigga Jerome or whoever turned you on ta da game will tell you you gonna get money, you gonna get rich. But it's more likely dat you'll go ta jail. And I don't care how much money you made, you lost! Same thing makes you laugh, makes you cry. Honestly, I'd like you ta quit, stop doin' whut you doin', but I can't make you. You damn near grown. You gotta start makin' sum decisions fa yaself. I'm not gonna be here all ya life, holdin' ya hand. You know right from wrong."

Destiny couldn't envision a life without her father. It was simply unimaginable. After all, he had been there all her life. Destiny had no reason to believe he wouldn't continue to do so.

But while she felt everything her father was saying, she didn't feel that he was being realistic. How could she just stop hustling now? The bills wouldn't just stop coming. She had found a cash cow and she was determined to milk it for everything that it was worth.

From the look in her eye, Ken-Ken knew that his daughter wasn't going to walk away from the game just because he said so. He didn't expect her to. He was just trying to warn her about the trappings of the street life. Suddenly it seemed like his role has changed. Ken-Ken went from being Destiny's crutch, her safety net in times of need, to a figurehead just doling out advice. Though he didn't like it, he had to accept it. The winds of change had blown through his household.

Ken-Ken sighed and bowed his head. After awhile he looked up at her again. "And I know you just ain't gonna walk away from da game dat easy, so let me give ya some advice.

"When you out there runnin' ya game, remember, never feel sorry fa a sucker. You can never cheat an honest man or woman, because they won't go fa da game you runnin' no matter whut you say or whut game you playin'. Always remember, neva hip a lame ta ya game. And most importantly, 'Everything ain't fa everybody.' "

That day would forever be etched in Destiny's mind. She would never forget the heart-to-heart talk they shared. But it served as a turning point in their relationship. Because of Destiny's criminal activities their close-knit relationship began to suffer. Heart-to-heart talks would become less common.

The following day, when Destiny saw Rome she told him everything that had happened between her and her father.

"Well, whut you worried about it for?" Rome asked her. "At least now he know. Why you buggin'?"

"I'm buggin' because I didn't want it to go down like dat," Destiny said. "Me and my popz iz crazy cool. He deserved betta than dat."

"OK, all dat's fine and dandy. I understand dat you got wild respect fa ya popz, but whut I'm sayin' iz, whut'z done in the dark will one day come to light. It's betta he found out now anyway. Whut'z da sense in hidin' it from him?"

Destiny could have talked to Rome till she was blue in the face and there was still no way he would ever see her side of the story. She felt like he was being insensitive. It wasn't a big deal to him at all. But to her it was.

CHAPTER 8

Now that the cat was out of the bag, Destiny saw no reason to hide her newfound riches. She transformed herself completely from an innocent victim of the ghetto, to a go-getter, a perpetrator, to a money-making machine. She didn't waste any time making a name for herself in the criminal realm. Whatever con game there was, Destiny and Rome had a part in it. They were like a one-two punch in the street.

Though Destiny was the main cog in Rome's wheel of crime, when it came to splitting the money, Destiny knew he always kept a lion's share for himself. It was Destiny's ass that was on the line most of the time, yet Rome reaped the biggest benefits. But in Rome's mind, he was entitled to a bigger piece of the pie, since he had groomed her for the game. The only reason Destiny didn't bother to complain was because whatever amount of money Rome broke her off with, it was more than she had before. She felt like Rome had saved her from an uncertain fate. Now she was making enough money to keep the bills paid and keep herself freshly dressed in the latest fashions.

Rome and Destiny were making close to ten thousand a week. That might have not been much to big-time criminals, but to these two it was more than enough. They were 'hood rich. And they spent money as fast as it came.

Ken-Ken didn't accept anything that his daughter's ill-gotten gains bought except the home attendant. He turned down countless gifts like new Jordan sneakers, big-screen televisions, and jewelry. He felt like if he accepted any of the expensive gifts from her, then it would send her the wrong signal, as if he was condoning her criminal acts. Ken-Ken was a man of principle, so that was something he would never do. It might only push his daughter to commit bigger crimes. And what if something happened to her during the process? Ken-Ken didn't want that on his conscience.

He explained, "The bills gotta get paid and I do need a home attendant, but don't do nuttin' else for me. I don't want none of ya dirty money. I still want more from you than the game has to offer."

Destiny heard her father and she didn't hear him. She was sinking deeper into the game and being blinded by all her material possessions. Now she had high-priced designer clothes by Jimmy Choo and Manolo Blahnik. But she never did away with the gold chain she had gotten from Makeba. No matter how much money she made or fine things she bought, there was no way she was going to part with that. It held too much sentimental value. Even though she now had several other gold chains of greater value, the one Makeba had given her was the one she was most proud of.

Rome knew he had a cash cow in Destiny and he wanted to keep her on lockdown. He still hadn't slept with her, though he could tell she was more than ready. He resisted the urge to sex her. Rome wasn't going to make the move until he felt the time was right. But tonight was the night he was going to mix business with pleasure.

After a long, hard week of hustling, Rome treated Destiny and Makeba to a night out. Rome pulled up to the block in a shiny burgundy Infiniti Q45. He had sweet talked his mother into renting it for him. After he picked up the girls they headed straight for the Whitestone movie theater in the Bronx. There was a blockbuster movie premiering that weekend. Rome knew there would be a lot of people out, so it was the perfect place to not only show off his newfound wealth but to flaunt his prized possession, Destiny.

"Damn this joint iz crazy crowded," Destiny said. "I hope they still got tickets left."

"Don't worry, dat movie iz showin' at three different theaters," Makeba said. "We bound to get into one of them."

Rome didn't have too much to add to their conversation. He was more concerned with his surroundings. He was dressed to impress and he had a dime piece under his arm. Nothing else seemed to matter. He had all the earmarks of a successful hustler—nice clothes, a fine girl, and a pocket full of money. Tonight he was that nigger.

After enduring the long movie line, they finally purchased their tickets. The movie turned out to be well worth the wait. Long after it was over they were still was talking about it.

From the Whitestone movie theater they went out to eat at Sammy's on City Island. They ordered the most expensive dinners on the menu. Before, during, and after dinner Rome drank heartily. He was living it up. But Makeba was alarmed. She felt if he didn't slow down, he'd be too intoxicated to drive.

Rome grimanced when she said as much. He was really feeling himself and Makeba had spoiled his mood. *Who was she to question him?* he thought.

"A, yo, check dis out, let me do my thang. You free ta leave if you don't feel comfortable. Ain't nobody wanted ya ugly ass to come along anyway," he barked.

Destiny was shocked by Rome's harsh reply.

"Rome, chill," Destiny cautioned. "Yo, dat shit ain't cool."

Makeba was crushed both by Rome's mean words and Destiny's flimsy defense of her. *Your man just disrespected me and dat'z all dat you can say?* she thought.

Makeba got up from the table and walked out of the restaurant. She couldn't stand to be in Rome's presence a minute longer. His insult had stung her more than he knew, because she had a secret crush on him.

"Yo, you didn't have to even go there wit dat. Dat shit wuz unnecessary." Destiny said.

"Yeah, whateva," Rome mumbled.

As far as Destiny was concerned she was done with the matter. She credited Rome's foul mouth to the liquor. She would smooth things out with Makeba later when everyone had a chance to cool off.

Meanwhile, outside in the parking lot, Makeba fumed. She paced back and forth till she calmed down. Still, she was too embarrassed to go back inside the restaurant.

They rode home in silence. Destiny drove. After dropping Makeba off, Destiny took Rome home.

"Yo, it's gettin' late, I'm about to go home." Destiny told him when they got inside. "I did my job, helpin' you up da stairs and in da house."

For Rome it was now or never. "Wait a minute. Follow me back here real quick. I got sumthin' I want you to see."

"Whut is it?" she insisted. "Can't it wait till tomorrow?"

"C'mon, now, stop actin' like dat," he announced. "Just follow me."

Doing as she was told, Destiny followed Rome's hulking figure down the hallway as he navigated his way through the dimly lit apartment. In no time they reached a doorway and then suddenly he made a sharp right turn into his bedroom.

"Well, where's it at? Whut you gotta show me so bad?"

"Dis." Rome said.

In one smooth motion Rome spun around and wrapped Destiny up in his arms. He pulled her close and began passionately kissing her. Things happened so fast that she didn't have time to protest. Soon it felt so good Destiny didn't want to.

In the middle of the room they stood engaging in a long French kiss. Now Destiny was completely into it. Her hands began to roam freely over Rome's upper body. Through the material of his shirt she could tell that he was in great shape. His pectoral muscles flexed repeatedly as she ran her hands over them. As she made her way down to his washboard abs his nature began to rise. Quickly Destiny gripped a handful of his manhood through the jeans.

Sensing the time was right, Rome began to undress. There was no shame in his game. Rome wasn't shy about exposing his body at all. His time spent in correctional institutions had helped him overcome any insecurity he may have had about undressing in front of people.

Destiny sat there frozen. Never in her life had she seen a man actually naked. Except for the time she and Makeba had snuck one of her father's porno tapes and watched while he was at work. Makeba seemed to get more of a thrill out of it than she did. She went so far as to ask Destiny if she could borrow some, and Destiny obliged. She always thought that underneath Makeba's nerd-like qualities was a freak.

As Rome stripped down to his birthday suit, Destiny noticed a tattoo on his chest. It read "JR" in cursive over his heart.

"You got kids?" Destiny suddenly asked. "Who's JR?"

"Nah, I ain't got no kids," Rome said. "Dat's my man. God bless da dead JR."

"Whut happened ta him?" she asked. "How he die?"

"It's a long story." he told her. "We can trap about dat later."

By now Rome was totally naked. His manhood was carelessly dangling in the air. To Destiny he look just like a porno star, big, black, and hung.

Again he pulled her close to him and began to remove her blouse.

"Wait a minute," Destiny said suddenly.

"Whut'z da problem? I do sumthin' wrong?" he asked.

"Nah, you ain't do nuttin' wrong," she quickly assured him. "I just don't want you to rip my blouse."

Hearing her response, Rome breathed a sigh of relief. He thought he had done something to hurt his own cause. He thought the party was over.

Slowly, as if stalling for time, Destiny removed her clothes, taking great care in doing so. And it wasn't because she necessarily cared about her articles of clothes. But this was her first time and she was nervous.

Laughing it off, Rome shook his head in disbelief. Quietly Destiny was taking most of the fun out of it. Rome liked to see what he was getting. He loved to admire a female's nakedness. Nicely shaped bodies like Destiny turned him on. The older he got the harder they were to come by. He would cherish every minute of this sexual encounter with Destiny.

Destiny was still a virgin. He knew he had to be patient with her. *Whatever floats ya boat!* he thought to himself.

In the middle of the room, Destiny and Rome stared each other down, like two gunslingers from the Wild West. Finally he made the first move, slowly yet deliberately. Reaching out, Rome grabbed her and pulled her close to him. His long arms lovingly embraced Destiny. Gently he began to kissing her. Inside her mouth, their tongues intertwined, doing a passionate dance.

Destiny immediately warmed up to Rome's sexual advances. She matched his high level of passion with some bottled-up aggression of her own. Her tongue found his hot mouth. She began kissing him hungrily, as if her life depended on it. Their kisses were suffocating and both of them could hardly breathe.

The foreplay was just beginning. Rome took his tongue and began to seductively lick her neck. Then he worked his way down her body, slowly undressing Destiny. His hands wandered all over her body, touching and feeling. Smoothly he reached for her jeans, loosening her belt, freeing her shapely hips.

They continued to passionately touch and kiss each other. Destiny took his manhood into her hand and began gently stroking it. Up and down, back and forth she let her hand run wild as she felt the length and the girth of his manhood.

How in the hell am I gonna handle all that? she thought. *Dis nigga iz really holdin'.*

Quickly Rome placed his hands on her hips and tugged at her jeans. With a little help from Destiny, they came off. She stepped out of her pants, kicking them to the side.

Destiny stood facing Rome in a nice black bra and panty set. The set called attention to her caramel skin tone. It was too bad her underwear wasn't sheer. Rome would have really gone wild for sure.

Rome's manhood stood at attention, his penis was rock hard. It pulsated for so long that it had begun stabbing at the air. A spurt of semen dripped from his penis onto the floor.

Quietly he hoped that he wouldn't come too fast. He wanted

Destiny's first sexual encounter to be a memorable one. He didn't want her to ever forget him. He knew if he did this right, he would always hold the advantage over her. He would have absolute control over Destiny. And that's exactly what he wanted. Whenever he said jump, she'd jump.

Finally Rome pulled her down onto his bed. Destiny tumbled on top of him, never breaking her lip lock. Only the sound of heavy breathing could be heard in the room. Through the rest of the house there was a peaceful silence.

Changing position, Rome began to run his wet tongue down Destiny's entire body, leaving a trail of saliva that led to her panties. He playfully licked at her panties. He wanted to give her a quick preview of what was to come.

On her back, Destiny closed her eyes and relaxed. She welcomed his long, warm, probing tongue. She enjoyed every minute of it. Her thighs began to quiver as Rome fumbled between her legs, touching her clitoris. Hungrily he tore her panties off till her virgin vagina was fully exposed.

Rome wasted no time burying his whole face between Destiny's thighs. The fresh scent that came from Destiny's vagina made the act of oral sex that much more enjoyable. In fact, it spurned him on, making him want her that much more. Eagerly Rome tackled his task. Pleasing Destiny really turned him on.

Destiny had frozen at the first lick. She didn't know how to react. The pleasure she was currently experiencing was mind-blowing. She began to moan. A shiver of pure passion ran up and down her spine. Forcefully she pushed his head between her legs, temporarily rendering Rome unable to breathe. He desperately gasped for air as his face was covered with a light coating of ejaculation.

"God damn!" she exclaimed. "Dis shit iz so fuckin' good!"

Never in her life had Destiny experienced something so physically pleasing. She was intoxicated with sexual gratification. Words couldn't explain this feeling. She was currently in a sexual trance, and nothing else seemed to matter. As Rome continued to work wonders with his tongue, Destiny inched closer and closer to an orgasm.

"OOOOhhhhh, *my God!*" she screamed. "I'm cumin'!"

"Cum fa daddy," he said softly.

Rome had Destiny right where he wanted her. Judging from her reactions, she was on cloud nine. He began to focus strictly on her clitoris, gently biting and sucking on it. The feeling made Destiny go wild. She furiously began to arch her back and thrust her hips in an attempt to meet his mouth. The first wave of ecstasy surged through her body. Once again he buried his face in her vagina till she climaxed.

After the first wave of ecstasy ran through her body, the second hit. Destiny felt her thigh muscles convulse. Uncontrollably she climaxed twice. During both times she closed her eyes and savored the feeling.

Just as Rome was about to enter her vagina, unprotected, Destiny quickly came to her senses.

"Plueezzze, don't go up in me raw!" she begged. "I ain't tryin' ta get pregnant or catch nuttin'."

As good as Rome made her feel sexually, it became clear he was going to penetrate her. She couldn't bear the thought of having a baby, or how disappointed her father would be in her.

What the fuck am I doin'? Rome suddenly pondered. *I can't afford ta get dis young chick pregnant. I got enough problems.*

Rome honored her request. There would be another time for that. Reaching up on his nightstand, he retrieved a handy condom. With his teeth, Rome tore into the protective wrapping, opening it. In one smooth motion, he donned the condom, unrolling it onto his penis. Now it was time to penetrate her.

Destiny lay motionless on the bed, still recovering from her trip to wonderland. Slowly Rome straddled her and began to feed the inches of his penis inside her vagina. With great care he inserted it only partially until a quarter of his penis was inside her. Immediately Destiny began to grimace in pain. She placed her hands on Rome's hips to prevent him from penetrating her all the way.

"Awww! Take it easy. You hurtin' me," she pleaded.

Destiny began to complain early and often. It was beginning to irritate and frustrate Rome. She sounded like a crybaby to him. He could never get a rhythm going. Every time he turned around she was yelling.

"Stop! Rome, take it out!" she cried. "It's killin' me!"

"C'mon, Ma. Don't do me like dat," Rome said, panting. "Work wit me."

"Stop!" Destiny shouted. "I can't take it no more!"

She shoved him off her and lay there in the dark, recovering.

Rome quickly got up and began to fumble around his room till he found his dresser drawer, flung it open, and launched a desperate search for something. He was not about to let this opportunity slip away from him like that.

After a brief search he found what he was looking for—lubricant. He took the K-Y Jelly out the drawer and carried it back with him to the bed.

"I got it, Ma. Everything gonna be aiight," he said. "A lil K-Y jelly and I'll slip right on in."

Destiny wasn't too keen on the idea of Rome trying to penetrate her again. But she didn't voice it. She lay in silence. From her position on the bed, she could hear Rome squeezing ample amounts of K-Y jelly out of the tube and applying to himself. Straddling Destiny again, Rome slowly inserted his penis inside her tight vagina. This time the results were a whole lot better.

It took some maneuvering and few oohs and aahs on Destiny's part, but finally he was all the way inside her. Rome couldn't have been happier. Destiny's vagina felt so wet and warm, wrapping around his penis like a vise.

No matter how much lubrication he used, she still was in was in a great deal of pain. Tears came to her eyes as Rome's penis began to stretch her virgin vagina to its limits.

Dis pussy nice and tight like a muthafucka, he mused. *I ain't have pussy dis good inna minute!* He couldn't believe how good it felt. Rome knew lots of girls who claimed to be virgins in an attempt to impress him. But there was no denying it, Destiny was truly a virgin. Her vagina was the real deal. Slowly Rome worked his way deeper and deeper inside her. He was careful not to hurt her. Rome knew one wrong stroke and the party was over.

Rome started slowly, till Destiny's vagina got wet. The added moisture made her vagina easier to penetrate. Finally he was able to build up his strokes into a good rhythm.

Rome was a sexaholic well versed in the art of fucking. If experience was the best teacher, then Destiny was about to get schooled. He began to place her in various positions, everything from missionary to doggy style, stroking her vagina from weird angles. He used a variety of pumps, thrusts, and strokes to reach places in Destiny's vagina she never knew existed. Rome hit spots that bought her extreme pleasure. At times, some positions hurt worse than others. To Destiny the pain never felt so good. She endured Rome's incessant grinds and strokes like a champ.

From the low, seductive moans coming from Destiny, Rome knew he was doing a good job. Though her cries of passion drove him bananas, Rome totally ignored them. He blocked out everything and focused on the beige bare walls. By doing so he went a long time without ejaculating. Time and time again Destiny climaxed. Several times he resisted the strong urge of climaxing.

After a while he was unable to control himself. The head of his penis swelled up to twice its normal size. The pressure inside the head of his penis was too great. He threatened to explode at any moment. Finally he couldn't hold it back anymore and ejaculated, filling the condom with sperm.

"Damn, dat pussy wuz da bomb!" he said. "We need ta do dat again."

Rome was so weak from the sex session that he collapsed on top of her. Destiny was too exhausted to complain. She endured the burden of his weight and lay there, totally drained.

That night they had sex over and over again. Each time it was a little bit better than the first, for both Destiny and Rome.

Sex with the Rome was off the hook, but what Destiny liked more than the physical part of their bond was that Rome listened. He listened to her hopes, her dreams, and her fears. He knew all her likes and dislikes, her favorite color, her favorite television show, her birthday. He knew when to hold her hand and when to give her space.

And with the slow deterioration of Ken-Ken's health, Rome dried her tears and slowly began to fill that void in her life. He showered her with attention when the world didn't seem to know she existed. Rome became her Rock of Gibraltar. He was Destiny's shoulder to cry on, her confidante, and her lover.

Another thing Destiny loved about Rome was his spontaneity. She loved surprises and Rome was full of them. Every day he would find some new way to show his affection for Destiny. He showered her with gifts. In the beginning it was the basics: cards, flowers, and candy. Over time the gifts became more expensive. He bought her Dolce & Gabanna, Movado, Kate Spade, fabulous jewelry like a three-carat diamond tennis bracelet, and much more. And each gift seemed to bring her closer to Rome. Best of all he hardly ever told Destiny no. Rome gave into all her whims or materialistic desires.

Rome also spoiled himself with a nice expensive gift. He bought a silver Mercedes Benz sedan, which he drove around the 'hood stunting on a daily basis.

When it came to public displays of public affection, Rome didn't falter. He proudly held hands and hugged and kissed Destiny in the street. To those other females who still wanted to get with him, he made it known that Destiny was his wifey. Rome left no room for doubt in her mind that he was her man. Her man was down for her and she was down for her man. Destiny trusted Rome with everything, from her money to her fragile emotions.

High above New York City, at the top of the Empire State Building, Rome and Destiny shared a tender moment. The trip had been Rome's idea. She had told him that although she had lived in the city all her life, she had never been to its landmarks. So here they were.

"Look over there, Destiny, there's da George Washington Bridge," he said.

"Wow! It's beautiful," she said. "Everything looks so different from up here."

The Empire State Building offered one of the most spectacular views on earth. Destiny was awestruck. She was a stranger to this side of New York. It was far less dangerous than the one Destiny had previously known.

"You know whut, Rome?" Destiny said suddenly.

"Whut?" he gently replied.

"Inna few years, afta we get our shit together, I could see myself havin' ya baby."

She had only just realized that she yearned for the security that a family could offer. She yearned for a normal life.

Her statement caught Rome off guard. Having babies was the last thing on his mind. He had other things to worry about. Still, he was flattered just the same.

"I ain't scared ta say dis to you, either. Rome, I love you. When I look at you, I don't see no one else. It's like the world don't exist. You my everythang!"

Suddenly Rome scooped Destiny into his powerful arms and kissed her passionately. At that moment they were oblivious to everyone and everything around them.

Much to their surprise, they were given a rousing round of applause. The tourists on the observation deck thought that Rome had just proposed to Destiny.

They broke apart, embarrassed.

"Oh, my God!" Destiny blushed. "These people are crazy! They're clapping for us."

Rome smiled, "Guess they know real love when they see it."

A few months later, Rome still hadn't curtailed his sheisty ways. He was still doing the least amount of work and taking the most money. For her part, Destiny pretended not to mind. In reality she did, but she justified this as paying her dues. Seemed like sex had changed everything, temporarily blinding her to what was wrong and what was right.

Then one day, while they were coming home from running some scams, Rome decided to hop the turnstile at the subway station. Wrong move. Undercover New York City transit cops arrested him. Since Jerome had prior criminal offenses on his record, they decided to send him through the system. The mayor of New York City had implemented a new get tough-on crime policy, called zero tolerance. The thinking behind it was that criminals committed small crimes on their way to committing big ones. Snared in their trap, Rome became a statistic.

Destiny watched helplessly as her man was taken away.

"Don't worry, I'll be out tanite!" he boasted. "It's a misdemeanor. A small thing ta a giant."

Unbeknownst to Rome, he had warrant pending against him for a parole violation. Somehow he had forgotten about reporting to his parole officer during his crime spree. He wouldn't be home anytime soon. Now Destiny must strike out on her own. It was sink or swim for her.

And for the first time, she would be doing it without Rome.

CHAPTER 9

With Rome locked up on a parole violation, Destiny decided to recruit Makeba as her new partner in crime. She had learned so much from her previous experience with Rome that she knew she had to be the one to call all the shots. She was never going to get rich working for somebody else. And that was her goal, to get rich or die trying. Since Destiny was aggressive by nature and Makeba submissive, it was a partnership made in heaven, or so it seemed.

Makeba was all too happy when Destiny asked her to become her new partner. She knew little or nothing about hustling, but with Rome out of the picture, she was so glad to have her friend back that she was down for whatever.

After a crash course, Makeba was more or less ready. She wasn't the ideal partner, but she was the only one Destiny had.

"Damn!" Makeba exclaimed. "Dis spot sure looks different, don't it, Des? It look way different from back in dat day when your father use to bring us down here ta see da karate flicks. Remember dat?"

"Yeah, whuteva!" Destiny replied, brushing her statement aside. "Look, let's get on our job and get dis money."

Now that she was on her own, Destiny had something to prove, mostly to herself, that she was as capable as any man. She knew she'd need another set of eyes to look out for the police, so Makeba was the logical choice. Destiny could only do so much alone. But sometimes she even wondered why she even bothered to put Makeba down. Though Makeba was book smart she lacked common sense sometimes. Her mind wandered to the wrong thing.

"Yo, Makeba stop actin' like a fuckin' tourist. Get ya mind right! We here on business," she said. "Now go stash dat in da rest room's garbage in Port Authority. Ga'head! Hurry up!"

When Destiny said to do something, Makeba hopped to it, no questions asked, like she was a flunky or something. At times that's exactly how she felt. Most times Destiny had a demeaning tone to her voice when she spoke to her.

Destiny watched as she headed in the opposite direction to do what she was told. Meanwhile, Destiny focused her attention on the sea of faces, looking for a mark. The hunt was on. She was a predator and the unsuspecting public was her prey. Forty-second Street, Times Square in particular was one of the most popular tourist attractions in all of New York City. Tens of thousands of tourist flocked there every day. They gawked at the spectacular million-dollar billboards that advertised everything from recording artists' new albums and designer clothes to exotic perfume. These signs seemed to clutter the midtown skyline. At night the neon lights lit up, creating a spectacular eye show. It was truly a marvelous sight to behold.

Underneath these very billboards Destiny placed the general public in her crosshairs. She had heard stories about the old "Forty-deuce." Back in the eighties it had been a gold mine for criminals. But that was back when "The Deuce" was filled with smoke shops, strip joints, and triple-X movie theaters. It was there that the worst of the worst converged to engage in lawlessness. Anything and everything was bound to happen on The Deuce.

The times had changed, and The Deuce had since received a much-needed facelift. All of the undesirable businesses were closed and the riffraff chased out. These businesses were replaced by more family-oriented establishments like a wax museum, restaurants like Red Lobster, the ESPN Zone, and a twenty-five-theater mega movie complex, to name a few.

Since tourism played a big part in New York City economics, police presence was now heavy. Plainclothes and uniformed officers patrolled the area night and day. Sometimes one couldn't tell who was who. City officials didn't want a repeat performance of the eighties, when Times Square was a free-for-all for criminals.

Destiny didn't care about the police. She believed that her presence would go undetected for a while. She knew there was money to be made down there and she was determined to make it. The whispers of what once was were too strong of an allure for her to ignore. To her, Forty-second Street was hers for the taking.

The only question that remained was whether she was brave enough or stupid enough to risk her life and liberty in an attempt to make a fast buck.

The search for a victim proved to be more formidable than Destiny first thought. But showing the patience of an expert fisherman, Destiny kept her fishing rod in the water and waited for a fish to bite.

All the walking up and down the streets had made Destiny hungry. She stopped at one of the hot dog stands and waited in line to buy a beef frank from the vendor. After devouring her makeshift meal, Destiny washed it down with bottle of spring water. It was now early evening, rush hour, and she hadn't come anywhere near hitting a lick. Destiny witnessed countless waves of people heading for the subway station, native New Yorkers and tourists alike. She began to feel as if she were losing money. Out of sheer desperation she stepped up her game, becoming more aggressive.

"Got dat weed!" she whispered, at any naïve face she saw. "Smoke! Marijuana! Got dat haze! Skunk! Chocolate!"

Any street name she could think of for marijuana she called it out. She only hoped that she spoke her customers' language and that they could decipher her street terminology.

"Hey, did you say something about weed?" a young white boy asked.

Quickly Destiny gave him the once-over. She looked for any signs that might blow his cover if he was a cop, like a bulge on his hip where his weapon would be. She saw none. So she proceeded with her con game.

"You ain't a cop, iz you?" she asked suspiciously.

"Are you?" he replied.

"Do I look like one?" they both replied in unison.

They both had to laugh at the timing of their response. It was like they could read each other's minds.

"Hey, dude, let's take a lil walk down one of these side blocks. I don't wanna do business all out in the open. If you know what-Imean?" she insisted. "Neva know who's watchin'?"

"Sure!" came the reply. "I don't wanna get busted."

Because the side streets were high traffic areas as well, the young white boy wasn't afraid to follow Destiny. He felt there were too many people around to get robbed. He thought a female wouldn't rob him, especially not in broad daylight. If worse came to worst he could always scream at the top of his lungs and have half the local police precinct on the scene. He knew the power of his shade of skin.

"Hey, what is your name, buddy?" Destiny asked in her "white girl" tone.

"Tommy! Tommy Taylor!" he admitted, giving her his real name. "Hey, what's yours?"

"Foxy! Foxy Brown!" Destiny said, as she fought the urge to burst out laughing in his face.

"Really? You mean like the rapper Foxy Brown?" he asked with his mouth agape.

"Oh, shit, you hearda me? I'm so embarrassed!" she went on. "I can't sell you dis weed. You're a fan. I can't do it."

"Pleeassee!" he begged. "I won't breathe a word of this to anyone, I swear."

"You promise?" she asked. "I can't."

"No! No! I promise!" he said.

"Okay, don't tell a soul. Remember you promised," she said. "Let's go in dis building's hallway."

Inside the well-lit hallway, away from prying eyes, Destiny whipped out a "real" nickel bag full of marijuana. Opening the small, clear baggie and waving it under his nose, she let him get a whiff. From the smile that spread across his face, it met his approval.

"How many you want?" she demanded.

"You wouldn't happen ta have a quarter pound on you? Would you?" he asked.

This kind of request again raised Destiny's suspicions. *What kind of kid smokes that much weed by himself?* Destiny thought. That said one or two things about him. Either he was a cop or a pothead.

"You ain't a cop, are you?" she asked again, readying herself to make an escape.

"For the hundredth time, no! My name is Tommy Taylor, I'm a twelve grader. I'm from Charleston, West Virginia. I'm here wit about four busloads of my classmates for our senior trip. That's the god's honest truth. I wouldn't lie ta you."

"Okay, okay, calm down!" she responded coolly. "I believe you. How much ya got ta spend?"

"Oh, 'round five hundred dollars," he said. "It mostly my classmates'. A few of my close buddies. I'm the only one brave enough to come out here and buy it."

Dollar signs began to dance in her head. Destiny knew this country bumpkin was as good as it got. He was ripe for the taking. She tried hard not to appear too overzealous to get her hands on his money.

"For dat I'll show you some love. I'll give you a whole half a pound. You and ya lil classmates can smoke till smoke come out yall ears," she told him.

"Wow, I guess everything I heard about New York was true. Everything costs more in the Big Apple. You know, I also heard like all the rappers are ex-drug dealers, thugs," he said.

With a blank expression on her face, Destiny stared at the stranger. She thought to herself, *White people are so fuckin' stupid. Where is this kid getting his information from,* Vibe *or* The Source *magazine*?

"You want it or whut?" she demanded. "Cause dis ain't *Deal or No Deal.* My prices are not negotiable."

"Sure, I'll take it," he said, caving into her high-pressure sales pitch.

Immediately Destiny got on her cell phone and called Makeba, who was already prepositioned in the Port Authority Bus Terminal watching the fake stash of weed. She told her exactly how much to bring and to get there with the quickness. This meant for Makeba to catch a cab before their mark has second thoughts and leaves.

The night before, Destiny had gotten some "dirt weed" from a local marijuana dealer, at a bargain-basement price. She mixed that with oregano to give it some weight. Then she processed it to bag up quarter ounces, half ounces, and ounces of weed. She left a half pound untouched. It was a good thing she did, too. Now it came in handy. Back in the hallway, the white boy was talking Destiny's ear off. Silently she wished that Makeba would hurry up before the cops stumbled across this odd couple lurking in this office building hallway.

"Hey, Foxy, you know you look shorter on TV. And a whole lot darker!" he said.

"It'z a camera trick. Don't you know da camera makes people look smaller than they actually are?"

"I thought it was the other way around. Doesn't TV make you look bigger than you actually are?" he asked.

Destiny snapped, "Listen, you heard wrong! You ever been on MTV? Aiight then!"

Just as the white boy was beginning to bombard her with all types of questions about the music industry, Makeba arrived with the stash.

"Here!" Destiny said. "Now gimme my dough!"

The white boy complied after he snuck a peek inside the book bag.

"Put dat shit away, you trying to send us ta fuckin' jail!" she warned. "Dat shit ain't a misdemeanor in New York City, buddy."

Destiny further dramatized the situation by sneaking a peek out the door to make sure the coast was clear. With her hand she silently signaled for Makeba and the white boy to exit the building. Then the girls went one way and he went the other. Had he bothered to turn around he would have seen them speed-walking to put some distance between them.

As they walked away, Destiny swore she heard the white boy talking on his cellular phone.

"Hey, dude, I just copped a half a pound from Foxy Brown. Yeah, the rapper, dude!"

On the subway home, Destiny and Makeba laughed so hard about the incident that their stomachs hurt.

Destiny ran her scams and con games to perfection all over the island of Manhattan. She met little or no resistance. She was getting over like a fat rat, too. There was nothing more she liked to do than match wits with squares, the nine-to-five types who swore they were getting over on her when it was the other way around. But by the time they found out that they had been swindled, Destiny was long gone and, more importantly, so was their money.

Some of her favorite ways of beating people out of money were selling slum jewelry as if it were the real thing. She would go to Canal Street in Lower Manhattan and buy fake gold stamped with carats of fourteen, eighteen, or twenty-four. The jewelry was so real in appearance that she would let customers scratch or burn it and it wouldn't change color, chip, or peel. Usually the jewelry went along with a sad song from her about her being from out of town, losing her all her identification, and needing the money for a bus ticket home. That usually worked hook, line, and sinker.

Destiny found out that the general public was a sucker for a sob story. If she came up with a good enough lie, they would literally shower her with big bills. So she told them exactly what they wanted to hear, perpetrating frauds left and right.

Though Destiny still lived with her father, she now began to see very little of him and conversed with Ken-Ken even less. She now relied heavily on her home attendant to take care of her father and trusted her so much that she began to think of her as part of the family.

CHAPTER 10

"Are you Mr. Greene's kin?" the doctor asked in a formal tone.

"Yeah, I'm his daughter. Now tell me, whut'z wrong wit my father?" Destiny barked.

While Destiny was out in the street hustling, the home attendant had called her and told her Ken-Ken wasn't doing well, that an ambulance was en route to take him to the hospital, and that she should meet them there.

"As you know, your father has been suffering from a severe case of bedsores as a direct result of his gunshot wounds," the doctor began. "As a result of those bedsores, Mr. Greene has contracted a condition called sepsis. It occurs when bacteria from an infected bedsore spreads to the bloodstream, thus spreading through the entire body. This causes organ failure. Which is why your father was rushed into the emergency room today suffering from a mild heart attack."

Destiny and Makeba both stared at the doctor for a few moments without saying a word.

"Is it fatal?" Makeba asked, as if she were reading her friend's mind.

"In almost half the cases in which a patient develops sepsis it's fatal," the doctor said gently.

The finality of the word "fatal" hung in the air. Destiny refused to accept it, though. She believed that her father would be home in a day or two, a week, worst-case scenario. Destiny knew all too well about hardships, suffering, and death. Unfortunately, it had become a way of life. She refused to believe it could possibly happen again. God couldn't possibly snatch another parent out of her life. Could he?

"If you would excuses me, ladies, I have another patient," the doctor said.

The sounds of the physician's shoes faded as he advanced down the long hospital corridor. Destiny helplessly watched the unimposing figure as if he was fleeing the scene of a crime and she was the only eyewitness. The bad news that he had given her had numbed Destiny.

Destiny and Makeba stood just outside her father's hospital room, contemplating what to do or say next.

"Yo, I'm goin' in ta see my dad!" Destiny suddenly said.

Without being told, Makeba automatically knew this was personal, a father-and-daughter moment. She didn't dare infringe on their privacy.

When Destiny walked into the room she was not prepared for what she was about to see. Lying motionless in the bed, in a semi-upright position, was a rail-thin man whose head suddenly looked too big for his body. It was then that she realized her father was on his deathbed.

She wondered how her father could have just withered away, right in front of her eyes, and she didn't take notice. How could she neglect the only man she loved in this way? She suddenly realized maybe she had her priorities mixed up.

Destiny cursed herself for being so selfish in the past, for not spending more time with him, for not seeing this coming. Since her inception into the game, Destiny had been in a 24-hour, 365-day grind, which kept her knee deep in the street life. It preoccupied her mind, and sometimes she totally forgot about her father.

As Destiny approached his bed, she noticed her father was hooked up to all kinds of medical monitors and machines. The soft sounds these machines emitted were the only noise in the room. They were like music to Destiny's ears and gave her hope. Destiny felt physicians don't hook up machines of life support to a dying man.

"Daddy?" she gently said, squeezing his hand. "Daddy? Daddy? It'z me, Destiny. Can you hear me?"

"Yeah, Des, I hear ya baby," he moaned. "I'm still here. I'm still alive and kickin'."

For a brief moment there was silence between them. Destiny merely raised her eyebrows and a big grin suddenly creased her lips, inviting her father to keep talking, encouraging him to keep breathing, keep fighting, keep living.

She came into the room to uplift his spirits and somehow he had uplifted hers. So far the signs were hopeful.

"Daddy, how you feelin'? You aiight?" She sat on his bed.

"I ain't so bad!" he said. "It could always be worse!"

"Daddy, don't worry, it'll be aiight," she insisted. "Dis a good hospital."

"Save it!" he interrupted. "Destiny, I'm dyin. I know it. They already told me."

Even in the weak condition that Ken-Ken was in, it would have been easy for him to simply lie to his daughter, to play along and give her hope where there was none. But that wasn't his style. He had never lied to his daughter before and he wasn't going to start now. He had always lived life on his terms. And now he was prepared to face death on the same terms, never compromising his principles. He was going to die with the same dignity that he had lived.

"Daddy, plueze don't talk like dat," she begged him. "You scarin' me right now."

Death and dying had always been Destiny's biggest fears. At times she wished she was never born so she wouldn't have to take that journey into the unknown. That's what she feared the most. Destiny didn't know if there was life after death. Or what lay in wait for her on the other side.

"Destiny, life iz what it iz. Not what we want it to be," he stated. "Death iz aparta life. I always told you when it'z my turn ta go, I won't fight it. Every man has been allotted a time on dis earth and I'm no different. I neva said I wanted ta live forever."

Destiny couldn't understand how her father could be so brave while looking death in the face. But she guessed that his bravery came from having his life on the line daily in the streets. Maybe it came from seeing so many senseless killings or being inches from death himself.

What she didn't take into account was all the pain and suffering he had been through since the shooting. At this point, Ken-Ken was thinking death had to be better than life. This couldn't be life, waking up to pain and going to sleep with it. Taking all kinds of medications that didn't work.

When will it all stop? he often wondered.

"Destiny, always remember da world iz no place fa a child! You gotta grow up and grow up quick! I raised you da best I could."

Ken-Ken refused to elaborate anymore. He held his tongue and gently shook his head. Tears began to trickle down his face. He knew the sands of time were dwindling away on his life. His only regret was that he was leaving his daughter alone in this world. He would no longer be there to protect her or to console her. Destiny would have to face the cold cruel world by herself.

Weeks after Ken-Ken's admittance into the hospital, he passed away, quietly in his sleep, from a massive heart attack. Destiny was right by his side when he passed. She wouldn't have had it any other way, either. She temporary curtailed all her street activities to ensure that she would be there for him in his time of need. Death had been a waiting game and now the wait was suddenly over. Now she could lay him to rest. Though her father was pronounced dead, there was still one final act the two had to share. This would be a testimony to the love that Ken-Ken and Destiny shared. Since this was the last time that father and daughter would ever be together, it would be her last act of love.

"Are you okay?" the mortician at the funeral home gently asked. "You sure you wanna go through wit this, young lady?"

"Positive," she responded. "I don't want anyone else doin' dis but me."

The old black man with leathery skin and sad, sunken eyes stared expressionlessly at Destiny, trying to gauge the young girl's mental state.

Could she handle it? he wondered to himself. Though she appeared to be physically fine, from his years of working as a mortician, he knew one could never tell how stable a person's mental state was when dealing with the death of a loved one. Over the course of time, he had seen some very strange things happen at his funeral home.

Destiny wanted her father to look his best, so she volunteered to braid her father's hair in cornrows one last time, just so he could look as presentable in death as he had in life.

At the entrance to the room, Destiny stood in the doorway as if she were frozen by fear. Her father's corpse lay stiff and lifeless on a cold, stainless-steel table. A thin white sheet covered his body. Underneath it he was naked as the day he was born.

Near his body were all the utensils Destiny would need to perform her task—hair grease, a large-toothed comb, and a wooden brush.

Once again, the mortician glanced over at Destiny to make sure she was doing alright. Finally he was satisfied with what he saw, a young, strong, black female. He admired the girl. She had nerves of steel. In his decades of work the man had never seen anything like this. The average person would normally be too spooked by death to even think about performing such a task, let alone going through with it. For that he took his hat off to her. Her action showed him the true power of love. She was willing to overcome anything in the name of it.

"Let me know if you need anything, young lady," the mortician said as he excused himself from the room. "I'll be in my office doing a little paperwork."

His absence gave Destiny the privacy she needed to perform her task. Destiny took off her coat, pulled up a chair, and began to do what she came to do. As she proceeded to braid her father's hair, she accidentally touched his body. Destiny couldn't help but notice how cold and hard he was. But his hair felt no different. It was as thick and nappy as it had ever been. With loving care Destiny managed to untangle his hair. Carefully she parted and greased it, then slowly she began to braid it.

She purposely took her time while performing her task because it was the last time they would physically be together. Destiny cherished every moment alone with her dad, just like she had as a child. A collage of memories rushed into her mind, and she seemed to remember things she thought were long forgotten. Flashbacks of her first step popped up in her mind. She remembered how her father had coaxed her along, the way she used to fall asleep on his chest to the sound of his heartbeat, and all the quality time the two had shared.

Before Destiny knew it, she had accomplished what she set out to do. More importantly, she hadn't shed a tear in the process. She remained strong, just like her father would have wanted her to. Now her reason for being at the funeral home was gone and it was time to go, time to re-enter the world of the living.

In her final act, Destiny lovingly placed a kiss on her father's forehead, like he had done so many times to her. Now she returned the favor. It was a small token of her love.

"I love you, Daddy," she said before turning to leave. "You did good. Rest in peace."

Word of Ken-Ken's death had spread quickly throughout the streets. As a result, hustlers, gangsters, and thugs, the underworld in general, past and present, came to the wake and funeral to pay their last respects to a fallen soldier. He was indeed well liked and beloved for his sense of fair play. The streets had lost a "good dude."

Destiny didn't know her father had been so popular. She had no idea he was so well connected. To be told how well known he was one thing. To see it was something totally different. She recognized a few young hustlers at the funeral. She had no idea they knew her father.

Though Ken-Ken had played the game, in the end the game

had played him. He died broke, like a bum on the street. Like most minorities, when Ken-Ken passed away, he left nothing for his daughter to inherit except bills, the biggest one being his funeral cost.

But thanks to Destiny's lawless ways, she had more than enough money to cover the cost. This allowed her father to keep his dignity, even in death. Destiny didn't have to call family member after family member and beg them to donate money for her father's burial costs. She was more than thankful for that since neither she nor her father really fooled with them like that.

"The Lord giveth and the Lord taketh away, the preacher intoned. Brother Kenneth Greene is in a better place now. He's departed God's green earth for that heavenly mansion in the sky. There will be no more hard times or bad times for that brother. No more pain and suffering. Only the living suffer!"

"Amen!" a woman shouted out. "Preach on! Preach on!"

In the cemetery, somewhere in New Jersey, on a bitterly cold winter day, Destiny and dozens of mourners stood huddled together over her father's casket as it was lowered into the frozen earth. Destiny blinked away a few tears as she silently said her last good-byes to a good man and a helluva dad.

As the funeral workers began to move in to do their job, friends, neighbors, and family members had already begun to quickly disperse. Some turned toward Destiny, offering their heartfelt sorrows, condolences, and words of comfort. Destiny stood there in the freezing cold taking in all their apologetic words. Unfortunately, she heard none of it.

The family gathered at her and Ken-Ken's apartment after the funeral and burial services. Some of the older women from the

Greene clan had whipped up some soul food dishes, and festivities began. All day long Destiny caught bits and pieces of conversations from well-meaning family members. It was sad to say, but not all of their comments were nice.

"Poor baby!" someone said. "She lost both her parents! That's a damn shame. She probably gonna end up just like them too, dead in the streets. Just like a common criminal."

"Girl, did you see how bad Ken-Ken looked?" another person whispered. "I don't care whut nobody say, he looked like he had the AIDS. Don't no bedsores make you shrink up like dat! He lost alotta weight. You know I ain't neva seen him wit no woman. Not since da child mother died. Wuz he gay?"

Destiny put up a brave front, enduring all the idle chitter-chatter for the sake of harmony. There were a few people she wanted to slap, just on principle. Her peaceful mood wouldn't last long, though.

After hearing the Reverend give the beautiful eulogy about family, togetherness, eternal life, and man's purpose on earth, Destiny had somewhat bought into the concept of getting to know her family. There was no bright side to losing a loved one, but Destiny viewed it like this—she lost her father but gained the family she didn't know in the process. It was all good, up until this point, but one family member stepped way out of line.

As Destiny made her way down the hallway toward the bathroom, she noticed the door to her father's room was slightly ajar. Silently she moved toward the room. Peeping inside, she saw one of her distant older cousins going through her father's closet, trying on his wardrobe. At that point she lost it, and all hell broke loose.

Totally engrossed with his thievery, the older man never heard the door open. Nor did he hear Destiny creep up on him.

Dis pair of pants should fit me, he thought. *I'm takin' alotta dis stuff. Shit Kenny don't need it no more.*

Destiny raised an empty bottle of beer she had found lying in the hallway and mercilessly brought it crashing down on his head.

"Nigga, whut da fuck you think you doin'? Huh?" she hollered.

Destiny was like a wild animal. She attacked her cousin with intent to do serious bodily harm. She took him by surprise and never relented. She landed blow after blow on the fallen figure, then began stomping him.

The ruckus in the next room drew the attention of the other family members. They came rushing into the room to break up the altercation. Much to their surprise, they found the man balled up on the floor, taking a beating. A few strong males intervened, saving the man from further embarrassment.

"All you muthafucka's get da fuck outta my house! Now!" Destiny screamed at the top of her lungs. Venom dripped from Destiny's mouth. Her disdain for her family members was clear. With that said, they exited the house and Destiny's life without even looking back. Most of them were never to be seen or heard from again.

When they left, she was alone. Only Makeba remained. Together they began to straighten up the apartment.

"Des, you aiight?" Makeba asked. "Ma, you really spazzed out!"

"I'm good," she said. "Them fuckin' triflin' niggas deserved it and more! They been stressin' me out ever since my father died. Actin' just like real fuckin' niggaz. Can I get dis? Can I have dat? These niggaz thought my father's funeral was a garage sale or sumthin'. They ain't have no fuckin' respect. Da man's grave ain't even cold yet and they hoppin' into his clothes. Oh, *hell fuckin' no!* I wouldn't give none of them niggaz a pair of socks. I'll donate all my father's clothes to Goodwill. I'm not givin' them leeches shit!"

"They foul! I'm glad you let 'em have it! How ya own fuckin' family gonna do some shit like dat? Man, niggas ain't right, I swear."

At the end of day, like always, Makeba and Destiny were together. They were side by side, to comfort and support each other.

Later that night, Destiny spent the first of many nights alone in the apartment. She felt that Makeba's presence was unnecessary. Besides it wasn't the dead who worried her. It was the living. They were the only ones capable of doing any physical harm to Destiny. On that note, she had removed her father's gun from his closet and placed it underneath her pillow, for protection. After all, she was a female, now living alone in New York City, which was no place for a single woman.

In the wee hours of the morning, Destiny suddenly was awakened by some unexplainable force. Something had gripped Destiny, rendering her unable to move. Try as she might, she was unable to break its grip. She opened her mouth to scream but not a sound came out. For minutes she lay in her bed, paralyzed by fear. She thought she was going to die. Destiny thought the grim reaper had come to take her soul too.

Her father shunned the church setting, reasoning that church people were some of the biggest hypocrites in the world. He never spoke of God, unless something tragic happened like death. He subscribed to the theory that, you only live once.

CHAPTER 11

It didn't take long for Destiny to get back on her grind. After her father's death she hit the streets with a vengeance. There was nothing that was going to hold her back. Around this time, she adopted a mantra from the street: "Life's a game like bread and meat. If I don't win then I don't eat."

"I got socks, you got feet! Whut'z up?" a hustler cried to passersby. "Two packs fa ten! Get 'em while I got 'em!"

Destiny burst out laughing when she heard the statement. She understood the money-hungry undertone of the man's wisecrack. At the ripe old age of eighteen she was every bit of the hustler he was and more. But unlike him, she wasn't stuck in that nickel-and-dime rut, the legal grind. She was scheming up different ways to get paid. With the success of each scam, Destiny climbed higher and higher up the criminal latter of success. At this point in time, life was definitely sweet.

Unfortunately, moments like these were fleeting. These same monetary gains, material ills, would one day be her downfall. It was only a matter of time.

Slowly but surely the game was changing Destiny for the worse. But she couldn't see it. She couldn't retain her innocence, her sense of fair play, while grinding daily in the struggle.

Here she was in the black man's mecca, the center of the Black Renaissance, Harlem, 125th Street. The hustle and bustle attracted all kinds of hustlers from near and far. It was there that hustlers congregated to hawk their wares. They sold everything from loose cigarettes and books to bootleg CDs and DVDs. If one had an ounce of hustle in them, 125th Street was the place to be.

Over the course of a short few years, the ethnic makeup of Harlem had changed dramatically. The process of gentrification was sweeping Harlem. Well-to-do whites were moving farther uptown because of the limited housing space in midtown. As a direct result, landlords began to raise their rents. This forced the low-income residents to relocate. But the sudden influx of cash attracted con artists galore. This was the nearest thing to the trickle-down theory the residents of Harlem would ever see.

This scent of money attracted Destiny like a bloodhound to the chase. She scouted out the area before devising a plan of attack. For days she stood around, watching, identifying the hustlers and cops alike.

Exiting the Number Four train on Lexington Avenue, Destiny and Makeba paired off into two teams, taking with them two little boys, Munch and Pop, from their neighborhood. They were the children of two local crackheads. They each went in opposite directions in search of potential victims. Destiny and Pop went to work the west side while Makeba and Munch worked the east side.

"Excuse me, how you doin' today, ma'am?" Destiny said in a proper tone. "My name is Shauna Tucker. I'm from the Seventh Avenue Baptist Church of Harlem. The church is trying to raise money for the boy's basketball team. So we're selling raffle tickets. We would appreciate it if you showed some support."

The older black woman was dressed in a beautiful peach-colored pantsuit and matching jacket, with a long set of pearls draped around her neck. She appeared to be a church-going, God-fearing woman. Seeing this, Destiny approached her.

At first the woman cast a suspicious eye at Destiny. She gave her the onceover, leery about who she gave her hard-earned money to. One could never be too sure who was on drugs these days. To her drug addicts were a crafty bunch who told some amazing lies. As a lifetime resident of Harlem, she had seen it all and heard it all. She was confident that she could spot a fraud from a mile away.

Dressed very conservatively in a white blouse, a long navy blue skirt, and flat black shoes, Destiny looked very much like the Sunday churchgoer she claimed to be. Her little partner, on the other hand, was dressed rather shabbily. The boy had on a pair of Nike Airs, cut-off jean shorts, and a holey New York Knicks jersey. His attire called attention to the fact that he was indeed one of the underprivileged youth that the church was sponsoring.

After she closely scrutinized the duo, the woman was satisfied that they represented the church. After all, this was Sunday, the Lord's day. Who would try to con her on a day like today? The woman opened up her heart and her pocketbook, seeking the Lord's blessing. She had just heard a wonderful sermon by her pastor about giving to the less fortunate.

"Chile, you're doing such a wonderful thing for the church. You know you don't see many kids your age even in church, let alone volunteering and taking donations," she said. "God bless your soul! How much are those raffle tickets anyway? And by the way, what kind of prize will I win, should I win?"

"Well, the church is raffling off a huge forty-seven-inch flat-screen TV. It's really nice, too. I think it's a Toshiba. And all we're asking is a small donation of five dollars per raffle ticket," Destiny said.

"Good God almighty!" The woman grimaced. "That's an awful lot of money for a raffle ticket. Back in my day raffle tickets were a dollar. My, times have really changed. Everything is so expensive."

Quietly Destiny began to fret. She thought she blew it by overpricing the raffle tickets. If the woman caught on to her scam she would simply move on to another lick. There was plenty of money to be made with all these tour buses coming to Harlem.

Destiny elbowed Pop. This was his cue. The boy shot the woman a pitiful look. His puppy-dog eyes seemed to beg her for a donation without his even saying a word.

"Sorry, ma'am, is that too much?" Destiny replied. "Cause if it is . . ."

"No, no, chile! It's alright! The church must be in need or the prize must be very expensive," the woman said as she dug into her purse. She removed two crisp, big-faced hundred-dollar bills, handing the money over to Destiny.

Inwardly Destiny smiled. She had gotten over again, outwitting another unsuspecting victim. Though the money wasn't a hell of a lot, it was a start. To Destiny every little bit helped.

"How many raffle tickets would you like ma'am? One, two, three?"

"Hush ya mouth, chile. Keep the money. That's my donation to the church," the woman explained. "It's the least I can do. I only regret I don't have more money to give you."

"Oh, ma'am, you're too kind," she gushed. "God bless. I'll say a prayer for you."

"You do that, chile," the woman said with a smile. "You do that. I need all the blessings I can get. I'm trying to see the Lord Jesus Christ. My lord and savior! Amen!"

With that the two parties exchanged pleasantries and parted ways.

On the east side of Harlem, Makeba caught her fair share of suckers. She was more than holding her own weight. And though she did make a great deal of money, it wouldn't compare to Destiny's take.

After hours of raping the Harlem community, Destiny and Makeba called it a day and headed back to the Bronx on the Number Four train.

Inside the comforts of Destiny's apartment, the two girls gave the young boys a hundred dollars apiece for their time and effort. The boys were more than happy with their pay. It was easy money. With it they planned to buy the latest video games. They collected their money and went on their way.

"Eighty, ninety, a gee!" Makeba counted aloud. "All tagether, dat's like twenty-seven hundred."

"Not bad!" Destiny said, nodding. "Not bad at all!"

The two longtime friends sat on opposite ends of the bed, counting and recounting their ill-gotten gain till they were sure that the count was correct.

Then Destiny reached into the pile and handed over a stack of money, which amounted to a little over eight hundred.

Makeba grabbed the stack and took a quick tally. Inwardly, she was more than disappointed. In her mind she felt like Destiny owed her more. She felt a fifty-fifty split would be fair. Makeba was getting tired of playing second fiddle to Destiny, never receiving her true props. When things went well, Destiny took all the credit. But when things went wrong, the blame was placed solely on Makeba.

Destiny, on the other hand, had personally thought up all the money-making schemes that they had participated in and made money off of. Had it not been for their so-called friendship, Destiny would have given Makeba her walking papers. She felt Makeba wasn't pulling her weight. Destiny could get just about anyone to play her position. But she felt they were already in too deep. Makeba had knowledge of her past criminal exploits and some of her future plans. She didn't want to stir any more unnecessary bad feelings between them.

Destiny, you one selfish bitch! Makeba thought to herself. *I hate ya fuckin' guts!*

A while ago, the two friends had had several heated arguments over money that nearly turned into fisticuffs. But Makeba didn't want to take on her friend in a fight. That was something she knew she couldn't win, so she just blew off the slight with a sly smile that masked her true envious feelings. Besides, earlier in the day, she had taken it upon herself to pocket a few extra hundred dollars. Makeba was determined to get hers, by any means necessary. Before she met up with Destiny, she had stopped in a McDonald's bathroom and stashed some money on her person. If Destiny wouldn't give it to her she'd simply take it. She had to even the odds.

Makeba felt she was the straw that stirred the drink. She felt her role in these cons was just as critical as Destiny's. Therefore, she deserved an even spilt. But in her heart she knew that would never happen, so since she couldn't physically beat Destiny, she decided to cheat her.

Because Makeba wasn't vocal, Destiny never knew what she was thinking. As far as Destiny was concerned, she was paying Makeba for experience, of which she had little or none. She wasn't giving Makeba a fish, she was teaching her how to fish, thus feeding her for a lifetime.

At times Makeba was placed in awkward positions and asked

to produce. She was left with one simple agenda from Destiny: don't fuck up. Destiny knew in time that Makeba would get better at committing crimes. But she would never be the catalyst or leader she was. In her book, a deer doesn't turn into a lion.

Oftentimes, during cons Makeba didn't do a convincing enough job on the "vic." Destiny would have to come to her aid, to assure that things went right. The streets were a place at times where Makeba didn't feel comfortable, where she didn't look like she belonged. Destiny used her awkwardness as the reason for the disparity in pay.

"Yo, I'm out. It's gettin late," Makeba said. "I got sumthin I gotta do at da crib."

"Aiight, see you later," Destiny replied. "Let yaself out and make sure you lock my door."

In a flash Makeba was gone. The sound of the slamming shut let Destiny know that now she was alone, free to count the loot she had hidden from Makeba.

If money was the root of all evil, it was causing an irreversible rift in their friendship. And soon it would threaten to tear them apart.

CHAPTER 12

All the time that Destiny spent apart from Rome was taking its toll on her. She was finding it hard to adjust to life without him. She had become dependent on him for everything and was used to interacting with him in some way every day. She really missed him. But at the same time Destiny noticed her lack of a social life. With all this time on her hands, she had to fill it somehow. She was going crazy sitting at home waiting on Rome's collect phone calls and his release from prison.

During a casual phone conversation, she decided to heed some advice from Makeba. She advised Destiny to live a little and enjoy her youth.

Right after that call Destiny reached back out to Makeba. She began hanging out with her on a daily basis. With the absence of Rome, Makeba became Destiny's "new" best friend again. In the process of reestablishing their bond, Destiny also recruited Makeba to be her new partner in crime.

For the first time in a long time, crime and making money wasn't the focal point of Destiny's life. Now she yearned to do some of the things her peers were doing. She began to hang out and shop. Together Destiny and Makeba began doing the things that kids their age were doing. Destiny started to enjoy the money she was making. Over the course of time she picked up a few new habits like partying, shopping for clothes, and even looking at the opposite sex.

It was a picture-perfect fall day in New York City. The weather was unseasonably warm. Destiny and Makeba found themselves in the SoHo section of lower Manhattan. This was home to all of the high-end fashion designers like Louis Vuitton, Gucci, and Prada. Destiny and Makeba frequented these stores and spent large sums of money in them as easily as they had made it. They truly shopped till they dropped, bogged down by a half a dozen bags.

"Hey, shorty, whut'z good? Can I speak to you fa minute?" A young guy said.

Destiny didn't even bother to turn around. She and Makeba kept on walking, ignoring his advances. Guys usually tried to talk to Destiny wherever and whenever they saw her. They liked what they saw. Makeba wasn't even an afterthought to them.

"Fuck you, bitch!" the guy cried out. "You ain't all dat anyway!"

Why I gotta be all dat? Destiny thought. *Just a few seconds ago you was trying to rap to me. Now I'm a bitch, huh?*

The name-calling usually happened after the guy was rejected. Usually this type of confrontation was reserved for the 'hood. Nowadays that 'hood mentality was everywhere.

"Ya mother's a bitch!" Destiny shot back. Makeba knew that was coming. There was no way in the world that Destiny was going to let anyone disrespect her verbally and not respond accordingly. The streets had raised her that way.

But the girls didn't let that hostile exchange of words ruin their day. They kept right on shopping. From there they went to Macy's department store on Thirty-fourth Street. By the time they left Macy's they had entirely too many bags of clothes to continue shopping, so they decided to hail a yellow taxi cab and go home.

Back in the Bronx, the girls relaxed at Destiny's house. They each took turns modeling the new clothes they had bought. After Makeba was finished it was Destiny's turn. She pranced about the room like a runway model. Every outfit she donned Destiny's body seemed to do it justice. The high-priced clothes enhanced her beauty. Makeba lay on the bed while Destiny strutted her stuff and was green with envy. Makeba could only wish to look this good or be that confident.

"Yo, I'm kill 'em wit dis. I'm rock dis iceberg shirt with the jeans. Bitches iz gonna be sick! I can see it now."

"Yeah, dat outfit iz fly!" Makeba admitted. "Watch somebody bite ya style, though."

"Yeah, I know." she added. "I'm often imitated, but never duplicated. I didn't know being me could be so complicated."

In response to her comment, Makeba merely smirked back at Destiny. In reality she thought the money and the high-priced clothes were going to her head. Makeba was beginning to see a side of her friend that she didn't necessarily like.

It was a Friday evening in the Bronx. Having already done their dirt for the day, Makeba and Destiny decided to go out. They were currently standing on a long line waiting to get into the local roller-skating rink. Up until now the only socializing they did was at school or with each other. Neither one of them was a social butterfly, each for different reasons.

Makeba suffered from self-esteem problems. Although she slept around, she wasn't really comfortable around the opposite sex. Most of her life she had been told that she was ugly, so she began to believe it. This left her feeling unwanted around them. Even though her clothes were now up to par, she didn't think she could compete with the other girls for the boys' attention.

In Destiny's case, her boyfriend Rome had forbidden her to go out. He kept her on lockdown. He didn't want the world to see what he had. He felt the longer he kept Destiny away from her age group the longer he could keep her. Not knowing any better, Destiny complied. But now that Rome was locked up, she began to feel the sudden urge to go out and this time Rome wasn't around to stop her.

The Skate Key roller rink was a popular weekend hangout in the Bronx. It attracted hundreds of African American and Hispanic teenagers from all over the Bronx and Harlem. It was a place to see and be seen, where boys came to check out girls and vice versa.

Tonight Destiny and Makeba had taken a day off from their life of crime, just to be regular teenagers for once. The line leading into Skate Key was long as usual. Destiny and Makeba patiently waited on it. They endured a quick search, paid their admission, and they were in. Once inside they were greeted by loud, blaring hip-hop music. Skate Key's sound system was definitely top notch. The music alone made Destiny want to have fun. "Rock, skate . . . roll, bounce . . ." some seventies or eighties R&B artist sang. The song was unknown to most of the kids. After all, they were eighties babies. Only a select few could sing along. But still, the music conveyed a message that Destiny responded to.

"Yo, I don't know about you. But I'm 'bout ta grab me a pair of skates and hit the floor," Destiny excitedly said.

"Ga'head, do ya thing." Makeba expressed. "I'll chill right here."

"Stop bein' a party pooper!" Destiny suggested. "Yo, grab a pair of skates and let's go have some fun."

Initially, Destiny hadn't come here to go skating. Not too many people did, except the hardcore skating fanatics. The majority of the kids there were into talking to the opposite sex and making fashion statements. Destiny decided to let her hair down and have fun. She didn't get too many chances to do that. She didn't care if the other females thought she was corny for doing so, either. She wasn't there to impress anyone.

"Aiight! But I haven't been skating in a long time." Makeba admitted. "So don't laugh if I bust my azz."

After exchanging their sneakers for roller skates, Destiny and Makeba locked their valuables in a locker and hit the floor. Roller-skating was like riding a bike to Destiny. She never forgot how to do it, no matter how long since she had done it. She had honed her skating skills on the potholed streets of the Bronx, so roller-skating on these smooth wooden floors was a breeze.

While Destiny glided effortlessly around the rink, Makeba stumbled along. Whenever she could she held on to the railing for support. Destiny was supportive at first of her attempts to skate. She held Makeba's hand a few times around, but when a group of cute boys passed by, she joined them.

This left Makeba open to the ridicule of other skaters. They laughed at her as she fell several times. Embarrassed, Makeba left the rink's floor, turned in her skates, and sat near the concession stand, fuming.

"I'm living the single, single life," the R&B group Cameo sang. "Single, single life."

As the song played the DJ suddenly made an announcement. "Singles only on the floor. Singles only!"

To Makeba's surprise, she spotted Destiny skating on the floor. Around and around she went without so much as looking Makeba's way. Makeba knew she saw her, too. This only infuriated her more.

Oh, you single, huh? she thought. *I bet Rome don't know.*

A few minutes went by and then the DJ made another announcement as he changed the song.

"OK, couples only on da floor. Dat's couples only!" came his booming voice.

Soon the skating rink floor was packed with people. Makeba was one of few who were excluded from the proceedings that evening. She felt like she looked left out.

If one wasn't looking for Destiny it would have been hard to spot her, but Makeba was scouring the crowd in search of her friend. And she spotted her too, skating closely with some kid. The boy was all in Destiny's ear, whispering sweet nothings.

Makeba was furious. Destiny always got chosen. She was the pick of the litter. She wished it were her.

For the rest of the evening Makeba sat in that very same spot. She only moved to use the bathroom. Her night was a disaster, and she was glad when it was over.

After the skating rink closed in the wee hours of the morning, the surrounding streets were flooded with minority youth. The police were out in numbers in order to keep the peace because over the years the skating rink had been plagued by a rash of shootings and even a few killings.

Destiny and Makeba were amongst the hundreds of kids trying to flag down a cab. They saw other cabs come and go, picking up other passengers, and were getting frustrated.

"Whut'z wrong wit you?" Destiny asked. "You been actin' kinda funny. You ain't said two words since we left Skate Key."

Makeba was caught off guard by the statement. She didn't realize her emotions were betraying her like that.

"I ain't feelin' too good!" she remarked. "My stomach hurt! I'm startin' ta cramp up. I think my period 'bout ta come. I'm tired, hungry, and sum more shit."

"Word?" Destiny replied. "I thought you wuz mad at me fa a minute there. I wuz like, whut I do ta you?"

The girls continued to be ignored by cab drivers. They were stopping only for overly aggressive customers. It seemed like they had to practically throw themselves in front of a cab in order for it to stop. Just as Destiny was losing hope and thinking about catching the subway home, a black Nissan Maxima came to a halt right in front of them. They couldn't see the occupants of the car through its smoke-black-tinted windows. When the window on the passenger side did roll down, neither Destiny nor Makeba recognized the face. It wasn't until the driver leaned over his friend on the passenger side that Destiny realized it was Ramel, the guy she had been skating with all night long.

Though Makeba didn't know him personally, she did recognize the boy from school. But Ramel didn't recognize her.

"Yo, whut'z good? Yo, you needa ride?" Ramel asked.

From the grimace on his friend's face, one could tell this stop wasn't prearranged. To him Destiny looked good, but her friend was a different story. There was no way he was going to end up keeping her company. He had already made up his mind he wasn't even going to talk to the girl or do anything to encourage her.

"Here you go!" he commented to Ramel. "I don't believe dis, dude. Whut you doin', man?"

Destiny wasn't too big on taking rides home from people she barely knew, but under the circumstances that rule went out the window. She was trying to get home just like the next person. She figured knowing the boy from school had to count for something.

"Hell, yeah!" Destiny admitted. "It'z crazy out here wit dis cab situation right now."

"Aiight!! Get in!" Ramel said. "I'll take you home."

"Son, you buggin' right now," his friend complained. "Drop me off! I ain't fuckin' wit you."

Ramel flashed him a devilish grin that let his friend know he was on a mission tonight. Ramel was trying to get into something, preferably with Destiny.

His friend, on the other hand, wanted no part of the situation. Suddenly he turned very antisocial. If Ramel was going at Destiny, he knew that he was going to end up with Makeba. And his rule of thumb was "Don't sleep with anyone you ashamed to be seen with." Because anything can happen, like a condom breaking.

Quickly Destiny and Makeba jumped into the back of the four-door car. The music was turned up so loud, they couldn't hear themselves talk.

"Yo, could you turn da music down a lil?" Destiny shouted.

Ramel responded, "Aiight, Ma. I got you."

"Yo, where you goin'?" Destiny said. "You don't even know where I live."

"Nah, I wuz gonna drop my man off first. He gotta go handle sumthin'," Ramel explained.

"Yo, whut'z ya friend's name? She real quiet back there," Ramel asked, looking through his rearview mirror. "You didn't even introduce us. Whut'z up wit dat, Destiny?"

"Oh, my bad. Her name Makeba," she told him. "Dis my peoplez."

"Yo, my man name—" Ramel began.

"None of ya fuckin' business!" his friend exclaimed. "Yo, let me out right here!"

Ramel was doing his best to keep a straight face. Still, he couldn't help it. He chuckled lightly. His friend's evil disposition was amusing to him, so much so he could hardly drive.

Everyone in the car could see that the boy was acting real funny.

Neither Makeba nor Destiny found it very amusing, though. Destiny could tell that the boy was being very disrespectful to her friend. The only reason she didn't address the issue was they needed a ride.

At the corner the kid hopped out and started walking aimlessly.

"A yo, I holla atcha tamorrow," Ramel called out.

"Fuck outta here!" came the reply.

Being that the car had stopped, Destiny got out and moved to the front passenger seat. From there she began to give Ramel directions to Makeba's block. When they arrived at her building, Makeba said her good-byes, then headed to her apartment. She had never been more embarrassed in her life.

Meanwhile, in Destiny's apartment, Ramel had managed to talk his way upstairs. He claimed it was an emergency, that he had to use the bathroom badly. If he just had to urinate Destiny would have made him do it right there in the street. But, since he drove her home, Destiny was kind enough to let him use her bathroom.

Pretending to use the bathroom, Ramel flushed the toilet a few times and sat on the commode. He even threw in a few grunts and strains for good measure. After a few minutes had elapsed, Ramel washed his hands and exited the bathroom.

"Thanks, Ma!" Ramel announced. "A nigga am't use ta blowin' up other people bathrooms but you know how nature calls."

"You gotta lotta nerve, my man. You gotta lotta nerve!" she joked. "Ain't no shame in ya game."

Ramel replied, "It be like dat sometime."

Ramel had promised to leave her apartment as soon as he finished using the bathroom. But that was just a game to get into the apartment. He really had no intention of leaving, at least not until he made a few sexual advances toward Destiny.

In an instant Ramel had made his way over to the couch. Now

he was suddenly sitting right next to Destiny. She couldn't deny there was some definite physical attraction there. Destiny had had feelings for Ramel for awhile, but the only problem was she never really saw him outside of school to tell him.

Before Destiny knew it, she was passionately kissing Ramel. To her surprise she was enjoying, too. She had a lot of built-up sexual frustration to let out. After Rome had gotten locked up, it left a void in her life, physically, mentally, and sexually. They had sex so frequently it was habit-forming.

Taking full advantage of the situation, Ramel was all over Destiny. His hands seemed to be everywhere at once. One thing led to another and before Destiny knew it, she was feeling hot and bothered. Her body overruled her head. She suddenly yearned to take it a step further.

"I want you, Ma!" Ramel whispered. "Lemme eat dat pussy."

Ramel meant every word he said. When it came to having sex, he was down for whatever. He always gave a female her way, hoping later he could get his. It was a trade-off, pure and simple.

Destiny didn't say a word. She was caught up in the rapture of the moment. Everything felt so good and she wanted to keep the good feeling going. Showing a momentary weakness, she conceded to his request.

After removing her pants, Ramel went down on Destiny. He ate her out like there was no tomorrow. He licked, sucked, and rubbed her clitoris in hopes that he would get her hot enough to let him penetrate her. Instead of being straight up and stating his intentions, Ramel sought to circumvent the system.

Hanging halfway off the couch, Destiny was going crazy. She didn't know whether she was losing her mind because of the way Ramel was eating her or because she hadn't had sex in so long. Maybe it was a little of both.

Just when Ramel thought he had her where he wanted her, Destiny came to her senses. Ramel still had his face buried in her crotch when she pushed him away.

"Whut'z wrong, Ma? Huh?" Ramel wondered.

"Nuttin'!" Destiny informed him. "But you gotta go!"

Quickly Destiny began to put on her panties and jeans. She had suddenly realized that what they were doing was wrong. Destiny knew she had violated the sanctity of her relationship with Rome. If she had thought about consequences of her act beforehand, she probably wouldn't have done it. Now she was sick with guilt.

"Yo, you can't be serious," Ramel insisted. "I know you ain't gonna do me like dat. Not afta a nigga just ate ya pussy."

"Yo, my man you got like five seconds ta bounce, 'fore I start screamin'!" Destiny coldly stated. "One, two . . ."

Instinctively Ramel wanted to punch Destiny in her face for threatening him with a rape charge. That was the worst thing a female could do to an innocent man. Ramel's reputation would forever be tarnished. He wouldn't get any respect in jail or his neighborhood.

"You stupid bitch!" he cursed on the way out the door.

"Ya mother!" Destiny spat.

When she was sure he was gone, Destiny locked the door. She began to pace her apartment floor, regretting what she had done. Her conscience was eating her alive. This was a secret Destiny desperately wanted to keep to herself, but she couldn't. Seeking the advice of her friend, she told Makeba exactly what had happened. She spared no detail. Together the two of them came to the conclusion to keep it to themselves. They decided Rome must never find out.

The next day Destiny and Makeba were out shopping again. Destiny was looking for some new clothes and Makeba was out searching for some new electronic gadget.

"Destiny, I'm ugly, ain't I?" Makeba remarked. "Look at me compared ta you! You got mad niggas sweatin' you. And ain't nobody even tryin' ta holla at me like dat. I could drop my draws fa a nigga and he'll hit it. But it seem like nobody wants to be with me fa me."

"You buggin' right now, Makeba!" Destiny commented. "Why would you even say some shit like dat?"

Destiny knew her friend suffered from low self-esteem, which was why she had always been used and abused by some more-than-willing male.

Destiny continued, "First of all, we're friends, I would neva compare myself ta you. Dat ain't cool! Dis ain't no competition! So why would you even say dat 'bout yaself, you 'ugly'! How dat sound? If you don't think highly of yourself, then who will? There's somebody fa everybody, you don't gotta play yaself."

"True," Makeba stated. "but I'm sayin' I'm tireda niggas steppin' ta da next chick or niggas hollerin' at me ta get at you."

Destiny explained, "Listen, whut you need ta do iz step up ya fuckin' game. Insteada buyin' all dat computer shit wit ya share of da loot, you should start spendin' money on yaself, start doin' more clothes shoppin'. And I ain't talk 'bout da Gap either. Spend some money on yaself, treat yaself, don't beat yaself! You ever heard that clothes make da man? Well, dat goes fa da women too! Just look at Venus and Serena Williams, they wuz busted when they came out! Member? Now look at 'em."

So, on Destiny's advice and under her supervision, they began a ghetto makeover of Makeba. They began going to trendy stores like Neiman Marcus, Nordstrom, and Saks Fifth Avenue. Suddenly Makeba went from wearing Nikes to rocking Prada. She went from urban wear to high-end European designers. With the drastic change in her wardrobe came the sudden change in her mentality. As Makeba began to build up her self-esteem, she acquired a confident swagger. The ugly moth had blossomed into a beautiful butterfly.

CHAPTER 13

Two years later

Destiny was so deep in the game that she had dropped out of high school to devote herself to hustling twenty-four/seven. Never mind that she was on course to graduate. It was all or nothing.

After years of grinding hard, Destiny had saved up enough money to move to a better apartment. She found one on a quiet, tree-lined section of the Bronx called Pelham Parkway. Makeba's parents signed the lease for Destiny's new place after the two friends concocted a story about Destiny inheriting the money from her deceased father's will. Makeba's parents gladly helped out.

Though she moved just a few miles away from her childhood home, the quality of life there was eons away from that on Davidson Avenue. For the first time in a long time Destiny felt safe, far removed from the savagery of the South Bronx streets.

Criminal activity would not be tolerated in this old Italian/Jewish neighborhood. Here the residents were even known to call the police for loud music. The noise ordinance, along with every other law, was thoroughly enforced. In the ghetto it was a known fact that cops seemed to police white neighborhoods differently from minority neighborhoods. Their response time was much quicker.

By moving, Destiny accomplished two things. First, she rid herself of the ghosts of her parents that seemed to haunt her nightly at her old apartment. At times she dreaded going home. Secondly, she now had peace of mind. Destiny didn't have to worry about would-be thieves breaking into her house and stealing some of the things she had stolen.

With her share of the illicit money, Makeba bought a used BMW, a 525I. Destiny was happy for Makeba, but wished she could do the same.

One of the biggest breaks in Makeba's hustling career would come from a missed opportunity by Destiny. Now the stage seemed to be set for a changing of the guard.

"Why you movin' way uptown ta da fuckin' white neighborhood fa?" Makeba questioned. "Whut, da 'hood ain't good enuff fa you?"

"Yo, I been in da 'hood all my fuckin' life. And dat's just how fuckin' long I've been tryin' ta get up out da muthafucka!" Destiny remarked. "Ain't nuttin' poppin' there, just muthafuckas tryin' ta pull you down wit em. I'm not gonna end up like my father and mother. Da 'hood won't be the death of me!"

"I know dat'z right!" Makeba remarked.

"It'z time fa me ta step my game up." She said. "Dis iz just aparta dat."

"Yo, Destiny, check dis shit out, I gotta power move fa us ta make. Peep dis, there's dis chick named Tracy from River Park Towers, in onna my classes, so da other day we get ta kickin it, 'bout blahzay, blahzay. Anyway, da bitch tell me 'bout some older African broad who makes checks. And how we could get on wit dat."

The years had brought about a change in more ways than one. Time had seasoned Makeba. Suddenly she wasn't this plain Jane, naïve little girl anymore. Suddenly, she was this fly, fashion-conscious, super slick chick who thought she had the game all figured out. Quite frankly, Destiny preferred the old "Keba" to the new one. At times she didn't know who she was or where she was coming from. Destiny felt Makeba was trying too hard to be something that she wasn't. And what she wasn't was a leader.

On the other hand, Makeba felt like it was her time to shine, to make her own moves with or without Destiny. Makeba had a once-in-a-life time opportunity and she was going to take it.

"Yo, I hope you ain't mention my name to dis bitch, durin' yall conversations!" Destiny barked. "Makeba, whut am I alwayz tellin' you'."

"Everything ain't fa everybody!" Makeba replied robotically. "Neva hip a lame ta ya game!"

"And our bizness ain't everybody bizness!" Destiny commented. "Niggas iz tellin' nowadays."

Silently Makeba fumed. She was tired of being brushed off or playing second fiddle to Destiny. She thought that her friend didn't and wouldn't ever recognize her as her own equal, which in her mind Makeba thought she was.

"Ain't nobody stupid. Don't worry, I neva mentioned ya name." Makeba stated. Destiny fired back, "Good! Keep it dat way!"

"I don't know 'bout you but, I'ma go fuck wit da lady. See if shit's official or not," Makeba insisted.

"You go right ahead, then. Don't be surprised if ya black azz get locked da fuck up either," Destiny commented.

"Don't worry, I got bail money," Makeba sarcastically remarked.

For now Destiny washed her hands of the situation. She would say no more about it. If Makeba wanted to risk her freedom, let her go right ahead. Still, she couldn't figure out why her friend would want to deviate from the plan this late in the game. It had always worked out well when she led and Makeba followed. If Destiny wasn't in control of the situation, she rarely wanted to be involved in the crime. That's just how she was. If she was going to take a fall, let it be from a mistake she made, not someone else's, she reasoned.

"Anyway," Makeba said, changing subjects, "Ya nigga Rome be home any day now, huh?"

"Yeah, his azz finally comin' home!" Destiny said. "I can't wait ta see my baby. Afta all these letters, collect calls, and visits, he finally comin' home. No parole or nuttin'."

"I know dat nigga gonna be all diesel and shit wit his fine self," Makeba gushed. "Shit, dat nigga dick game gonna be bananas afta all these years. He gonna tear dat pussy up! Wish it wuz me."

As soon as the words left Makeba's mouth, she realized what a mistake she'd made.

"Bitch, whut da fuck dat'z suppose ta mean?" Destiny snapped.

"Yo, you buggin'. Takin' it da wrong way," she countered. "I didn't mean it like dat. My bad! It'z not how it sounded."

Destiny wondered, *Where did that come from?*

She started to delve even deeper into Makeba's choice of words, then let it go. But she made a mental note to keep a closer eye on Makeba. Her friend had definitely changed, for the worse. Destiny couldn't help but wonder what role she played in creating that monster.

Destiny tossed and turned in her sleep all night long. She was never quite able to get comfortable enough to fall into that deep sleep Finally, she stopped even trying. How could she when she was having anxiety attack? The only man she'd ever been with, in all her years on this earth, was coming home today. He was coming to her. While Rome was locked up, Destiny had continued to divide up the money from her scams as if he were there. Only the money was spilt, equally. She did so partially out of gratitude. After all, he did put Destiny on to her current way of life. The other reason was, she was madly in love with him.

All those jailhouse love letters had worked wonders on her. In those letters, Rome had pledged his undying love for Destiny. And he had promised to straighten up and fly right, once he got out, if she promised to stay loyal to him. Destiny had more than lived up to her end of the deal. The question was, would Rome hold up his? Still, Destiny didn't doubt him for one second.

Slowly the sun began to rise and the living with it. Destiny began to hear the sounds of city buses going to and fro. Car engines roared to life and school buses could be heard as they passed. Morning turned to afternoon with no sign of Rome. Soon evening came and he still hadn't show up.

The slightest sound she heard inside her apartment made her run to the door. Each time she fully expected to see Rome's face; each time she was disappointed. Finally, Destiny had had enough of walking on eggshells all day and she sat down at the computer to get to the bottom of this.

Destiny was living in the information age. Anything she wanted to know, she knew the answers were right at her fingertips. The days of an inmate lying about his release date were over. She logged on to www.inmatelocator.com and then went to the Web site for the New York State Bureau of Prisons. She punched Rome's government name into the computer, along with his prison identification number. Within seconds the screen told her what she already knew. It read: Jerome Wells *released.*

Then where the fuck is he? she thought. Still, she wanted to give him the benefit of the doubt. If she was in his shoes, she would want the same. She would wait until tomorrow before she started making any phone calls trying to locate his whereabouts. That night Destiny ran through a gamut of emotions, from loving Rome to hating him, from worried sick to not even caring. But in the end, she couldn't deny her true feelings for him. She was in love with Rome. Destiny's day ended just as it had begun—stressed out.

She couldn't remember when or how she got to sleep. But somehow she did.

The next morning, Destiny's sleep was rudely interrupted by some loud pounding on the door. Still half drowsy from burning the midnight oil, Destiny stumbled to the front door. Her heart damn near stopped when she saw who was on the other side of the peephole. It was Rome.

"Yo, you gonna let me in or whut?" he playfully asked. "Is dis da right house?"

In an instant the locks were unfastened. Destiny threw the door open and stood there with a perplexed look on her face. It was clear she had an attitude.

Meanwhile, Rome stood in the hallway, flashing a killer megawatt smile that revealed two rows of straight white teeth. His body was buffed up from excessive weight-lifting in the prison yard. He was in the best shape Destiny had ever seen him in. But it would take more than a pretty smile and a nice build to get him out of the hot water he was in.

For a brief moment they stood staring each other down. Rome gave Destiny's body long, lustful looks. Her body had filled out fully. Destiny had an hourglass shape that clung to the material of her blue tericloth robe. In Rome's opinion father time had definitely blessed Destiny with a body to die for.

"Nigga, where da fuck you been?" Destiny spat. "I wuz waitin' all nite fa ya fuckin azz ta show up!"

"Here you go," he coolly replied. "Where da fuck iz da love at? Whut happened ta all dat love you had fa me in them letters? Huh? C'mon, Ma, you ain't even give a nigga a chance to explain. Damn, hear me out first. Cauze one day you might want it. Word!"

His words seemed to have a calming effect on Destiny and relaxed a little. Suddenly she moved from the doorway and allowed Rome to enter.

Following her lead, Rome walked in behind her and closed the door. Inwardly he smiled to himself. Rome knew if he just got Destiny to listen long enough while he ran his game, then everything would be okay. He didn't know exactly what he would say next, but he figured he would improvise.

"Yo, where wuz you at? How come you ain't come here yesterday? Huh?" she questioned. "I went on da computer, so I know you got released yesterday!"

"Yo, I ain't even gonna lie," he began. "I did get released yesterday! But not when you think. Them crackers fucked up my paperwork. They wuz claimin' dat I had a fuckin' detainer on me. Come ta find out it wuzn't me. By da time they got dat straightened out, all da fuckin' buses were gone. I had ta sit in some fuckin' hick town, all da fuckin' day, till da wee hours of da mornin', till a Greyhound bus came and brung me ta da city."

"So, wuz dis ya first stop? Or you went to go see onna ya jumpoffs first?" she demanded.

"A, yo, ga'head wit da bullshit!" he suggested. "A nigga ain't even thinkin' 'bout no fuckin' jumpoffs. I went ta go see Ma Dukes first. No disrespect but dat's my momz. If I did anything else, I'd be outta line."

Rome was lying his ass off, but Destiny seemed to be buying it. He couldn't believe how easily she fell for his game. Rome ran game all day every day, from the streets to prison. He was fond of saying, "I got game for days" so much so he didn't know when to turn it on or off. He didn't know how or when to be honest, even with himself.

Hearing her boyfriend's explanation relaxed Destiny. It eased her all the fears she had of him being with another woman. She couldn't bear the thought because she had sacrificed time out of her life to be with him. He wasn't the only one locked up. She did time right along with him.

"I'm sorry," she apologized. "But you gotta understand my position, nigga. You ain't here when you suppose to be. So naturally I'm goin' think sumthin funny. You been locked up a minute, too. You probably fiendin' fa some ass."

Rome didn't even bother to reply to her latest comments. He simply just let her vent. He sat there taking the admonishment like a man.

"Yo, I'm hungry!" he exclaimed.

"You hungry?" Destiny suddenly asked. "Gimme a minute and I'll hook you up sumthin' right quick."

"Nah, Ma, dat ain't whut I'm hungry for." He smiled.

At that moment the last thing on Rome's mind was food. He yearned for Destiny's body. His eyes hungrily roved every inch of it, as if he would devour her at any minute.

"C'mere, Ma," he commanded. "Let me show you all dat good shit I wuz tellin' you in my letters."

It was amazing how quickly Destiny's harsh sentiments and ill feelings disappeared. Now she was wrapped in her man's strong embrace and nothing else seemed to matter. This was the moment she had lived for all those long months and lonely nights she endured while he was in prison. The animalistic sex they were about to have was the culmination of all that.

Rome threw Destiny up against the wall, pressing his pulsating penis against her private parts. Like two snakes mating, their tongues intertwined, doing a strange sensual dance inside their mouths. This only heightened their sexual expectations.

With his free hand, Rome explored the inside of Destiny's robe. Quickly he ran his hand up and down her leg until he found her vagina. He then pressed his index finger against the flimsy material that made up her underwear till he discovered her clitoris. Sticking his hand inside her underwear, Rome rubbed on it furiously. Destiny moaned ever so slightly from the pleasure she was receiving.

Finally Rome broke the viselike grip he had on her mouth. In one smooth motion he dropped straight to his knees and began savagely tearing at Destiny's underwear. Not wanting him to ruin a good pair of panties, she assisted him in taking them off. Rome's tongue began to flick in and out of his mouth nonstop, licking Destiny's clitoris. She was so responsive to the oral sex she received, Destiny grabbed the back of his head and buried into her vagina. This only excited Rome more, encouraging him to keep up his feverish pace.

Destiny was in a complete sex trance. She began licking her lips and fondling her breasts. Suddenly her knees buckled. She was standing on spaghetti legs as she climaxed in Rome's mouth. He willing lapped up her love juices as they drenched his mustache and beard. Destiny was in a sexual utopia. She had orgasm after orgasm. When one ended another quickly began.

"Fuck me!" Destiny begged.

The statement was music to Rome's ears. His penis ached with anticipation. Getting up off his knees, he quickly stripped himself of his clothes while Destiny took off her robe. When they were done there were clothing items and undergarments everywhere.

Taking Rome's hand, Destiny attempted to lead him to the bedroom. But it was a trip they would never make. Rome manhandled her, wrestling Destiny to the floor. On the plush dark blue carpet, Rome began to take control. Straddling her from behind, Rome put Destiny in a doggy-style sexual position. He began slapping her playfully on the behind, watching it jiggle, as he entered her vagina. Her warmth and wetness was inviting to Rome. He swore to himself that he had never had any pussy this good. From this position he watched as Destiny's butt cheeks shimmered with each thrust of his hips.

"Throw dat ass back at me!" Rome spat. "Show how much you missed me."

Destiny did just that. She began bucking her hips wildly and bouncing her butt off Rome's pelvic area. Meanwhile, he drove his penis ruthlessly inside her vagina, pounding away. Sweat began flying off their bodies, as if they were exercising.

Wild grunts and moans could be heard from the couple. The head of Rome's penis began to swell. He could no longer contain himself. Faster and faster he pumped his hips till he exploded inside Destiny. In tune with his body, she began to shake uncontrollably, climaxing along with him.

The two lovers crumpled right there onto the floor. For a few minutes they were unable to move. They both savored the hot sex, committing their recent act to memory. It was truly unforgettable for both parties.

All day long Destiny and Rome had sex, in strange places, on countertops, behind the couch, and in weird positions. For the next few weeks this went on. The couple had unprotected sex without giving the consequences a second thought.

While Destiny was in her own little world of domestic bliss, Makeba was hustling hard. Finally she had gotten away from Destiny's control and she was making the most of it.

First Makeba started out bouncing checks here and there, before she realized that that was a sure way to go to jail. It didn't take long for her to hook up with her classmate, Tracy.

Tracy took Makeba to meet a middle-aged African lady in Yonkers, New York. The lady told Makeba what to do. First she instructed her to report to the Department of Motor Vehicles that her driver's license was lost, so she could receive another. Then she successfully altered her new license, changing some critical personal information on it. Then the lady began making out bogus checks to Makeba.

It didn't take long for Makeba to start doing her thing in department stores. The naïveté Makeba had about her now worked in her favor. The cashiers never suspected any fraud on Makeba's part. They never saw the wolf in sheep's clothing coming.

Makeba met little resistance, and as a direct result she was able to surpass Destiny in the amount of money she made off each caper. Makeba began feeling herself. Nobody could tell her anything, least of all Destiny. She was the shit and she knew it.

As a way of paying back the African woman, Makeba would get her gift cards of the largest monetary value she could find. For some reason the woman had a strange feeling the police would be closing in on her soon, due to the vast number of young girls she had working the streets. All of them didn't share the same good fortune Makeba had. Quite a few young girls had recently gotten popped in different parts of the city. In light of that, the lady informed all parties involved that she was shutting down and going on the "down low."

The woman had taken a liking to Makeba, because in the short time they did business Makeba had become one of her top money-makers. So in hopes of some day hooking up with her again, the African woman told her how and what she did. She instructed Makeba on which computer programs to buy, what kind of printer, and what type of paper she would need to pull this hustle off. Makeba's book smarts had finally come in handy in the streets. She was now able to use her math skills and working knowledge of the computer to her advantage.

The rest was history. Makeba began making her own checks and recruiting her own criminal team to bust them for her, with the spilt being sixty-forty her way.

With her newfound wealth, Makeba began to step up her game to a whole new level. She was 'hood rich and proud of it. She began dressing better and living better. She finally left her parents' house and moved into a townhouse in Teaneck, New Jersey.

Now that she was an established player in the game, Makeba noticed something very strange. People began to treat her differently. Suddenly she was what's poppin' in the 'hood. Chicks who used to look down on her were now looking up to her. Dudes who wouldn't give her the time of day now were trying to holler at her. Now that she was making money, everything seemed to be better, life was better, the water was colder, and the money was greener.

Seemingly overnight she was thrust into a position of power. Makeba went from just another face in the crowd to a star in the 'hood. With the death of the drug game, Makeba was at the forefront of a new money-making machine. Guys and girls alike were dying to "eat" with her. Law enforcement authorities had made hustling on the street too difficult. Suddenly the risks were high and the rewards were low. The 'hood had finally picked up on what white America had known all along, that white-collar crimes were the way to go. These crimes yielded high rewards for minimal work.

Soon she began to abuse her power, too. She began sending the females she didn't particularly like on the riskiest missions in some of the hottest spots. To her these people were nothing but leeches. They were expendable. If they got caught, then she wouldn't even waste her money bailing them out, because there were more where they came from. As a matter of fact, Makeba had an endless supply of flunkies.

For the guys who thought they were too cute before, Makeba had a trick for them, too. She would have casual sex with them, with the promise of getting some money together later. It was an empty promise because she never followed through. She was smart enough to see they were just using her. In the process of using them, Makeba became a nymphomaniac. She dogged guys out and then changed her phone number, just like they had done to her.

Makeba became a tyrant. She actively sought out anyone who had ever offended her, whether it was real or imagined. The success she was enjoying hadn't made her this way. It merely exposed her real self, revealed it just like a truth serum. And the funny thing was, she liked the new Makeba.

One would think, with all the monetary success she was having and the revenge she was extracting, that Makeba was happy. But she wasn't.

CHAPTER 14

For the first few months of Rome's release from prison, Destiny was totally happy. Finally she was reunited with the man she loved. The void that had formed in her life while he was away had now been filled. The bitterness she felt toward the world and life in general after her father's death had been replaced with hope and happiness. Rome was beginning to define Destiny's happiness and she didn't even know it.

Recently some of the happiest moments of her life were shared with Rome. It seemed like she couldn't eat or sleep right unless he was somewhere in the vicinity. Unfortunately for her, Rome had begun to show his true colors. He started becoming quite promiscuous, "creeping" with other females. This led to more time being spent away from Destiny. His mind became more preoccupied with each of his sexual conquests. He began to neglect home base, coming in later and later, then some nights not at all. As a result the arguments began, then became early and often.

"Nigga, where da fuck you been?" Destiny shouted.

Rome calmly strolled through the apartment, completely ignoring Destiny. He found this to be a more effective tool than engaging in a heated argument. But sometimes this method didn't work. Destiny left him no choice but to confront the issue. And today was one of those days.

She continued, "Muthafucka, I know you fuckin', hear me?"

"A, yo, how many fuckin' times I gotta tell you I wuz out grindin'?" He barked. "I'ma grown-azz man! I ain't use to explainin' myself ta nobody."

Rome wasn't used to being questioned by a woman. In his house, he wore the pants and called all the shots. It was a dictatorship not a democracy. He was used to coming and going as he pleased. What he did wasn't open for discussion, plain and simple.

The only problem with that picture was, Destiny paid all the bills in this household. She took care of Rome's broke, jobless, nonhustling ass. Out of respect for that he bit his tongue and ran his game. But lately he had been running it into the ground. His game was getting old, quick.

"Since you wuz grindin' all nite, show me a few dollars and I'll leave it alone." Destiny explained.

This request threw Rome for a loop. He didn't have a dollar to his name. As a matter a fact, he was just about to ask Destiny for a few dollars until she began talking all crazy.

"Man, listen, I ain't got time fa ya muthafuckin' games. I'ma grown-ass man. Destiny, I done been there before with another crazy-ass bitch. If I shown you some dough, whut'z it gonna prove? Taday it'z dis, tomorrow it'll be sumthin' else. So, nah, I ain't showin' you shit. You gotta calm ya nerves sum other fuckin' way!" he growled.

Rome hoped his lame explanation was enough to quiet Destiny. He had never in his life seen a broad who was so worried about his whereabouts.

He added, "You need a fuckin' hobby or sumthin'? Stop watchin' me and watch some TV. Damn! I ain't neva seen no shit like dis in my fuckin' life."

His last comment infuriated Destiny. She exploded into a tirade.

"Oh, nigga, you got da game fucked up now!" She spat. "Nigga, I'm da one holdin' dis household down. You ain't contributin' shit. If anything you take away from dis household, stressin' me da fuck out and shit! Ya da one dat needs a job. You can't even hustle right. When you do come up on a jooks, you spend all of da money on god knows what? I'm startin' think ya azz on fuckin' crack or sumthin'. Nigga, where da fuck iz all ya dough? You stay in da street till all hours of da night and never got nuttin' ta show fa it! Huh? And you call yourself a hustler?"

Destiny's verbal attack ripped right into Rome's thin skin. He couldn't take her challenging his manhood, even though she was 100 percent correct. Rome's blood boiled from her vicious comments.

Without warning it happened. Rome quickly brought up an open hand and smacked the shit out of Destiny. The blow caught Destiny off guard, causing her to stumble against the wall.

Quickly she shook off the stunning force of the blow and went on the offensive. She came back at Rome, something he hadn't expected, with a flurry of blows. The first blow grazed his face. He was able to successfully ward off the other punches with a series of blocks, bobs, and weaves. Rome was good with his hands. He could hold his own with just about anybody in the street. This fight could have been over at any moment had he really wanted to end it, and though Destiny could fight, she was no match for a man, especially Rome.

As Destiny attacked Rome, she began to look around the apartment for something to hit him with. She really wanted to hurt him. She wanted to scar him so he would never again put his hands on her. Fortunately for Rome, they were fighting in the hallway, so there weren't any household fixtures she could hit him with. Rome simply backpedaled and let her continue to throw blows till she got tired out. Then he grabbed her, holding her arms so she wouldn't strike him.

"Nigga, I'ma kill ya fuckin' azz! I don't believe you just hit me. My father neva even fuckin' hit me!" she cursed.

"Shut up!" he playfully said. "You gonna kill nuttin' or see nuttin' die! You ain't tuff."

"Nigga, lemme go and we'll see! Lemme go!" she ordered.

Rome decided to play it safe. He continued to hold her as if his life depended on it. After awhile Destiny saw it was useless to struggle against his brute force, so she simply relaxed till her body went limp in his arms. Sensing that her anger had subsided, he loosened his tight grip. Like a caged animal Destiny tried to attack him again. Once again he subdued her.

"A, yo, c'mon now, Ma. Cut da crap!" he suggested. "It'z ova already. Take it as a loss."

"It ain't neva gonna be ova, nigga! Not till I bust ya shit!" she fired back.

Quickly Rome decided to try another tactic. As Destiny spoke he stuck his tongue down her throat and began kissing her.

Destiny's first response was to clamp down on his tongue with her teeth. While she held on to a pit bull–like lock on his tongue, Rome shrieked in pain. He regretted even attempting to smooth things over with a kiss. Suddenly Destiny let go of his tongue and began to passionately kiss Rome. Before they knew it they had stripped off their clothes and engaged in animalistic sex. Then came two sudden knocks on the door. From the pattern of the knocking, Rome knew it was the police. He could feel it in his bones. The couple looked at each other, puzzled, as if to say "Who da fuck iz dat?" Quickly they began to gather up their garments, knowing the answer to the question.

"Who iz it?" Destiny called out.

"Open the door ma'am, it's the police," a voice replied from the other side of the door.

Destiny desperately tried to make herself look presentable as she made her way toward the door. She straightened out her clothes and fixed her hair. Meanwhile, Rome hurriedly pulled up his pants.

Destiny opened the door Two white officers stared her in the face. One officer began to speak while the other scoured the immediate vicinity for anything illegal or any signs of a scuffle.

"Ma'am, we received several complaints saying there were loud noises coming from this apartment, possibly a domestic dispute. Is there a problem?" he asked.

"No sir!" Destiny stated. "I don't know whut you're talkin' about. Me and my boyfriend just walked in da door a few minute before you arrived. Ya'll must have da wrong apartment, officer."

Like most minorities, Destiny was distrustful of the police. Where she was from the cops were not your friends. They were more like public enemy number one. The authorities were seen as invaders in an occupied land. Their daily intrusions into the residents' lives were unwanted. So there was no way in hell Destiny would turn her boyfriend over to the man. It didn't matter what he did to her, she wasn't about to tell on him. She couldn't live with herself if she did.

"Is that so?" the officer replied. "Are you sure everything's okay?"

"Yup!" she exclaimed. "Musta got da wrong apartment! Everything just fine here."

The policeman turned to his partner, shooting him a suspicious look. He then shrugged his shoulders as if to say, "Let's go."

"Okay, ma'am, sorry for the interruption. Have a nice day," he stated.

"You too, officer," she replied, shutting the door. "Good-bye!"

As soon as they left, Rome and Destiny picked right back up where they left off. The scent of sex was in the air, so thick you could cut it with a knife.

Having wild sex with Destiny was a way for Rome to get Destiny's mind off him smacking her. It was a way for him to control her. If there was one thing Rome could do, and do well, it was fuck. Growing up, he didn't have any hobbies or talents. So while other kids ran around playing games or going to practice, Rome fucked. Like anything else, practice made perfect. The more Rome had sex, the better he got at it. If he couldn't do anything else he could make a female climax, and in Rome's book that was all he needed to do. Once he did that he knew he was in. And once he got in, it was over. The unfortunate female was in for it. She would be taking care of Rome and putting up with his shit for a long time. Rome would drink from her well till it was dry. Whatever chick was doing good in the 'hood, Rome was going to find a way to get with her.

"I'm sorry!" he said. "I ain't mean ta do dat. I don't know whut got inta me."

Silently Destiny listened to Rome cop a plea. She didn't buy one word of it, either. Destiny thought back to something her father once said; "If you let a man hit you once, he'll do it again."

Right now Destiny was confused. She didn't know what to think. Good sex had clouded her judgment. She wasn't able to separate Rome from the act he committed against her. At this point she didn't like him. She decided she needed a little time to herself.

"Rome, you gotta go!" Destiny suddenly said. "In need ta be by myself for a few days. Get out!"

Destiny's decision stunned Rome. He had never been kicked out of a female's apartment before. Reluctantly he got dressed and left the apartment without saying a word.

After a few days alone, Destiny regretted her decision. She missed Rome more and more each day. Destiny caved in and called him. She begged Rome to return. Rome said he would but he didn't.

Like a fool, Destiny took Rome's word that he would return. She waited for days. Still there was no sign of Rome. He didn't even have the decency to call. Her worries turned into anger. Feeling disrespected, Destiny wanted to disrespect him back. She thought they were better than that.

Turning her attention to his clothes, Destiny went to work. First she cut nice, neat holes in all of Rome's shirts. Every day he was absent from her house, she moved on to another article of clothing, like his underwear. After running out of clothes to damage, Destiny thought of something else to do. She removed all of Rome's expensive sneakers and poured urine in them, then used a blow drier to dry them. Finally, she packed all his stuff up, took it to his mother's apartment, and set the bag in front of her door.

When Rome got wind of Destiny's actions he was furious. His initial reaction was to go over to Destiny's house and beat her up. She had ruined thousands of dollars' worth of clothes. But on the long ride over he reconsidered his actions. He didn't agree with what she did, but he could understand.

After an extended lovemaking session, the couple joked about how crazy Destiny was.

You could take Rome out of the street but you couldn't take the street out of Rome. Though he didn't live in the 'hood anymore, he often frequented it. On any given day, he could be found on 174th and Davidson Avenue, doing much of nothing. He hung on the block so much, people started to believe he had moved back in with his mother.

To Rome there was nothing like being on your block, where everybody knew your name, where everybody gave him props for who he once was, not who he was now. Davidson Avenue was where he was still king, and it was where people still paid him homage and stroked his ego.

On this day, as fate would have it, another familiar face was seen on the block, one that he readily recognized. The face belonged to Makeba.

Makeba cruised the block in a pearl white Lincoln Navigator. Her truck sat on twenty-four-inch, chrome, deep-dish rims. They were so shiny you could see your reflection in them. All eyes were on her.

Through a pair of dark oval Gucci shades, Makeba scanned the block for any familiar faces. She loved to stunt on people she knew from the past. Out the corner of her eye she noticed Rome. He was standing with a group of hasbeens, reminiscing about back in the days. As Makeba slowly rode by, all conversation ceased. Someone in the crowd happened to mention, "There go dat ugly bitch Makeba."

Rome almost broke his neck to catch a glimpse of her. *Damn!* he thought to himself. *That bitch done came up!* Immediately his wheels started turning. *What the fuck is she doing?* he wondered. *I should stop her.*

Acting on his thought, he broke away from the crowd. Rome didn't care what they would say or think about him for shouting out Makeba's name. She was getting it and he wanted to be down.

"Yo, Makeba! Makeba!" he yelled.

At first Makeba pretended not to hear him. But after the second calling of her name she slammed on the brakes. Putting her truck in reverse, she smoothly pulled up to the curb.

"Who dat?" she asked, pulling off her shades.

"Yo, it'z me, Rome!" he exclaimed. "Whut, you don't remember me no more? Oh, it'z like dat, Ma?"

Of course she knew who Rome was. How could she forget him? He was another pretty-boy type who only messed with the top-of-the-line females. He was the type of guy who wouldn't look her way, who only had eyes for Destiny. She remembered Rome clear as day. Makeba knew his style. She knew how he got down.

"Ooohhh, yeah, dat'z right, Rome! Oh, snap, when you get out, nigga?" she asked. "Last I heard, you wuz still up north."

"You know they can't keep a good man down!" he bragged. "I been home 'bout a few months now."

Makeba recklessly eyeballed Rome's body. She had to admit he was looking good. Soon her mind began to wander as she wondered what that dick of his could do. After making money, having sex ran a close second in things Makeba liked to do for fun.

"Yo, Rome, how's Destiny doin'? You still fuckin' wit her? Huh?" she questioned.

By this time Rome was half in Makeba's truck, leaning through an open passenger side window. Rome was sizing her up. From this view she looked and smelled like new money. Like the bloodhound he was, Rome was all on her.

"Nah, it ain't really like dat no more," he lied. "Shorty had too many issues. She wuz stressin' me out. I had ta bounce."

"Oh, fa real?" she gasped. "I ain't think she wuz on it like dat. Dat ain't a good look."

Makeba knew he was lying through his teeth, but she didn't say anything. She just let him think he was gaming her. But he wasn't fooling anyone. She had spoken briefly to Destiny, and she had told her Rome was home.

He replied, "You tellin' me? But enuff said 'bout dat. Whut'z up wit you? You look like ya doin' big thingz! I'm sayin' how can I be down?"

Makeba gave him a sly Cheshire-cat grin and thought, *If only you knew.* If only Rome knew how Makeba really got this car and the other luxury vehicles that she had. Makeba was switching cars like most people switched clothes. This made it appear like she was getting more money that she really was.

If the truth be told, these luxury cars were tagged, which meant they were stolen, but the car's vehicle identification number was altered to match the registration. This kind of thievery couldn't be detected by a routine traffic stop. No, it would take a more in-depth investigation to discover the truth.

"Yo, you don't look like you're doin' too bad yaself," she commented. "I wanna be down wit you."

"I try. You know whutimsayin'? I gotta do me," he insisted. "I ain't like da rest of these bum-azz niggas round here. I ain't lookin' fa a handout. I'm lookin' fa a hand-up. Ya heard!"

Makeba was feeling him more than she cared to admit, so she decided to end this cat-and-mouse game.

"Yo, Rome, whut you doin'?" she suddenly asked. "Get in da car. I got sumthin' ta tell you."

Her statement peaked Rome's curiosity. He wondered exactly what it was that Makeba had to say to him and jumped in the truck to find out. He sat back comfortably in the passenger seat.

He didn't care where they were headed. All he wanted to know was, what was the big secret she couldn't talk about right there?

As soon as the door closed, Makeba hit the gas, quickly putting Davidson Avenue behind them. They had driven a block when Makeba got straight to the point.

"Yo, Rome," she began. "I hope you ain't still fuckin' wit Destiny. I know how you niggas are. But, anyway... I don't know how to tell you this... but... if you still fuckin' wit her I think you should know. She ain't been keep it real wit you."

"Whut?" Rome complained.

"Hope you ain't tryin' ta wife her," she continued. "Da bitch ain't wifey material. While you wuz away she was fuckin' wit other niggaz. But she don't want you to know that. She want you to think dat she was holdin' you down. But..."

Makeba glanced over at Rome to see how he was taking the news. Though he tried to keep a straight face, it was obvious that he was hurt. Makeba smiled inwardly, glad to be the bearer of bad news.

She was willing to do anything to mess up Destiny's relationship, willing to do anything to have Rome.

Rome couldn't believe what he was hearing. Never in a million years did he think that Destiny would betray him in such a manner. Anybody but her, he would have shrugged it off. But he had true feelings for Destiny.

Makeba continued to carry a one-sided conversation, with her talking and Rome listening. Makeba mixed lies in with the truth. She inflated the number of guys Destiny slept with from one to five. By the time she was finished she had successfully depicted Destiny as a "hoe" in Rome's eyes.

Later that day, Makeba and Rome ended up on the other side of the George Washington Bridge, at the Best Western Hotel in Fort Lee, New Jersey. Rome was angry, so he took out his frustrations on Makeba's vagina. It turned out to be the best fuck Makeba ever had.

Though physically Makeba wasn't his cup of tea, Rome pretended she was. He sexed her down like a man possessed, as if he had a point to prove. For Makeba it was a point well taken. She didn't have to whore herself around in search of that good dick. Rome had it right there.

From day one Rome knew he had her open. He would continue to bed her, just as long as she took care of him, that is, giving Rome money. "One hand washes the other, but they both wash the face," he was fond of saying. He had bigger plan, too, like weaseling his way in on her hustle. Rome knew thugs like him were always good for such a woman to have around. It was good for business. He would discourage a lot of things, like robbers. There were many people, guys and girls alike, plotting on Makeba. It was the beginning of a torrid sexual affair.

CHAPTER 15

Rome went back to Destiny with the sole purpose of dogging her out. Though he never breathed a word about her affair, he began to treat her differently. He could only pretend not to know so much. He wanted to say something so badly, but Makeba had sworn him to secrecy. He didn't want to blow her cover.

As the weeks went by, Destiny's home situation only worsened. Rome's disappearing acts became more frequent than ever, only now he was producing cash that seemed to justify his whereabouts to Destiny.

He had to be doing something, she reasoned. Still, she had her suspicions. Rome was getting sloppy. His game wasn't as tight as it once had been. When he did come home, he would smell of a fresh shower. If you were out in the street grinding all day, it was highly unlikely that you would smell as fresh as he did. If it wasn't that, he often smelled of different fragrances of soap. Little did Rome know that women paid very close attention to patterns and details. Maybe these bad tendencies just escaped Rome's attention. Or maybe he just didn't care.

"A, yo, guess who I saw da other day?" Rome asked. "You gone bug when I tell you who."

"Who?" Destiny flatly asked.

"You'll neva fuckin' guess inna million years," he commented.

Every day Makeba had been putting more pressure on Rome to have Destiny contact her. Somehow she had misplaced her home number, so she couldn't reach out to her. Rome was hesitant at first to relay the message. He feared that Makeba would do something scandalous, like reveal their secret relationship. Only after she kept persisting did he relent. Now finally he found a way to bring up Makeba's name.

"Who?" she asked again, clearly agitated.

"Makeba!" he replied.

Destiny took a nonchalant attitude at the mention of her friend's name. She hadn't heard from her in months. Still, she didn't think any love was lost. She had no reason to. Destiny thought she was doing her thing and Makeba was doing hers, and didn't coincide. Sometimes life could be funny like that. It was known to pull friends in different directions.

He continued, "Yo, dat broad iz gettin' some serious cheddar too. I be seein' her in all kinds of whips. Yo, here. She said dis her new number to call her! I'm out!"

Before Destiny could even get a meaningful conversation out of Rome, he was gone. He hadn't been home a good hour before he rushed back to the streets. Destiny didn't even get a chance to break the news to him that she suspected that she was pregnant. She wondered, would it make a difference? Would he even care? Was Rome a family man? Could he make the transition from street thug to working man, like her father had? These questions gnawed at her soul.

Shit!" Destiny exclaimed.

This was the third time she had taken the test. It came up

positive each time. Finally it sunk in her head that the home pregnancy test couldn't be wrong.

It was quite ironic. Destiny found herself in almost the same position her mother had been in some two decades ago, pregnant and in desperate need of money. She had temporarily stopped hustling when she thought she might be pregnant.

The money she had stashed away had dwindled severely. Being the lone bread winner of her household, she was responsible for paying all the bills. The fact that Rome wasn't even man enough to assist her with that didn't bother Destiny at all. She was independent. Destiny was going to take care of herself regardless.

For weeks she had contemplated calling Makeba. She knew she could count on her, if nothing else, to help put money in her pocket. Finally she made the call.

After a brief conversation with Makeba, the two decided to meet. The reasons for Destiny taking part in the meeting were purely financial. She had to replenish her stash. In the back of her mind she worried about who was going to provide for her baby. And how was she going to do it? Destiny decided to take her destiny into her own hands. From the streets she came so to the streets she returned. Out of desperation she returned to the game.

Where da fuck iz dis bitch?" Destiny cursed.

Standing in front of Bronx Community College on University Avenue, Destiny felt stupid. She had been waiting on Makeba for a little over an hour. If it was one thing she hated, it was waiting on somebody. Destiny was impatient. She liked to do what she came to do, when she came to do it. But the problem was, she was no longer in control of the situation. Makeba was calling the shots, so they were working on her time, not Destiny's.

Before Destiny could spot Makeba, she had made her out. Even from a distance, she could see the agitated look on Destiny's face. Her body language, arms folded across her chest, spoke volumes. Makeba couldn't help but chuckle to herself. She knew how much Destiny hated to be kept waiting. That's why she did it. *Fuck her!* She thought.

A midnight black Nissan 300ZX with dark-tinted windows came to a halt directly in front of Destiny. For a moment she stood there just looking at the car. Then her New York survival instinct kicked in and she began to twist up her lips and roll her eyes in disgust, hoping that would be enough to stop the driver or passenger from trying to rap to her. Guys pulled up on her in nice cars all the time in hopes of impressing her enough to get her number. But dudes had to come better than that. She felt that method was for hoes or chicken heads and she was neither. Destiny never exchanged words with guys unless they got out the car and approached her like gentlemen.

Since Destiny couldn't see through the dark tints, she didn't know who was driving or what their problem was. In a second or two she was going to give them a piece of her mind, though.

"Bleep! Bleep!" The car horn sounded.

Destiny stood defiantly on the sidewalk with a look on her face that said, "I know you ain't talkin' ta me." She thought to herself, *You better speed on fa you get peed on!*

Then suddenly the passenger's window came rolling down. Since the sports car was so low, Destiny had to bend down to get a peek inside. Finally the window revealed the driver's identity. It was Makeba.

"Girl, you ain't changed a bit!" she gushed. "C'mon, get in!"

Destiny couldn't believe her eyes. To hear that someone is making money, then to actually see it, were two different things.

She was impressed. Inside, Destiny kicked herself for initially not making the move with Makeba when the opportunity presented itself. Now she would undoubtedly have a greatly reduced role in the criminal act. There was no way in hell that Makeba would cut her in as a partner. Destiny had to keep it real with herself. If the shoe were on the other foot Destiny knew she wouldn't.

As soon as Destiny got into the car, Makeba shifted into gear and they shot down the block. Immediately the factory-fresh fragrance of a new car infiltrated her nostrils. There were two type of smells that Destiny loved, the smell of new money and the smell of a new car. Destiny inhaled the scent deeply, appreciating every breath.

"You doin' it like dis, huh?" Destiny smirked.

"Whut can I say? I hit a nice lick!" she replied. "You think dis sumthin, you should see my truck. Dat's my pride and joy there."

Destiny couldn't help but feel a tinge of envy in her heart. Her feelings were not necessarily a bad one. Envy can make people do one of two things. It can inspire them to work hard to attain the material item the other person has, or conjure up an ill feeling in that makes them think that the person doesn't deserve that material item and lead them to take it. Destiny's feelings had inspired her to make money like Makeba, too.

"Word? Ya truck iz like dat?" Destiny marveled.

Makeba was brimming with confidence. It seemed like she had been waiting her whole life to shine, to be a leader and not a follower, to hear Destiny sing her praise. From the looks of things she would have to wait a whole lot longer.

No matter how happy Destiny may have been for Makeba, she couldn't bring herself to verbally express it. She couldn't bring herself to give Makeba her props.

All Destiny kept thinking was, *If Makeba is doing it up, imagine what I'm going to do.* In the past she always had thought of Makeba as her inferior and that hadn't changed.

Makeba began, "Yo, I think you know whut I'm into already. In case you don't, I'm fuckin' wit them checks ta make my paper. If you wanna make some dough, I'll hook you up wit a few checks. You bust 'em and we split 'em sixty-forty."

Destiny's back was against the wall. She was in no position to bargain with Makeba. She knew it wasn't right, putting her free-dom at risk for a few hundred. The risk she was now about to take was like the one she had taken when she first started out, as a Three Card Molly dealer on Fordham Road. Makeba's proposition showed Destiny just how much she thought of her.

Things had definitely changed between the two friends, and they knew it despite their best efforts to pretend otherwise. There was a friction in the air. Makeba and Destiny both felt awkward in each other's presence. It seemed difficult for them to find the words to make smalltalk. Somehow they didn't find the words to update each other on their personal lives.

After they finished discussing their business, Makeba dropped Destiny off home and they went their separate ways.

As she drove home she thought, *My, how the mighty have fallen.*

Makeba continued to drive on the Cross Bronx Expressway with thoughts running wild through her head. In her heart she knew that Destiny would never take direction from her former underling. Her ego was too big. In the past it had always been about Destiny, and Makeba had no reason to believe it would be different. Now she even regretted offering her a position. But there was a way to take care of that problem.

The kicker box in back of the white Lincoln Navigator had the entire inside of the sports utility vehicle rattling as it blasted loud rap music out of the expensive stereo system. It attracted a lot of attention and annoyed just as many people. Rome could care less, though. He was stunting right now and he wanted the world to see him.

This was the type of vehicle he wanted to be seen in. When he got his money together, this was the exact same whip he was going to buy. It looked like a beauty and handled the road like a beast.

Rome had had Makeba's truck practically all day, and during that time he had driven through or by practically every project, live drug block, or happening place in the Bronx. Before he took the car back to its rightful owner, he steered it in yet another direction.

Restricted to his room, a little black boy sat in the window watching the cars go by. Anthony was currently on punishment. His mother had removed his television, an X-box video game system, and his radio from his room for bringing home poor grades on his latest report card. An occasional car passing by was his only form of entertainment while he did his homework.

"Oh, shit!" Anthony cursed. "Dat fuckin' truck iz bananas."

With his eyes Anthony followed the beautiful white truck as it glided up the block. Much to his surprise, it stopped right in front of his building. Double parking in the street, the driver put on his blinking hazard lights and proceeded to exit the truck. Even from that distance the kid automatically knew who it was. The man's walk was unmistakable.

"Daddy's here!" he screamed at the top of his lungs. "Daddy's here!"

In the kitchen, his mother busied herself frying chicken for tonight's dinner while his sibling watched reruns of *Jimmy Neutron* on Cartoon Network, seemingly unaffected by his brother's hysterics.

His mother, on the other hand, heard all the commotion. As the boy passed, his mother snatched him up by the collar of his shirt.

"Whut da hell you doin' outta ya room?" she demanded. "And why iz you screamin' like a goddamn fool, Huh? Didn't I tell you ta stay in dat room?"

"Yes, Mommy, but it'z Daddy!" he blurted out. "Daddy's here! I just seen him gettin' outta a big white car."

"I should whup ya black azz!" she warned. "Number one, fa bringing ya azz outta dat room before I told you to. And number two, for lyin' ta me. Whut I tell you bout lyin' ta me? Huh?"

Kim Harris-Wells didn't know what she was going to do with her elder son, Anthony. The boy had been showing out in school and acting up at home. It was like he would just get in trouble for the extra attention he received. She believed her son was acting out as a direct result of missing his father. He worshipped the ground his father walked on. It was a pity she had picked such a poor choice in a man to be her children's father and her husband.

Just as she was severely reprimanding her son, there was a sudden knock on the door. Kim looked strangely at her son and then released her grip on him. Curiosity led her toward the front door. Silently she removed the peephole cover and peeked out. *Well, I'll be damned! He wasn't lying after all,* she thought. *Look at this nigga here.*

Quickly Kim undid the locks and opened the door. Rome stood in the doorway, tapping his hand against the door frame, impatiently waiting for admittance. Rome acted as if he were the man of the house coming home from a hard day's work.

"Well, look whut the wind blew in," Kim said sarcastically. "To whut do we owe dis pleasure? Kidz, ya'll know dis nigga?"

Kim was the bitter type who constantly involved her children all in her marital problems. She used her kids every chance she got to get back at her husband. If Rome didn't straighten up and do right, she planned to put the man on him. Taking him to court for child support was her trump card that Kim played to perfection, especially when Rome got out of line.

"Here you go! Don't you ever get enuff of dat shit? You's one angry black bitch!" he barked.

"Ya mother!" she replied. "Call out my name again! Muthafucka! I dare ya azz!"

Kim walked toward Rome with her fist balled up in a threatening manner. She took offense to Rome threatening her.

Rome chose to ignore her rather than argue in front of the kids. Besides, he knew if he verbally insulted Kim anymore, she was libel to attack him. She was crazy like that. Over the years Kim had done everything to him, including stabbing him and shooting at him. If they got into another physical alteration, Rome knew he would probably have to damn near kill her, just to stop her from hurting him.

He didn't come here today for a fight or an argument. Rome came here to see his kids. He could care less about his wife's attitude. He came to give them money toward their support, thus ensuring the kids would have a good Christmas. One thing about Rome was that when he was doing good, his kids were well taken care of. The only problem with that was, he did bad more than he ever did good. So their financial support fell solely on Kim.

"Daddy! Daddy!" Anthony screamed.

Rome kicked the apartment door closed and bent down to scoop up his little man in his arms. The boy smothered him with hugs. Kim stood down the hallway stewing in anger. No matter how hard she tried there was nothing she could do to break their bond. "Daddy! Daddy! Is dat ya car? Huh? Can you take us fa a ride? Huh?" Anthony excitedly asked.

"Nah, I can't right now," Rome told him. "I gotta get ready ta go somewhere. I'll come back another time and take ya'll fa a ride."

Kim erupted, "Stop sellin' my fuckin' kids dreams! Nigga, you know you ain't comin' back no time soon!"

Rome didn't even bother to put up an argument because he didn't know when he was coming back. But he would be back one day, that he was sure of. These were his children, the only ones he had. But since they were boys, he felt they could withstand the pressure of not growing up with a father in their household. Rome felt they had to "man-up" just like he did. Rome was going to do little or nothing to break the cycle of the absentee father in the black family.

He always said that the woman who bears him a daughter would be the woman he would be with for the rest of his life. Rome felt that having a daughter would make him a different man. But the truth of the matter was, Rome would be a dog regardless of the gender of his child, and he would continue to sow his wild oats.

Rome placed Anthony down and quickly scanned the apartment for signs of his other son. He saw none.

"Kim, where Junior at?" he politely asked. "I don't see him."

"He right there in the livin' room watchin' TV," she replied. "Ga'head on in there, you'll see him sittin' on the couch in the corner."

When Rome entered the room, his younger son acted as if he wasn't even there. He continued to watch television, even though his father blocked his view. Jerome Wells Jr. was mildly retarded, but his father preferred the word "special." That's what Junior was to him. He was so special Rome tattooed "JR" across his chest. No one else had managed to get that achievement. His mother didn't get it, his wife, or Destiny. His son was a special kid, so Rome showered him with special love. It hurt his heart to see his son in this state, especially when he didn't ask to be brought into this world. Rome couldn't help but feel partly to blame for his condition, though he didn't even know why he felt that way.

"Junior," he called out. "It's daddy, boy!"

Suddenly the boy lit up with excitement. He began to chuckle uncontrollably when he recognized the man standing before him. He got up and ran, jumping into his father's arms.

"Yeah, dat's my boy," Rome said. "I love Junior! I swear I do!" He engulfed the boy in his arms and squeezed him lovingly. Then he placed him back down. He began jumping around excitedly after being lethargic only few minutes ago. It was as if the child had gotten hold of a bunch of candy bars and ate them all.

"I don't know why you come up in here gettin' dat boy started," Kim commented. "And you know you 'bout to leave. I hate ya black azz. I swear."

Though that was a harsh statement for Kim to make, it couldn't have been further from the truth. Her big, bad talk was just a front. Who was she fooling? She certainly wasn't fooling Rome. He knew she still loved him. And most importantly, she did, too. This was real. No matter what Rome did to Kim, he could always return home. Her door was always open for him. Kim's love was unconditional. It had no boundaries, no time frame, and no restraints.

"Yo, here you go, Kim," he said. "Dat's a lil sumthin' fa da kids."

Rome proudly handed Kim a healthy wad of cash. She couldn't believe her eyes. Her greed wouldn't let her resist counting the money. She wondered, *Where in the hell did his broke ass get all this money?* Yet she accepted it and didn't bother to ask. Soon it came time for Rome to leave. He quickly said his good-byes and left the apartment. Rome felt a little guilty. Feeling he had to do what he had to do to provide for them, he was off to a secret sexual rendezvous in New Jersey with Makeba.

CHAPTER 16

God damn!" Destiny cursed.

After vomiting for what felt like the thousandth time that morning, Destiny knelt over the toilet bowl, too weak to move. She was battling a severe case of morning sickness. Her body had been going through strange changes. She was sick so often, she swore to herself she would never, ever get pregnant again.

Destiny dragged herself down the hallway and back to bed, feeling like shit. The sight of her child's father lying carefree in the bed angered her. She wanted and needed his unconditional support. As it stood now, though, he didn't even know she was pregnant. Now was the time, she told herself, to tell him. Now was the time to see just what he would say.

"Rome! Rome! Wake up!" she told the sleeping figure.

"Whut? Whut'z wrong?" he groggily asked.

It was a rare morning that Rome could be found in Destiny's bed. He seemed to be on the go, more than ever before. Knowing this, Destiny seized the opportunity to talk.

"We gotta talk," she firmly stated.

"Dis shit can't wait till later?" he wondered. "I'm tired than a muthafucka! Fa real! Could you please leave me da fuck alone?"

Destiny began, "Look, Rome, I don't know how to say dis, but I'm pregnant."

"Pregnant? You don't look pregnant," he replied. "Pregnant? By who?"

Destiny never thought Rome would stoop this low. How dare he ask her that? He was the only man she had sleeping been with.

"You's one lowdown dirty rotten nigga!" she spat. "How you even gonna fix ya face ta say some shit like dat, huh?"

For Rome it was quite easy. He knew Destiny's dirty little secret. Now it was payback time. He was going to do everything in his power to make her miserable. On the flip side of the coin, Rome knew in his heart the child was his, but he had to do everything in his power to try to discourage Destiny from having this baby. To him, another child by another woman would further complicate his life. If, God forbid, his wife Kim found out about this, he was going to jail for sure. He was positive that his impregnating another woman would push Kim over the edge. She would surely take him to court for child support and he would go to jail because he didn't have the money to make any payments. He was living off someone else.

"I wuz just playin'!" he announced, seeing her violent reaction.

"Nigga, don't fuckin play wit me like dat!" she warned. "Dis ain't no fuckin' laughin' matter. Now I wanna know how ya azz plan ta support dis baby!"

Rome lay in the bed, dumbfounded. He didn't have anything to contribute to the conversation. He knew he was in no position to feed another mouth. He could barely feed the two he had and himself.

"Oh, we ain't havin' no baby. I'm leavin' you if you have dis kid," he harshly stated. "I ain't ready fa no fuckin' kids!"

If Rome was bluffing, she decided to call his bluff. At that point, Destiny could have laughed in his face. That was a joke, it had to be. Destiny hardly saw him as it was.

"Nigga, you man enuff ta do all dat fuckin', then you should be man enough to support dis baby!" she remarked harshly. "You know whut? You's a real bitch-azz nigga! I can't believe dis shit."

Rome's temper quickly flared up. She had insulted his manhood one time too many. Before Destiny could utter another word, he struck. One powerful blow from his fist caught her on her right temple. He knocked Destiny out from the force of the blow. She hit the floor with a loud thud and remained motionless for a few minutes. He immediately rushed to her side to try and aid her. Suddenly he regretted what he had done. Her vacant stare scared Rome. He thought he had killed her. Frantically he ran around the apartment, looking for a first aid kit, but he found none. So he went and doused a towel with ice-cold water and applied it to her head. Slowly she began to come to.

"I'm sorry, Ma," Rome admitted as he gently cradled her head. "I didn't mean ta do you like dat."

Destiny was still woozy. She remembered little or nothing of what had just happened. This was partly because she never saw the blow coming. What she did remember was the sudden flash of a bright light. She couldn't recall what it was from, though. All Destiny knew was that she was stretched out on the floor.

Slowly she began to gather her senses. Destiny was no dummy. She put two and two together and came to the conclusion that Rome had struck her again. Though the blow had taken the fight right out of her, it hadn't stopped Destiny's heart from breaking from disappointment. Rome had broken his promise.

"Yo, you lied ta me," she moaned. "You promised neva ta hit me. Why you hit me? Nigga, I'm kill you when I get off dis floor."

"Ummm, I didn't mean to," he explained. "It wuz an accident. I swear! My anger got da best of me."

Repeatedly Rome copped a plea to Destiny. Now he realized he could be in serious trouble if Destiny chose to press criminal charges against him. With the new laws in place for domestic violence issues, Rome knew he could do some serious time for something he considered real petty. He couldn't see himself back in jail for domestic violence or anything else, for that matter. He was really enjoying his time on the streets. It would kill him to go back to jail now. He'd be the most miserable prisoner ever.

"It wuzn't no accident," she insisted. "Nigga, you meant ta do dat. Pack up ya shit and get out!"

"Des, why you doin' me like dis? We can work it out, nahmean?" he replied.

"Nigga, don't put da blame on me. You did it ta yaself!" she stated.

Destiny rose to her feet slowly and watched the only man she had ever loved, her unborn child's father, gather his things and leave her apartment. She never thought things would turn out like this. She never thought Rome would just leave without at least begging to stay.

In effect, what she had just done was chase him out of her house and into Makeba's bed full time.

The date and time that Destiny and Makeba had planned to hook up had come and gone without so much as a phone call from Makeba. Destiny dared not place a call to Makeba. She didn't want it to appear like she was sweating her. Nor did she want to seem pressed for some money when actually she was.

In the meantime, Destiny just moped around her apartment,

thinking about Rome. His absence dominated her every thought. There was nothing she could do to take her mind off him.

Though Rome wasn't physically in her household anymore, she maintained a line of communication with him. Destiny couldn't completely cut him off, considering her situation. Rome's calls were more like inquiries. He wanted to make sure Destiny didn't press any charges or that there wasn't a warrant out for his arrest. Other than that he could care less about Destiny.

Another day came and went with still no word from Makeba. Destiny gave her the benefit of the doubt, though. She just hoped Makeba hadn't been arrested, at least not till she got "put on." Being broke was every hustler's worst nightmare.

Then one day, out of the blue, Makeba called.

"Yo, I'm ready when you are!" she proclaimed. "Sorry 'bout da holdup, but shit happens."

The shit wasn't what really happened. She told a totally different story, something far from the truth, that she ran out of a specific kind of ink that she used to make the checks. But she didn't want to get into details over the phone because one never knew who was listening.

"Dat's a small thang," Destiny responded. "I'm been ready, I wuz just waitin' on you. You know me. It'z whuteva wit me."

Makeba remarked, "Aiight, so tomorrow I'll bring you them thangs. Early in da mornin'. Tomorrow's da first so they'll be crazy busy at da bank."

Destiny hung up the phone, excited by all the possibilities tomorrow held. When it came to crime, the only thing that motivated her besides the money was the excitement of outwitting someone. It was the thrill of the hunt that got her blood flowing, the thought of matching wits with people or established businesses that really gave Destiny an adrenaline rush.

Makeba delivered the fraudulent checks early that day as promised. She instructed Destiny where to go to cash them, advising her which banks were hot and which banks were sweet. Armed with that knowledge, Destiny proceeded to get dressed and prepared herself mentally for what she might encounter. Destiny replayed certain scenarios in her head, over and over again. She visualized her success, just like she had read successful people do. Satisfied, she left her apartment and embarked on her mission.

On the first of the month, normal, working-class America dreaded this time because it meant that they had bills to pay. But for ghetto America, especially those on public assistance, it meant their welfare checks were in the mail. As a result, the banks were excessively crowded. Bank tellers were pushed to their customer's-always-right threshold while they dealt with ghetto mentalities and attitudes.

Destiny looked stunning in a form-fitting dark blue business suit, black pumps, and a long leather trench coat. Though this getup wasn't necessary, Destiny thought it was. Like any great actor she wanted to sink into her role, and this costume was part of getting into character. She figured, how could she attract money if she didn't look half decent?

"Good morning! How can I help you?" the bank teller asked.

Destiny immediately produced a check from her purse, along with her identification and a pen, as the young black male teller studied her physical form through the thick bulletproof glass. He liked what he saw.

"Excuse me, miss, you mind if I ask you a question?" he inquired.

"No, go right ahead," she said as she signed the check. "Shoot!"

"Umm, you married?" he asked.

"Do you see any rings on these fingers?" she answered, showing him her hands. "Are you married?"

"Nah, I ain't married," he confirmed. "But I'm in da market, though."

"I hear you," Destiny joked. "You find anything you like?"

"No doubt!" he admitted. "I'm lookin' at her."

The young man smiled as he took the check from Destiny and began to process it. His mind was totally off his task. He never really closely examined the check like he was trained to. He was too busy making eyes at Destiny, so cashing the check took a little longer than usual. The young man didn't mind. He would have kept Destiny at his window as long as possible till he got want he wanted, which was her number, but the people in line didn't share the same sentiment. After seeing all the other tellers quickly dispose of their banking transactions, the natives became quite restless.

"Whut da fuck iz takin' da nigga so long?" one woman questioned.

Someone else shouted, "Do ya fuckin' job! Dis ain't da muthafuckin' club! Handle dat shit afta business hours."

"You got people on line tryin' ta get they money too!" someone else added.

With all the ruckus the people in line were causing in the bank, the young man quickly decided to speed up this transaction before the branch manager got wind of what he was doing.

"Write down your number," he mouthed. "Hurry up, they hatin'!"

Destiny quickly complied with his request, writing down some fake digits on a deposit slip, and he slid the money under a slot in the window in a banking envelope. "I'll call you later!" he promised.

It was that kind of day for Destiny. Though she had never done this before, she thought there was nothing to it. With each check she cashed, Destiny got a false sense of security. She thought, *Only an idiot could fuck this up.*

After meeting success time and time again at different banks scattered across the Bronx, finally Destiny was down to one last check. She had no reason to believe that things wouldn't turn out like they had previously. Though it was close to the end of the banking day, Destiny decided to take this one last chance.

This bank branch was crowded, like so many others she had visited throughout the day. Slowly the bank began to clear out. The bank manager locked the door, signaling the branch was closed. No more customers would be admitted, the few that remained would be serviced, and after that the bank employees could go home. Destiny was amongst some of the last customers in line. Out of nowhere she suddenly caught a bad vibe. *I'm going to jail,* she mused to herself. Destiny quickly dismissed the thought. She had come too far, she was already in the bank, and turning back wasn't an option.

"Hello, how may I help you, ma'am?" the elderly white female asked.

"Yes, I'd like to cash a check," Destiny replied.

She produced the check, signed the back of it, and slid it under the window. Destiny expected this transaction to be as easy as one, two, and three. But it wasn't to be. The woman on the other side of the glass had over twenty years of experience in banking. She had seen banks come and go and banking systems installed and rendered obsolete. She had a keen eye for frauds.

The minute the woman picked up the check, Destiny realized

she had picked the wrong teller. The woman began to scrutinize the check. The thing that jumped out at her were the inconsistencies in the check numbers. The one on top didn't match the one on the bottom.

"One moment, ma'am." The teller excused herself.

The teller left her window, and that drew Destiny's suspicion. She watched closely as the teller went over to the bank manager and whispered something into his ear. The manager and teller had a brief discussion before the teller returned to the window. Destiny grew very worried when the branch manger left her sight.

"What's the problem, Miss?" Destiny questioned. "Is there something wrong?

"No. No," the teller assured her. "I didn't have enough cash to cover the check."

The teller glanced around nervously, as if she was expecting something to happen. She was a poor liar. Destiny read her like a book. Her mouth said one thing, and her body language said another. Her actions made Destiny feel uneasy, but still she kept her cool. Destiny thought to herself, *If this chick even look like she gonna call da police, I'm out!*

But she couldn't. The front door was locked.

Simultaneously, from her peripheral vision, she saw two white men, clean cut, undercover police types, appear at the bank entrance. Suddenly the branch manager reappeared and opened the door.

Destiny's heartbeat began to escalate at an erratic pace. Her eyes desperately searched for another escape route that didn't exist. The only way out of the bank was the door behind her, and the police had that blocked. Her heart began pounding in her chest, almost drowning out their footsteps. The long arm of the law was closing in.

The teller smiled with glee, satisfied that she had foiled Destiny's plot to defraud the bank.

Destiny's facial expression showed her pain. A look of defeat appeared across her face. There was nothing she could do now. Destiny knew she was caught and the game was over for the time being. She decided not to put up so much as a fuss.

What Destiny didn't know was that her friend had set her up. Makeba had indeed gotten busted and flipped on everybody she employed to save her own skin. Now she was a confidential informer, working for the district attorney's office.

She was a rat in the lowest sense of the word. She had willingly participated in the crimes, but when she got caught, rather than face the consequences of her acts, she turned in her friend.

The firm grip on her arm let her know that she was now in police custody.

"Destiny Greene!" the detective announced. "You have the right to remain silent. You have the right to a lawyer. If you cannot afford one, one will be appointed to you."

Destiny Greene. His words rang in her ear. It was strange hearing him call out her legal name, especially when she was using an alias to commit her crimes.

The rest of his words were a bunch of mumbo jumbo as far as Destiny was concerned, because she didn't hear a thing. Her world went blank.

CHAPTER 17

All day the overcast, dark grey skies held the impending threat of rain. After a few false starts, light showers here and there, suddenly sheets of rain began to fall with a vengeance, pounding everything in its path. The unrelenting rainfall limited the visibility of every person driving a vehicle. It forced all drivers to reduce their speeds.

The highways, the city streets, and the intersections were beginning to flood, reducing traffic to a crawl. For a moment the city was at a virtual standstill. As the rain continued to fall, a pair of high-beam headlights poked their way through the torrential downpour. Slowly but surely it eased its way through the now flooded Major Deegan Expressway in the Bronx. It continued on its way to the Triborough Bridge and through the toll. Nothing short of an act of God, a traffic accident, or armed gunmen could stop it.

"God damn!" Destiny exclaimed as she cast her eyes up at the dark sky. "It's rainin' fuckin' cats and dogs!"

The stormy weather matched Destiny's emotions. She had just gotten the equivalent of a railroad in court. Though it was her first time getting caught for a crime, albeit a felony, she had been charged with several counts of fraud and grand theft larceny. Destiny had been remanded by the court to Riker's Island.

Judges are human, too. They work off emotions just like everyone else. This particular one, Thomas A. Harper, whom Destiny had the misfortune to be arraigned in front of, was having a very bad day, so he took out all his frustrations on her. He could have easily sent her home on her own recognizance, but he didn't. He ignored the flimsy argument Destiny's public defender put up. As it stood, Destiny was in for the ride of her life.

The letters painted on the side of the multicolored, white, blue, and orange striped bus read NEW YORK CITY'S BOLDEST DEPARTMENT OF CORRECTIONS. Before one even read that, the sight of bars on every window were an ominous sign that this was no ordinary school bus. And this trip wouldn't end at an amusement park.

Its destination was Riker's Island penal colony, New York City's county jail. There the bus would deposit its precious cargo, criminals remanded by the courts in lieu of bail or sentenced to serve time for their crimes against humanity.

Destiny pressed her face hard up against the glass, straining to see out of the dirt-stained, bar-covered windows. She was absorbing her last moments of freedom, at least until someone came up with the bail money. She didn't have a clue who would bail her out. With the ransom note she had as bail, she might have to sit for awhile.

If her father was alive there was no question he would have bailed her out. She probably wouldn't have made it this far. But since her dad was dead and gone, her prospects of getting bailed out were shaky.

Destiny snapped her fingers, suddenly remembering something. If she could get in contact with Makeba, she'd bail her out.

According to the rules of the game, Makeba had to do so. It was sort of a common courtesy amongst criminals that someone gets arrested for you while committing a crime, the person on the street has to bail you out. To Destiny it was a given. She would be out in no time. Surely Makeba would track her down in the system and post bail. She already knew her real name, so it would be real easy to find her.

Getting arrested had taught her a very valuable lesson—to save some money for a rainy day. Up until now, she had been hustling ass backwards. Destiny made lots of money, but she spent it just as fast. It was easy come, easy go. She had absolutely no money for a lawyer or bail. Now she knew she had to curtail her bad spending habits. Either that or change her lifestyle.

No matter how terrible the weather was outside, Destiny would give anything just to be in it. But as things stood she was on her way to jail and no amount of wishful thinking could change that.

Bits and pieces of the loud conversation in the bus filtered through Destiny's ear. She let them pass in one ear and out the other. Through it all she remained neutral and emotionless. She wasn't in the mood to hear anything funny. She was in dire straits and her current situation was no laughing matter.

Destiny told herself over and over again to hold her head up and make the best of a bad situation. Everything was going to be alright, she reasoned. It could be worse.

One glance around the bus revealed a group of seasoned, hard-core female criminals. Amongst these battle-scarred, hardened faces, her baby face seemed out of place. She looked too pure to be corrupted by the evil ways of the world. She looked innocent enough to be on a Girl Scout bus trip. Her appearance didn't fit in with these career criminals. Yet here she was amongst them.

But looks were deceiving. Destiny had been breaking the law for a while now. The only difference between them, the haves and the have-nots, other than their age and rap sheets, was the kind of crimes they committed. Destiny committed white-collar crimes while they committed everyday crimes of survival that fed their families or their drug habits.

In the past Destiny had always reaped the game's rewards, never suffering the consequences of her crimes. Now she was going to see how the less fortunate and the unlucky at crime live. Or better yet, where and how they lived. Now it was time to pay her dues. Her father had always said jail was an unavoidable consequence, something that happened to the best of them. It was only a matter of time. Sure enough, her time had come.

Maybe this is God's way of showing me down, she mused to herself. Then she quickly pushed the thought out of her head. *God ain't got nothing to do with this,* she reasoned.

Over the years, Destiny had had a hell of a run. She successfully pulled numerous capers without arrest. In all actuality she wasn't mad, she was a bit relieved. She promised herself this was her first and last time in jail.

To break up the monotony of the drive, two correctional officers began to, as prisoners say, kick the bo-bo or shoot the breeze.

"Yo, Smitty, whut you doin' tanite? You layin' up again wit dat old freak of yourz or whut?" the young corrections officer asked. "Or you gonna come clubbin' wit me? I'm goin' ta Justin's ta grab a bite ta eat. Then ta da Fort-forty club or Roseland. You know they got hoes by da truckloads down there."

The two men were longtime partners. Matter of fact, it was Officer Smith who broke in the young man, Officer Harris, when he first began working for the Department of Corrections. They shared a unique bond. The young man kind of looked upon the older man as a father figure. He was very fond of him. So Officer Smith going to the club with him was an ongoing inside joke to both parties, something that would never happen, due to their vast difference in age.

"Man, I ain't fuckin' wit them young bitches," he commented. "I'm keepin' my little state pay right in my pocket! Gimme an older broad any day of da week. They don't want much, maybe da phone or light bill paid. Me and a young broad wouldn't work. Shhhhhii-iittttt, I like nice things too. Them damn young girls want too much! Look, I done been there and done that. I got dat shit and I'm not goin' back!"

"I can't tell! Nigga, you tighter than fish pussy wit ya money," the young corrections officer joked. "Lemme find out back in da day you wuz a sugar daddy! Lemme find out, Smitty. I always knew you had some trick potential in you! I knew it!"

Officer Smith replied, "Nigger, I ain't never ever bought a bitch nuttin' but a ham sandwich. And dat was so she didn't pass out on me. And if I remember correctly, I made dat myself. So dat don't count! Nigger, you ever seen da movie *Da Mack*? Well, dat was da story of my life. They stole it from me. I put da "M" in mackin'. Befo' I come along it was actin'. You understand? Listen and learn, youngn'. Stop bein Captain Save-a-Hoe."

The slick comment made the young corrections officer break out into a wide grin. He loved it when the older man talked like this. In fact, he said things to him to garner that type of slick response. It was comical.

"Yeah, keep talkin' dat talk!" he replied. "I hear ya! I hear ya!"

Officer Smith fired back, "Are you listenin', young buck? There's a big difference. You know I can save you from a whole lotta pain, sufferin', and aggravation wit them women. And most importantly money. You young boys fuckin' da game up. Ya'll spoilin' these hoes. Thinkin' yall can buy every goddamn thing. Ain't yall ever hearda da sayin', da best things in life is free?"

"I ain't gotta buy a bitch nuttin' ta get in them draws," he commented. "I ain't no ugly muthafucka."

"You's a liar! Hate ta bust ya bubble, son, but you gotta face only a mother could love," Smitty kidded.

"Fuck you, old man!" he responded.

"I might be old but I ain't ugly! And furthermore, I get more pussy by accident than you do purpose," Smitty countered.

The officer's last statement caught the ear of a few signifying criminals and they broke out into laughter. At that point the younger man decided to kill the conversation. He didn't even bother to reply. He knew Officer Smitty was on a roll and when he got like that sometimes he could get out of control. He could make him look real silly. It was all in good-natured fun, though, and the younger man understood that.

What really made him end the conversation was the laughter. Though criminals were his bread and butter, he didn't like to fraternize with convicts. He was a clean-cut, hard-working, party-going kid from the suburbs of Brentwood, Long Island, who didn't understand the criminal element. He didn't understand the underworld that lay side by side and sometimes merged with the nine-to-five society. All he understood was hard work, overtime, punching a clock, and a pension.

As Destiny continued to stare out of the bus window, a gigantic green sign caught her eye. It read WELCOME TO QUEENS. After taking a few turns, the bus made its way to the entrance of the infamous Riker's Island.

After momentarily pausing at the guard booth, where a corrections officer waved them through, the Department of Corrections bus began to accelerate as it crossed the narrow bridge that led to the correctional facility. The bright light from the individual housing units revealed an island alive with pain and misery. This was not a sight for sore eyes. Riker's Island was a place that even the most seasoned criminal despised. Suddenly all the inmates' idle chit-chat came to an end, as if the harsh reality of their imprisonment had finally sunk in. The prisoners' worries and fears seemed to push to the front of their thoughts.

As the bus continued to ramble over the bridge, Destiny spotted several airplanes flying at low altitudes. Upon further inspection of the area, she noticed that LaGuardia Airport was on her immediate right, a stone's throw away from the jail.

Pulling up to the main gate, a corrections officer at the guard post slowly opened the twenty-foot metal fence topped with razor-sharp barbed wire. Now they had officially entered the belly of the beast. From left to right the inmates viewed various other housing units. Then suddenly the Women's House of Corrections came into sight and the bus came to a halt.

"Alright, ladies and gentlemen," Officer Smitty joked. "Ya'll ain't gotta go home but ya'll gotta get up outta here."

In a single file the women were led off the bus, shackled and handcuffed to each other, and marched like cattle into a large well-lit reception area. There they were taken out their shackles and handcuffs. All the while they were being closely scrutinized by a handful of corrections officers and a female sergeant.

Once freed from her restraints, Destiny began to massage her aching wrists. She hadn't noticed before, but her handcuffs had been placed on so tight they had left indentations on the skin of her wrists and suddenly her wrists were throbbing in pain. The sergeant walked around the receiving room with an air of arrogance, like she owned the place. There was no doubt who was in charge here. She gave each inmate an icy stare as she tried to intimidate them.

"Listen, ladies, I'm only going to say this once," she announced. "I don't care who you were on the streets. You are not in the world anymore. You are not in New York no more. Out there you were so-and-so or such-and-such. None of that shit matters to me. Out there you were the shit! In here *I am the shit!* This is my house! And when you in my house you gotta obey *my rules!*"

She went on rambling about this and that, sprinkling the institutional rules in with her rhetoric. The inmates were forced to listen to her whether they liked it or not. She ran things in the jail.

After the long speech, the inmates were then strip-searched, photographed, and fingerprinted again. They were given a written copy of the prison rules, called the inmate handbook, along with a bed roll that consisted of two sheets, a pillow, and a wool blanket.

When the receiving process was done, they were taken to a housing unit called New Admissions. This was temporary housing for new inmates until more permanent housing became available. Amongst the prisoners this dorm was called the New Jack Dorm. They would be housed there for a week and a half or until they got bailed out.

As the inmates were led into the dormitory, Destiny couldn't help but notice the buzz of excitement in the air, as if their entrance was some strange form of entertainment.

"Fresh meat!" someone called out. "New jacks in da house!"

All eyes seem to fall squarely on Destiny. She appeared to be the object of many women's desire. Try as she might, even Destiny couldn't ignore the lesbian overtones in the dorm.

These bitches barking up the wrong tree! she thought. *I ain't the one! Ain't nuttin' funny 'bout me! Ya heard.*

Inside the dormitory, another female corrections officer assigned each person a bunk. It was a piece of thin sheet metal held up by four steel legs, which masqueraded as a bed. Destiny threw her meager belongings on her paper-thin mattress and flopped down on it. Never in her life did she realize that something so uncomfortable could feel so good. After days of sitting on a hard wooden bench or sleeping on the cold cement floor in roach-infested, urine-scented cells in Central Booking, her bunk felt like a waterbed.

On the bunk, Destiny closed her eyes and relaxed. It had been an eventful few days. Things had happened so fast—her arrest, her arraignment, her betrayal. She lay motionless, pondering her criminal case and her current situation, desperately trying to make sense of it all.

Meanwhile, other inmates unpacked their things and began to settle into their surroundings. Most of them realized that they were going to be there for a while, so they made the most of a bad situation. Some inmates even went to the day room to watch TV while others joined card games and the rest socialized with other inmates.

Destiny's peace and quiet didn't last long. Before long another inmate approached her, tapping her on the foot. The move roused Destiny out of her thoughts. "Whut'z up wit you?" Destiny asked defensively. "Don't touch me!"

"Calm down. I just came over to talk to you. See how you wuz doin'. You looked a lil lonely over here. Whut up? My name iz Latoya. But everybody call me Toya. I don't know if dis ya first time in jail or not. Sometimes new jacks have a problem adjustin' ta jail. You'd be surprised ta know how many girls hang themselves in here," Latoya said. "They be seriously depressed but lookin' at 'em you'd never be able ta tell."

Opening her eyes, Destiny sat up on her bunk. She wondered what this was all about. She didn't know the woman or vice versa, but immediately she had a feeling that the woman was up to no good. Destiny's street instincts told her so. She felt like Toya was a predator, a wolf in sheep's clothing.

Destiny was correct in this assumption. Toya had a bad reputation on Riker's Island. She had sexually turned out many young unsuspecting inmates during her tenures there.

Destiny knew the woman was full of shit. She could "peep game" a mile away, and the woman was hiding her true intentions. But instead of verbally attacking her, she sat back and listened to find out where the woman was coming from.

Latoya continued, "Whut'z ya name? Where you from? Whut you in for? You from da Bronx? Ya face look mad familiar. Word! You Puerto Rican or black? Or both?"

One after another she asked Destiny personal questions in an attempt to get familiar with her. Destiny just stared back at her blankly. For awhile she didn't say a word, but her patience soon began to wear thin.

"Listen bitch!" Destiny snapped. "I don't know whut da fuck you up to, comin' round here tryin' ta get familiar and shit. But you betta go try dat dumb shit on somebody else. Don't worry 'bout my fuckin' name or whut I'm in for. Or anything else about me. Mind ya bizness. I don't know whut type of bullshit you bitches iz on, but I don't play dat. I ain't wit dat gay shit! Ya best bet iz ta go find somebody else ta play wit. Cauze I will fuck one of you bitches up in here! You ain't gotta take my word for it either. Try me!"

Upon hearing Destiny's reply the woman's whole facial expression changed. Immediately her jaw dropped in disbelief. She hadn't expected such a strong response. Quickly that expression was replaced by a wicked sneer that spread across her lips. She cut her eyes evilly at Destiny. She had never had her sexual advances rebuffed like this, especially not by some new jack.

"Oh, you's a tough bitch, huh?" she shouted. "Yo, everybody, we gotta gangsta in da house! We gotta real live gangsta bitch in here!"

The announcement caught Destiny off guard. She wasn't prepared to possibly offend the entire dormitory. She knew she could beat the woman in front of her in a fair fight. But there was no way she could take on the whole dorm and win.

Immediately numerous heads began to turn toward Destiny's direction. The woman had successfully called attention to Destiny and turned a few inmates against her in the process.

"Bitch, you ain't seen da last of me. I'ma get at you! Watch! We gone see just how fuckin' tough you are," she commented. "You betta wrap up what you don't want broke up!"

"Any time, hoe! Me and you one-on-one!" Destiny fired back. "Ain't nuttin' between us but air and ya fear!"

Though Destiny put up a brave front, the consensus around the dorm was that Latoya would beat Destiny in a fist fight. Everyone felt that it wouldn't even be a fight due to Latoya's manlike appearance. If looks counted for anything, then surely she would have her way with her.

The woman rolled her eyes and sucked her teeth before walking away.

With her eyes Destiny followed her every move. She could see her in the day room huddling up with some more of her lesbian friends. From the animated way the women acted, Destiny guessed that she was telling them what had just happened. She could care less.

Good! Destiny thought. *Tell all ya fuckin' friends I ain't gay.*

Her encounter with the woman made Destiny take a sudden inventory of everyone around her. As she glanced around the dorm, she began to see pairs of women secluded in different sections. Some were cuddling up and others were holding hands and openly displayed signs of affection. Now that she was looking for it, she could see it everywhere. It amazed her how many women in the dorm were gay. For some it was quite obvious. Their physical appearance gave them away. But there were some feminine-looking ones, too. That really surprised her.

They were regular, ordinary looking women. Destiny didn't worry about the ones she could spot; she worried about the ones she couldn't. She didn't want to encourage or give them any hope by speaking to them or socializing with them. From this point on, she vowed to be antisocial, talking only when she had to, preferably to the correctional officers.

"Count time!" a correctional officer yelled out.

Inmates began to scramble back to their bunk area, from the day room, bathroom, or other parts of the dorm. No inmate in her right mind wanted to mess up the count. In any jail in America that was a serious offense and surely a one-way ticket to solitary confinement. Since she was new to the system, Destiny couldn't understand the big deal. In time she would. She slowly walked back to her living quarters, to everyone's dismay.

After the count, it was bedtime. The lights in the dorm were dimmed and the volume of chatter lowered. Most inmates began to get underneath their blankets and settle in for a good night's sleep. Destiny wouldn't be so fortunate. She pressed her back against the divider, waited, and watched. She had beef, but with whom she didn't exactly know. Still, she wanted to be prepared if any signs of trouble should appear.

CHAPTER 18

The sun's red streaks broke through the light blue morning sky. On Riker's Island, for some inmates, this signaled the arrival of a new day. Hopefully it was a day closer to going home. For other inmates in the dorms and cellblocks, awaiting trial, hearings, bail adjustments, or new indictments, it signaled breakfast time. This was their first chance to quell the hunger pains that had nagged them throughout the night. Like zombies, one by one inmates began to rise out of their sleep.

From her bunk, Destiny watched the parade of inmates as they headed toward the bathroom to tend to their hygiene. Some nasty inmates with no sense of good hygiene merely lay in their beds and waited for the chow line to be let out to the mess hall. Destiny shook her head at these types. *Unfuckin' believable,* she thought. *Same way in jail, same way on the streets. These bitches are nasty.*

Destiny had already taken care of her own personal hygiene, washing her face, brushing her teeth, and combing her hair in the wee hours of the morning to avoid contact with the other parties. She did this so her adversary couldn't launch a sneak attack.

In not so many words, Destiny had been threatened. After she had been issued the threat, Destiny found it impossible to fall asleep or to function as she normally would have. Her nerves wouldn't allow it, so she didn't even try. She just watched and waited for a confrontation that never came. Still, she wasn't about to throw caution to the wind. In her book it was better to be safe than sorry. She wasn't putting anything past anyone. She was from the street. Where people didn't take threats lightly, no matter who they came from.

Destiny looked miserable in her new surroundings, like a fish out of water. She didn't want to be there and her body language said so. She crossed her arms against her breasts and her facial expression consisted of a mean scowl. It became clear to everyone to stay out of her way. Other inmates seemed to avoid her like she had an infectious disease. This wasn't due to all the mean mugging she was doing. No, the word was out that somebody was going to check her hard. Destiny had drama on her hands and nobody else wanted to be a part of it.

"Chow!" the female corrections officer shouted. Then she stuck her giant turnkey into the locked steel gate, opening it up. On cue, dozens of inmates began to march out of the dorm toward the mess hall. Destiny spotted Latoya and her little entourage as they exited the dorm. Destiny was amongst the last few stragglers to leave. She did so because she didn't want anyone walking behind her and possibly launching a sneak attack. She was security-conscious while most inmates were only worried about filling their bellies.

When Destiny entered the mess hall, once again, all eyes were on her. Inmates in the general population from other cellblocks and dormitories seemed to stare at her. In particular the gay inmates were drawn to her beauty. Destiny could hear the whispers and see all the commotion her presence caused. Still, she pretended to ignore it. Like the numerous inmates in front of her, Destiny endured the long chow line only to be rewarded by a brownish sauce with chunks of meat. Also on the tray were two slices of toasted bread, a cup of weak coffee, and a small carton of low-fat milk. The main course this morning was commonly referred to as shit on a shingle by the inmates. It was the worst meal on the menu, bar none.

After Destiny received her tray, she was directed by a corrections officer to sit at a random table. Sitting down, Destiny looked down at her meal in disgust. There was no way she was eating that. She was fresh off the street and still had a taste for real food, good food. Her tastebuds hadn't taken a hit yet. If she stayed in jail too long there was little doubt that she would either lose weight or begin eating a lot of junk food from the commissary. There was no way she was going to subject herself to this every day.

Destiny grabbed the cup of coffee off her tray along with the few packets of sugar the Department of Corrections provided. She opened the packs and poured them into the coffee. Then she shoved aside the tray, content with sipping on the lukewarm coffee.

"You gonna eat dat?" a greedy inmate asked.

"Nah! I ain't eatin' dat shit. I don't know whut dat shit iz," Destiny snapped. "If you want it, you can have it!"

"Good lookin' out!" she replied as she grabbed the tray and emptied its contents onto hers. She wolfed down the meal as if it were a delicacy. From directly across the table the woman was heavily scrutinized by Destiny. In less than a minute she knew her whole M.O. By the looks of her puffy, needlemarked hands the woman was a stone-cold dope fiend. Her hands were probably the biggest thing on her body. The rest of her was frail. The woman's clothes literally draped off her.

On the street, the woman was on a steady diet of dope. She had abused her body, often going days without eating. Now while she was in the penal system, doing a skid bid, she was attending every meal religiously and devouring every morsel in sight in a desperate attempt to get her weight up. Eventually she would put on some weight, but to no avail. It would come back off as soon as she hit the street, where the woman would renew her lifelong affair with heroin.

The inmates were only allotted a precious few minutes to eat. This was evident when the corrections officer came over and tapped on the table, signaling their time to eat was up.

Reluctantly Destiny got up and headed for the mess hall exit along with the other inmates while several wolfed down the rest of their breakfast. She shook her head in disgust at the rush job being placed on them. Destiny thought, *I gotta get da fuck outta here. I ain't usta takin' all these god-damn orders. Dis shit ain't fa me.*

Once again, Destiny was the last inmate back to the dorm. The steel gate was slammed shut and locked behind her.

"Hey, Greene," the regular housing officer said. "Ya ass better start movin' a lil bit faster to and from chow. We don't play dat slow-motion shit around here."

Whatever! Destiny mused to herself, totally ignoring her. *Next time, make me, bitch!*

As she re-entered the dorm she immediately noticed the place was a little bit livelier. That garbage breakfast had energized virtually everyone. Ignoring the idle chitter-chatter, Destiny scoured the vicinity in search of her foes. She found them congregating by another new jack's bed. Undoubtedly they were applying pressure to her.

Destiny saw this but as far as she was concerned that was the new jack's problem. Destiny was not going to rush to her aid, just as surely as no one came to hers.

When Destiny finally reached her bunk, she immediately saw something that sent her into a fit of rage. A chocolate Snickers candy bar had been placed there. As green as she was, even Destiny knew that she was being sexually propositioned. If she ate the candy bar she would belong to whoever placed it there.

With all her might she swatted the candy bar off her bunk. Then Destiny scanned the dorm for signs of the guilty party. After icily staring down a few known lesbians, Destiny lashed out verbally.

"I wish I woulda caught da bitch dat put dat candy bar on my bed," she yelled out. "Bitch, if you bad, step up and do it now! While I'm standin' right here!"

Standing there defiantly, Destiny waited for someone to accept her challenge. But no one took the bait. They just watched her vent.

Still fuming, she sat on the edge of her bed in silence. From afar she could hear a few snickers here and there. The noise was mostly from instigators anxious to see a fight. Destiny ignored them. To her the bitches were cowards. They were the types who never fought but always knew who was about to fight.

Suddenly it was time for the inmates who performed the daily sanitation duties in the dorm to get to work. Loud sounds of brooms and wet mops being put to use could be heard throughout the dorm as the sanitation team performed their assigned jobs of cleaning the bathroom, day room, and dorm.

It took a while before Destiny could calm down and get her mind right. She couldn't believe that someone had tried to play her out with that old prison homosexual ploy. The fact that they did it out in the open for everyone else to see infuriated her even more. There was no way in hell she was going to let that stunt slide. Destiny knew if she did, it would have a snowball effect on the rest of her stay. She made up her mind right then and there that if she found out who did it, she was going to make an example out of them. The laws of the place dictated her actions.

Right after breakfast, the whole dorm went back to sleep, everyone except Destiny. She was too hyped up to sleep. Instead she just sat up in her bunk, preparing herself for anything.

Shortly afterward the phones were turned on and inmates were allowed to walk around the dorm freely. Destiny was dying to use the phone. She practically ran to it. The possibility of being bailed out of jail excited her so much. She almost forgot Makeba's cell phone number. Somehow she managed to dial her seven-digit number. With her ear glued to the phone, Destiny waited for a ring that would never come.

"The number you have reached," the automated voice stated, "in area code 718 has been disconnected. No further information is available."

As the automated recording repeated itself, Destiny listened, dumbfounded. She couldn't believe her luck. Any thoughts she had entertained about getting bailed out were now dashed.

I know this bitch ain't cut off her phone, she mused.

With her head held low, Destiny walked back to her bunk, dejected. She didn't know what she was going to do now.

As Destiny cooled off on her bed, she heard her full name called out by a corrections officer. First she thought she was hearing things. Then she heard it again.

"Destiny Greene!" The officer shouted. "Greene, visit!"

Destiny jumped off her bunk, exhibiting more energy than she had since her arrest. As she bounced up the aisle, her eyes met with the envious stares of other inmates. She paid them no mind, focused on getting out of her current predicament. Inmates could be like children at times. They became jealous when one inmate got more privileges than another. These were the types that stared

Destiny down, especially the ones who knew they weren't getting a visit anytime soon due to their foul ways and actions while they were on the streets.

Unlike the rest of the inmates, Destiny didn't get all dolled up to go on a visit. She came as is. The blue pantsuit she wore looked atrocious. It was wrinkled beyond belief, but Destiny could care less how she looked. She wasn't out to impress anybody or being important in jail, because she was already somebody on the streets where it really counted.

After stopping at the inmate control booth, Destiny received her visitation pass and proceeded to the visiting room. Her mind began to wonder who had come to see her. In heart she hoped it was Rome, but there was no way she thought he would even look for her, let alone find her. She had only been missing two days.

As Destiny walked the long corridors that led to the visiting room, she prayed that it was Rome and that he had some good news for her. She wanted off of Riker's Island badly, not that she was afraid of anyone or anything, but because this was her first time she had been incarcerated, mentally she wasn't handling it too well. Besides, Destiny was a boss. She wasn't use to taking orders. In jail they told you when to eat, sleep, and use the bathroom. For appearance's sake, she looked like she had adjusted to her new surroundings, but inside it was killing her.

After walking through a series of checkpoints, showing her identification and pass, Destiny was finally admitted to the visiting room. Quickly she scanned it, looking for a familiar face. If there was one it was lost in the tidal wave of inmates and visitors.

"A, yo!" a familiar voiced cried. "I'm right here."

When Destiny spotted Rome her face broke out into a wide grin. This was a pleasant surprise. Suddenly all the drama of the past few days disappeared, along with all the personal problems they had been having. For the time being, all that was in the distant past and nothing else seemed to matter. They were genuinely happy to see each other. It didn't matter that their reunion had taken place within the confines of a prison visiting room. Suddenly not even her pregnancy was an issue.

"Yo, kid, whut'z up? You lookin' a lil ruff! Look like you had a fight wit an iron and you lost!" Rome joked before embracing her.

"Nigga, you know how it iz. I ain't tryin ta impress nobody," she replied.

Though their embrace was brief, it was quite intense. They both squeezed each other tightly as if their life depended on it. Destiny was the first to break their embrace and reluctantly Rome followed suit, taking his allotted seat.

There was a long period of silence between Rome and Destiny as they sat directly across from each other. The only thing that physically separated them was a miniature wooden table that stood at knee level.

They locked eyes for what felt like an eternity. Each set of eyes seemed to sing a sad song. Rome's seemed to say, *You fucked!* Destiny's seemed to say, *Bail me out please!*

Rome didn't come to see Destiny out of love or compassion, but out of respect. He felt he owed her at least one lousy visit after all the times she'd written and come to see him upstate. There was no sense in rubbing it in her face, or in kicking her when she was already down. Once again he bit his tongue and didn't mention her cheating ways. The time wasn't right for that quite yet.

"How you doin'?" he asked, faking concern. "You aiight? Right? I'm sayin' ain't nobody fuckin' wit you? Are you still havin' da baby?"

"Iz dat's whut dis iz all about? Huh?" she barked. "Let's not talk about dat right now. Let's talk bout gettin' me out. Anyway, how you find me?"

"Well, when I didn't hear from you inna few days, I figured sumthin wuz up. When a muthafucka come up missin' da first place I look iz jail," he commented. "I made a couple of calls and I found you. It wuzn't hard."

All the effort Rome put forth in finding Destiny seemed to tell her one thing—that he really loved her.

He continued, "I left a couple dollars in ya commissary. And I bought you up some clothes from da crib. You got a sweatsuit, socks, panties, and few magazines in ya package."

The thought of Rome's thoughtfulness brought a smile to Destiny's face. She needed these things in the worst way. Now at least she could be comfortable. But what she really was focused on was getting bailed out.

"Yo, Rome, you gotta get me up outta here," she confessed. "Da judge played me. My bail iz five thousand dollar cash. No ten percent. Can you do sumthin' fa me? If you got it could you bail me out? If not, I need you ta find Makeba fa me."

If it had been anyone else, Destiny would have felt stupid asking for money for such a low bail. But since this was her man, she didn't feel bad at all. After all, she had taken care of him. Now she felt it was his turn to return the favor. She didn't feel that her bail was that heavy of a burden.

"Dat'z all?" Rome inquired. "Shit, I'll have you outta here inna couple of hours. If not, then definitely by tanite."

"How?" Destiny asked. "Where you gonna get dat kinda money? Huh?"

"Stop doubtin' ya man!" he said. "I don't doubt you. Now I said I got you."

Upon hearing that news, Destiny's hopes began to soar. Instantly her mind flashed back to thoughts of the streets. Destiny couldn't wait to see the look on Makeba's face when she found out she was out. Her whole situation was starting to feel funny.

Unfortunately, Rome was bluffing her. There was no way he was bailing her out. He felt the longer he left her in there the more discouraged she would become about having the baby. Now all he needed was a reason to justify what he was about to do to Destiny. It seemed like the perfect time bring up the past.

"Yo, you know dis kid named Ramel?" he suddenly asked.

"Who?" she replied.

"Some kid named Ramel," he reiterated.

Rome studied Destiny's face for any signs of betrayal, but he saw none. What he saw was a genuinely puzzled expression. He watched as Destiny searched her mental Rolodex for an answer.

"I don't know no nigga named Ramel!" she insisted. "Why?"

Rome replied, "Word? Dat'z funny. He say he know you. Real good!"

Destiny snapped, "Yo, whut you tryin' ta say?"

"Whut I'm tryin' to say iz, you know dis nigga. You fucked him. Member da kid from Skate Key dat took you home?" he demanded.

Destiny's whole facial expression changed from defiant to worried. Her heart pounded wildly in her chest.

"Didn't think I'd ever find out about dat, huh?" Rome stated. "Don't worry Ma . . . it'z all good. I ain't gonna do you like you did me. I got more respect fa you."

"I'm sorry, Rome! It wuz a mistake. We didn't really do nuttin," Destiny said.

She was a pitiful sight. Expressionless, Rome pretended to sympathize with her, but in reality, he could care less. In his mind he was done with Destiny. Though he had cheated on her plenty of times, he still held Destiny to a higher standard. He operated under the rule of "Do as I say, not as I do."

Rome was brutal. If a female didn't make him completely

happy, he cut her out of his life like cancer. In Rome's book if women couldn't be used by him, then they were useless.

Time flew by. Before they knew it, visiting hours were over. Once again Rome and Destiny shared a passionate embrace. Then she went back to her dorm, worried and confused.

When Destiny arrived back at the dorm, she immediately drew the stares of her adversaries. By the looks on their faces and the way they were huddled in the back corner, she could tell they were up to no good. Their body language suggested that they were scheming, but on what or who Destiny didn't know. She decided it was in her best interest to be on guard and keep an eye on the group, just to be on the safe side.

Fully clothed, Destiny walked to the shower with a bar of soap, towel, shower slippers, a pair of white-on-white Nike Airs, a sweatsuit, and a change of underwear in hand. She did this just in case somebody tried to try something on the way to the shower. She wanted to be fully prepared.

For all her extra added measures of precaution, she knew she was still most vulnerable in the shower, but there was nothing she could do about it. Taking care of her personal hygiene was mandatory.

Destiny stripped down to her birthday suit, cautiously looking around as she did so. There were no signs of the female band of goons, so Destiny stepped into the tiny shower stall and began to handle her business. She moved quickly, like time was of the essence, getting completely wet and soaping up everywhere except on her face. She didn't want to chance getting soap in her eyes. That would have made things too easy. She knew that in this type of hostile environment it was a quick and easy way to get your ass kicked. She wasn't about to make this easy on anybody. When they stepped to her, they'd better come correct.

In the middle of Destiny's shower, out the corner of her eye she noticed one of Latoya's soldiers rapidly approaching. Expecting a confrontation, she quickly stepped out of the shower, kicked off her shower shoes, and prepared to fight in the nude. The woman laughed at the sight of Destiny standing stalk naked before her. She was glad to know that Destiny was on pins and needles.

"It ain't me you gotta worry bout, Shorty!" she remarked before going in a cramped bathroom stall.

Destiny stood silently watching. She didn't feed into the woman's comment.

While rinsing off, Destiny never took her eye off the woman. In exchange, the woman continued to use the toilet as if she were at home alone, completely ignoring Destiny, taking a crap and smoking a cigarette.

Quickly Destiny dried herself off and dressed. The brand new-velour Rocawear sweatsuit felt like silk to her skin. After days of being trapped in that sweaty business suit, she felt liberated. She was more comfortable in sweats, jeans, and boots anyway. After that refreshing shower, she began to think differently. Destiny mused to herself, *If I can just stay out these bitches' way for a few more days, everything will be all good. This is their world, anyway. I belong on the streets. I got bigger fish to fry.*

Destiny returned to her sleeping area and relaxed on her bunk. She was relaxed by the thought of going home soon. To her nothing else seemed to matter. But when Destiny opened her locker she realized something was seriously wrong. Her locker was completely empty. She had been robbed. Everything had been taken and disbursed throughout the dorm, making it difficult to locate her things.

Destiny was furious. All the positive thoughts she had earlier went out the window. Somebody had to pay for this. She wasn't going out like that. Destiny had never been robbed and she wasn't about to start now.

Instead of telling the correctional officer who worked the housing unit about the incident, Destiny kept it to herself. She wasn't a snitch in the street and she wasn't about to become one in jail. She didn't even bother to ask anyone who did it or if anyone had seen anything. She knew no one would tell her even if they did. Destiny didn't care who did it. She knew Latoya was behind it. And she was the one Destiny was going to make an example out of.

The time Rome set for bailing her out had come and gone. This further infuriated Destiny. Waking up in jail made her angrier than she had been the day before.

For the next few days, Destiny walked on eggshells, not because her stuff had been stolen because she had been expecting to be bailed out soon. But with each passing day she grew more and more frustrated. The bad thing was, she couldn't get in contact with Rome.

The longer Destiny sat in jail the more violent and angry she grew. She began to scheme on Latoya. Every day Destiny would study her, making notes on her tendencies and habits, where she went and with whom. Much to Destiny's dismay, she couldn't catch Latoya alone. One thing she did notice was that Latoya had a regular bowel movement every day. That's when she finally realized that there was one place everyone went to by themselves—the bathroom.

She would have to catch her in there.

Later that afternoon, Latoya came strolling through the dorm with a cigarette in her mouth and a newspaper in hand, headed toward the bathroom. This was the opportunity Destiny had been waiting for. Quickly she stuffed a block of lye soap in a sock and placed a towel around her head, hiding her identity, and casually walked to the bathroom.

"Fuckin' Knicks lost again! God damn!" Latoya exclaimed. "Fuckin' bums! Muthafuckas ain't win a championship since Elvis was alive!"

Latoya sat comfortably on the toilet, totally engrossed in the sports section of the newspaper, unaware of the imminent danger she was in.

The rest of her clique was currently in the recreational room either playing cards or watching *Soul Train* on TV, so Destiny was able to slide into the bathroom undetected by both parties. With her head lowered, she entered the bathroom. She quickly turned left toward the shower area in an effort to fake Latoya out just in case she was watching her. Unfortunately for Latoya, she hadn't paid her any attention.

Destiny peeped out the side of the towel to see if she had been spotted. Once she realized she hadn't, she silently crept toward Latoya's toilet stall.

The sudden appearance of a pair of feet standing directly in front of her was the first sign to Latoya that something was terribly wrong. She looked up and the sight of Destiny's sinister smile confirmed that thought.

In a flash Destiny raised her weapon and bought it down, intending on doing some serious damage. Before Latoya could raise her hand in self-defense, the weapon found its mark. Pain exploded inside Latoya's head as she was repeatedly clubbed.

"AAAAhhhhhh!" Latoya screamed. "Help! Somebody get her off me!"

"Na, bitch, can't nobody save you now!" Destiny cursed. "Ya azz iz mine! You gonna wear dis ass-whuppin'!"

All the loud noise in the dorm, from the television volume turned all the way up and the numerous obnoxious card players, made it virtually impossible for anyone from her clique to hear Latoya's cries for help and come to her aid.

Destiny continued to administer a beating that Latoya would not soon forget. All the hatred she felt toward her seemed to surface at this moment.

Destiny was careful to stay on the offensive. Since she was pregnant she couldn't afford to take a blow to the stomach. Once she got the advantage on Latoya, Destiny kept it. She beat her till she passed out. Then she beat her some more, bringing her back around.

Unbeknownst to Destiny, a neutral inmate with no alliances to either party happened to stumble across the savage beating. She silently walked back out of the bathroom and informed the corrections officer on duty.

Within seconds numerous corrections officers came charging into the dorm. They burst into the bathroom, and what they saw was not a pretty sight. Latoya lay sprawled out on the slimy bathroom floor. Her head was severely lumped up and blood oozed from a gash on her forehead.

Some corrections officers laughed at the sight of the victim, though it was clear this was no laughing matter. Those who didn't find the situation so amusing busied themselves by subduing Destiny. A group of corrections officers converged on her, disarming Destiny of her makeshift weapon.

"Okay, dat's enough, young lady!" one corrections officer shouted.

All the commotion had attracted the attention of practically the whole dorm. They came rushing to the scene, getting as close as they could before the corrections officers prevented them from getting any closer.

They were just in time to see a hyped-up and handcuffed Destiny being escorted to solitary confinement by several officers. Latoya's bull dyke girlfriends stared at her menacingly. Some even went as far to issue threats right in front of the corrections officers.

"Bitch, don't think dis iz ova!" someone warned. "You gonna get yourz!"

Another inmate spat, "We'll see you when you get ta population, hoe! You gonna catch a bad one!"

Destiny returned their menacing stares with one of her own. She refused to engage in any tough talk, preferring to let her actions speak for themselves. She would rather be about it than talk about it.

Because the fight happened over the weekend, it would be a few days before Destiny would be seen by the prison officials and punished for violation of institutional rules.

Solitary confinement was a lonely place, a place where many inmates went on purpose to gather their thoughts, but not Destiny. With nothing to keep her mind off going home, she began to fret daily. Not being able to contact anyone, due to the temporary loss of her privileges like the television and telephone only made matters worse.

"You down wit OPP, yeah you know me! Who's down wit OPP every last homie!" one inmate rapped.

The improvisational rap concert that had broken out in solitary confinement had caught Destiny's ear. She found herself singing the hook to the popular song by the rap group Naughty by Nature.

It was so dark in solitary confinement there was no telling just how many inmates were there. If the number of voices that joined in on the hook was any indication, then the place was packed.

"Yo, sing dat muthafuckin song I like. Dat old school joint," Trisha commanded. "You know my favorite! Da one by whatsher-name? I always have you sing it."

Trisha was an older, bossy inmate, a seasoned veteran of the penal system, whose criminal record stretched far back. The younger inmates in solitary confinement not only respected her, they listened to her, and some even looked to her for guidance. All day and night the other inmates called her name for one thing or another.

The inmates sang everything from rap songs to R&B slow jams. Often the group stopped to take requests.

"As we lay, we forgot about tomorrow as we lay," an inmate soulfully sang, her rendition of a Sherly Murdock song. Even Destiny had to admit the woman could really sing and that there was a lot of untapped talent in jail. The woman would give most professional singers a run for their money. Destiny lay in her bed and listened without saying a word. One thing she loved about music was how an old song bought back memories. She recalled vividly being a little girl and how her father would take her to the movies or just spend quality time bonding.

For a brief moment Destiny wasn't in jail. She was an innocent little girl once again, in awe of her dad. Destiny would give anything to bring those days back, right now. Life was so simple then. Her struggles in life seemed to make her grow up quicker.

Trisha rudely interrupted, "Aiight, enuff of dat! I'm tryin' ta hear sumthin' else. Why don't y'all sing some Christmas carols! It is Christmas time, you know."

One inmate cried out, "Damn, Trish! Fuck us, huh? It's all about you."

"Dat's right! Whoever don't like it can press their bunks. Lay ya tired ass down," Trish fired back.

The young inmate's plea for fair play fell on deaf ears. Trisha simply ignored her, as did the designated songbird. She sang the songs Trisha had requested.

"You better not shout, you better not cry, you better not pout, I'm tellin' you why," someone sang down the hall.

Suddenly Destiny was reminded it was the holiday season and here she was, incarcerated. If her luck didn't change, she would be locked down for New Year's Eve too.

From previous experience the year-end holidays, like Thanksgiving and Christmas, had been anything but happy for Destiny. They were among the loneliest times of the year. And this year appeared to be no different. To Destiny Christmas marked another joyless day, since she didn't have anyone in her immediate family who was alive to share it with her.

As time went on, one by one the inmates involved in the makeshift concert began to fall back on their bunks and the noise on the tier started to die down. Everyone settled in for what would be another long night. Suddenly another group of inmates took to their cell doors, only they weren't into singing and entertaining people. Their talk was exclusively about crime.

"Yo, I'm tellin' you da drug game is gonna be over soon!" one inmate insisted. "They formin' all these task forces and agencies to lock up niggers sellin' drugz. You know why? Because they can't control it. They can't tax drug sales and if they could, it would be a different story."

"Aiight, Minister Farrakhan!" another inmate joked. "If da drug game iz dead, whut'z da next move, then? How can a bitch really eat? Ain't no money like dat crack money!"

"Word up!" Someone else added their two cents. "You ain't lyin' bout dat."

"You bitches call yaself hustlers? Ya'll wuz gettin' money on da streetz?" a booming voice inquired. "You bitches iz handicapped. Ya'll can't do nuttin' but sell drugz. Ya'll don't even do dat cauze good drugz sell themselves."

The voice came from nearby, in the next cell if Destiny was hearing correctly. It belonged to the wise old convict named Trisha. She had dominated all forms of communication since Destiny was placed in segregation. Destiny was impressed by the wisdom in the woman's voice. It peaked her interest. From Destiny's vantage point there was a lot of sense in her message. Even if nobody else was taking the woman seriously, Destiny was all ears.

"To get real money, you gotta think like da white man. You gotta commit fraud! Gotta play dat paper game. It's where da real money at! Whitey been doin' it for centuries and gettin' away wit it. Muthafucka's been stealin' billions of dollars and don't get no jail time. They get fined! And pay their fines wit da money they stole! Ain't dat some shit?"

Destiny smiled to herself. The woman had confirmed what she already knew. She knew that busting checks was where the real fast money was. And she already knew that white people were amongst some of the biggest crooks on earth. History had recorded that fact. The Michael Milliken junk-bond sandal was just one of the most recent and infamous to rock the American economy.

The woman continued, "When I wuz gettin' down fa my crown, I put tagether a lil team. I had somebody dat made up da fake IDs, somebody dat stole da checks, and I had a bunch of bitches dat busted da checks fa me outta town. We usta go out ta Texas, Ohio, and alotta other spots in da Midwest. Da shit wuz sweet."

Fraud was Trisha's calling card. She knew the ins and outs of the check game. As much as Destiny was impressed by the expansive knowledge the woman possessed, later she would be even more impressed by the woman's wisdom. When it came to the game of life, her level of wisdom didn't take a drop-off there.

Laying on her bunk, Destiny listened to the older woman drop jewel after jewel on the younger convicts, but they all seemed to take offense to it as one by one they began to drop out of the conversation and go back to reading or sleeping. Everyone except Destiny.

"Trish, lemme ask you sumthin'," Destiny began, explaining the suspicious nature of her arrest.

Trisha was all ears, soaking up every deal of the incident. A time or two she stopped and asked Destiny a question to better fill in the blanks.

Destiny continued, "Don't dat shit sound funny? How Po-Po know my name? Huh?"

"You know whut happened?" Trisha commented. "I smell a rat. In not so many words you said it yourself."

"Think so?" she replied.

"Know so!" Trisha fired back. "I'd bet my life on it. Let me tell you sumthin', you ain't got no friends in da street. When it comes ta dat money, people tend ta do some change things."

"Yo, Trish, you ain't neva lied," she said. "Tell me whut you think about dis."

Destiny spilled her guts to Trisha. She didn't care who was listening, telling her everything from the pregnancy, to Rome's disappearing acts, his lack of money, to the beatings she received at his hands. Destiny even told her about her act of infidelity and its discovery. By talking about all her drama Destiny felt a sense of relief wash over her. Trisha's heart ached for Destiny, because she too had been fiercely loyal to a "no-good nigger" in her younger years, only to have that loyalty be rewarded with vicious beatings. So she definitely felt Destiny's pain when it came to men. Trisha felt it was her duty to give her "the real" on the matter.

"Yo, I hate ta say dis but . . . leave dat nigga immediately, if not sooner. He don't mean you well. Dat nigger ain't nuttin' but a leech and a woman beater. Whut you need him for? You can do bad by yaself," Trisha told her. "Don't ever let a man define ya happiness. Make yaself happy! If he don't make you happy, leave. Besides, y'all relationship ain't neva gone be da same now dat he know you cheated on him."

"Dat'z easy fa you ta say," Destiny remarked. "But it ain't just about me and Rome no more. It's about dis baby I'm carryin' in my stomach. Plus, he love me and I love him."

"Destiny, you ain't no weak chick. If worst come ta worst, have ya baby and raise it by ya damn self. It's been done before, with a whole lot less. Trust me," Trisha insisted.

The confidence the woman bestowed on Destiny brought a smile to her face. She actually began to fathom the thought of raising the child on her own.

Though Destiny couldn't see it, Trisha was in the next cell just shaking her head out of pity. She had been there before, trapped between a rock and a hard place.

She interrupted, "Destiny, I've been listenin to you talk fa a while now. You say you love dis guy, you ain't never say you're in love wit him. There is a big difference, you know. One more thing, love don't hurt. I don't know whut kinda relationship ya'll got, but it ain't a lovin' one."

Just then, Destiny suddenly realized how much she missed having a mother. All the advice that Trisha doled out to her was of the motherly nature. Trisha had just made the void in her life that much noticeable. Never in her young life did Destiny have that kind of support system to turn to for advice. Her father could only teach her so much. What he couldn't do was show her how to become a woman.

Somehow the topic of their conversation suddenly switched. Trisha and Destiny started speaking about other aspects of life, reflecting on their past.

"Des, if there wuz anything bout ya life, other than your parents dying, that you could change, what would it be?"

The question had taken Destiny by surprise. She took a few minute to ponder it. She wanted to make sure she expressed herself correctly.

She replied, "Like you said, other than me not gettin' a chance ta meet and know my mother, and my father dyin', I wouldn't change a thing. I'd do it all again. Minus messin' wit da dude."

"Then you crazy!" Trisha snapped. "Get ya mind right!"

"Why?" Destiny asked.

"You mean ta tell me dat you have no regrets? There's nuttin' in ya life you wished you wouldn't have done? There's no incident dat you wished would have gone ya way? Look where you at. You in jail!" Trisha said. "You failed somewhere along da line."

"Trisha, I don't live my life like dat. Wit a bunch of regrets and shit. I made my bed, so now I gotta lay in it," she admitted. "Hey, I did whut I did. And I can't change dat. I ain't gonna beat myself up over it, either. Everything dat I been through made me who I am. Change dis or dat, I wouldn't be me. Da streetz made me who I am."

Trisha knew very well just what the streets could do to you. It could rob you of your innocence. It made you someone else, totally. In the concrete jungle you had to be an animal to survive.

"Not fa nuttin, we just speakin' hypothetically, just passin' time," Trisha explained. "But check it out, you got in da game young. You placed yaself in adult situations while you still were a child. So in essence you robbed yaself of ya own childhood."

Quickly looking back on her life, Destiny realized she was one hundred percent correct. So she did indeed have regrets. If she could change one fact about her life it would be that.

"You right," she confessed. "If I could go back dat'z sumthin' I would change. Most definitely!"

On the streets Destiny knew she had been exposed to so many things. She had seen life-altering things like death, human lives taken for little or no reason. Destiny had no idea how it had affected her, but it had. It hardened her heart.

What Trisha was attempting was to get Destiny to look at other options, other walks of life. Running the street and playing the game weren't as natural as she made it out to be. There were other ways to live she needed to explore. Trisha felt she was too young to be restricted to a life of crime.

"Destiny, I heard you say sumthin else. You said dat da streetz made you who you were," Trisha stated. "Well, who are you? Tell me exactly who you are, witout tellin' me ya race, nationality, or religion."

Trisha's thought-provoking question had put Destiny in a soul-searching mode. Destiny racked her brain, trying to find the proper words that would define just who she was. But none came to mind. Soon she realized that there was no clear-cut response to Trisha's question. It required a lot of thought.

"Yo, dat'z a deep question, fa real. I'ma need ta sleep on dat," she answered.

"Dat'z whut you suppose ta do. You don't gotta get back at me wit da answer, either. Dat'z a question you need ta ask and answer yaself," Trisha remarked. "Just think about it. And think about whut you doin."

Over the next few days, Destiny and Trisha would talk more and more, to the point that other inmates in solitary confinement began to get jealous of their relationship. The longer Destiny stayed in jail, the clearer she began to see things and the more focused her thoughts became. The beat went on for Destiny. To her, jail was just a minor setback. Suddenly Destiny wasn't burdened by thoughts of what Rome might or might not do. She concentrated all her energies on herself and the unborn baby. If Rome bailed her out, he bailed her out. Destiny promised herself never again to worry over things she couldn't control. She was trying to forget all the things he put her through.

Every day Destiny Greene found herself staring at the wall for several hours, just thinking. There were times she thought about everything, and there were times when she thought about nothing in particular. Mostly, Destiny reflected on the unexpected detour her life had taken. On the streets she didn't have time to clear her mind and think. So for that opportunity she was thankful.

After a few days in solitary confinement Destiny was finally seen by the institutional adjustment committee. She was given a light slap on the wrist for the fight. Destiny came to enjoy the solitude that solitary confinement offered, not to mention Trisha's company. Over a short period they had become very attached to each other. So at her hearing Destiny decided to do something crazy to get even more time in solitary. Besides, all the drama that lay in wait for her in inmate population weighed heavily on her mind. She was in no condition to be fighting all of those goons. Destiny had her child's health to think about.

Throughout the jail the word about her had already spread, and everyone was just waiting for Destiny to be released from solitary confinement. Every day it seemed like a new threat made its way to Destiny, issued by some unknown foe. If this kept up, she would have to fight the whole jail. Never in her wildest dreams did she know that Latoya had this much backup or pull in the jail. Destiny knew she couldn't survive in the prison population, not with this many inmates gunning for her head. Realizing that the person she assaulted was well connected in the jail, she had to find a way out or she was in deep shit.

"For the institutional infractions against you, we sentence you, Destiny Greene, to time served. You'll be placed back into inmate population later today."

Destiny sat in the chair with a defiant look on her face. After the prison official had finished talking she erupted.

"Muthafucka, you and dis fuckin' kangaroo court, I shoulda neva been here in the first place. Whut da fuck I do, except defend myself against sexual advances?" she shouted.

"Miss Greene?" a prison official interrupted. "Miss Greene? Refrain from using that abusive language."

"Nah, fuck dat! I'll say whut da fuck I wanna say, when I wanna say it! I heard you muthafuckas out, now hear me out!"

The entire room of prison officials looked at each other in amazement. Never in their life had they seen anything like this. Immediately they thought Destiny had mental problems. As the corrections officers rushed in to restrain Destiny, they sentenced her to sixty extra days in solitary confinement. That was music to her ears, just what Destiny needed to get her mind right.

Back in solitary, Destiny retold her story to a standing-room-only audience. All the inmates in solitary confinement stood at their doors, making sure they heard every word.

"You shoulda saw those muthafuckas' faces. Da white muthafuckas turned red and da black muthafuckas turned white," she joked.

For the moment Destiny could breathe easy; she was safe. But eventually she too would be moved to population. The thought of that scared her, though she would never admit that to anyone but herself.

CHAPTER 19

In New York City, the Hunts Point section of the Bronx was known for two things. By day this area was alive commerce. Trailer trucks arrived empty and departed with fruit and vegetables to be transported all across the Eastern Seaboard and beyond. By night it was alive with a different kind of commerce—prostitution and strip clubs. The area seemed to be overpopulated with both. At times it seemed as if Hunts Point wasn't even patroled by the police department. It was an open market for a sexual smorgasbord of activities. Any sexual act under the sun was committed here, in the privacy of cars or in the wide open. It was a modern-day Sodom and Gomorrah.

On an abandoned Bronx street, Rome and Makeba sat in a dark, desolate area inside of one of Makeba's tinted-windowed cars, watching and waiting. Their purpose for acting in such a shadowy manner was to collect an unpaid debt. A stripper named Shavon, who Makeba had been doing business with, had run off with her money. For weeks phone calls went unanswered until one day she got tired of Makeba calling her cell phone. Their brief conversation quickly turned into a heated argument. Curse words and threats were exchanged. The stripper vowed not to give

Makeba shit, as she put it. Makeba didn't take too kindly to that. So she turned to Rome to try and retrieve her stolen money. She wasn't about to let Shavon get away with talking to her like that. Makeba wanted the stripper to be punished and Rome was the perfect person to do it.

Rome was her own personal mercenary, enforcer, or whatever she wanted to call him. As long as Makeba was taking care of him, there was nothing he wouldn't do for her, including beating up a female.

Tracking Shavon down was easy. Makeba knew she worked at the infamous Golden Lady in the Bronx. One thing she knew about strippers was that they were some greedy, money-hungry people, so sooner or later Makeba knew Shavon would show her face. Tonight Makeba was in luck. She spotted Shavon's white Toyota Camry parked nearby. Now it was just a matter of time before she surfaced.

It was the wee hours of the morning and the Golden Lady was still open. The club showed no signs of shutting down anytime soon. Rome and Makeba had staked out the club for so long that Rome had dozed off. Makeba stood vigil while her companion slept. Now her alertness would be rewarded.

"Rome? Rome?" she hollered. "Nigga, wake up. Here she come."

"Aiight! Aiiight!" he replied. "I hear you!"

Clearly Rome was more than a little bit annoyed. He awoke angry at the world. He hated for his sleep to be interrupted for any reason. Slowly his eyes began to focus on the shapely figure quickly advancing toward his car.

Shavon was amongst one of the first strippers to exit the club. Tonight had been a rather slow night, and she had left the club in search of money elsewhere. The cold winter winds caused her to walk swiftly toward her car, unaware of the imminent danger that lay in wait.

Before Shavon could reach her car, Rome sprang from the shadows and took her by surprise.

"Shavon?" he called out softly.

Shavon froze in her tracks, paralyzed by fear. She didn't know who was behind her. Not knowing whether to run or turn around and face this stranger, She chose the latter.

As soon as Shavon turned to confront him, her face was greeted by a hard black fist. The force of the blow caused her to stumble to the ground.

"Bitch, you like robbin' people, don't you?" he spat.

From the ground, Shavon strained through one eye, to get a glimpse of the big black brute who had just attacked her. His face wasn't registering in her memory bank.

"Who are you? Nigga, I don't know you," she screamed. "Why you doin' dis ta me?"

Before she could make another sound, Rome began to rain down on her body forceful stomps and kicks from every angle. Shavon never stood a chance.

From the cozy confines of her car, Makeba watched in glee. Rome's barbaric actions couldn't have made her happier. She laughed the whole time as he unmercifully beat her. *That's what you fuckin' get, bitch!* she mused.

If it weren't for the loud sound of sirens in the distance, Rome might have done some serious damage to Shavon. As it stood, the sudden noise spooked him, even though it was only a passing ambulance, and Rome ceased beating Shavon. He hopped in Makeba's car and they sped off.

Unbeknownst to them, a half a block away, two federal agents were photographing their every move.

Much to Makeba's relief, the airplane landed without incident. For the entire ride to Puerto Rico she had clung to Rome's muscular arm like a scared child. Though she had taken countless airplane trips as a child with her parents, that didn't meant she liked them. She merely tolerated air travel as a necessary evil, to get her where she wanted to go. And right now that was out of the city.

As a token of her appreciation for his ruthless act, Makeba had booked her and Rome a cruise. This was her way of thanking him and to see if she really wanted to be with him. She figured on an eight-day cruise you would really get to know a lot about a person.

Since it was wintertime, no cruise ship would enter the frozen waters of the Hudson River, risking damage to their vessel, so Makeba and Rome had to fly out of JFK international airport in New York City to the warm waters of San Juan, Puerto Rico. From there they would depart on a Carnival cruise ship.

After gathering their luggage, the couple quickly changed from their heavy leather coats into more suitable attire. Then they jumped into a cab and made their way to the cruise ship.

"Damn, dat fuckin' ship iz big," Rome announced. "A nigga could get lost on da ship fa real!"

Clearly Rome was in awe of the humungous cruise ship. He continually gazed at it from inside the cab.

For her part, Makeba was tickled pink that she was turning Rome onto some new things, the finer things in life. She was glad it was her and not Destiny who was introducing him to another side of life outside of the 'hood life he knew. Through the entire process Makeba felt as if she was civilizing a savage.

The first time Rome had ever left New York City was when he was sent to prison in upstate New York. He didn't hide that fact from Makeba. The facts were what they were with him. He wasn't ashamed of them.

After hours of waiting in long boarding lines, Makeba and Rome were finally allowed to board the cruise ship and settle into their suite.

"Yo, dis room iz crazy!" Rome stated. "How much dis shit cost?"

"Don't worry 'bout dat. Money ain't a thing," Makeba bragged. "You like it, huh?"

"Like it?" Rome asked. "Is dat a question?"

The room Rome referred to was actually a luxurious suite. It was built like a posh penthouse at some fancy hotel and was every bit spacious as it was spectacular. It seemed like every luxury known to man was provided. There was a state-of-the-art entertainment center, a separate living room and dining room, a whirlpool, and floor-to-ceiling-sliding glass doors with a breathtaking view of the ocean.

Inside the suite, Rome felt like a king occupying his palace. Makeba had hoped that this romantic setting would inspire him to do what he did best—have sex, early and often.

"Yo, when we leave I'm takes me a few these robes," he stated. "A nigga sure could use a few of these joints at da crib."

Out of Rome's sight, Makeba just shook her head in disbelief. She couldn't believe how petty Rome was.

From their veranda deck, Makeba and Rome watched as the cruise ship finally embarked, much to the other passengers' delight. With the ocean breeze softly caressing her skin Makeba couldn't help but feel romantic. On the privacy of their veranda Makeba and Rome had a quick, torrid sexual session.

After going through the emergency evacuation procedures, the couple settled back into their suite and rested up for a fun-filled evening on the ship.

"Whut'z on da agenda fa nite?" Rome enquired. "Whut we gone get into?"

"Well, I wuz thinkin' afta we go get sumthin ta eat, maybe we'll go hit da casino," she replied.

"They got a casino on dis joint?" he questioned. "Word?"

"Didn't you read the brochure I gave you?" she asked. "It told you all there is to see and do on the ship."

Makeba could see she was in for a world of stupid questions, which all could have been alleviated by him just reading the brochure. If there was one thing she hated it was stupid questions.

"I musta missed dat part," he said. "But anyway, I'm hungrier than a muthafucka. Let go get sumthin' ta eat."

"Yo, before we leave, could you please do me a favor?" Makeba politely asked. "Could you take dat do-rag off ya head, please."

Rome snapped, "Fa whut? I ain't out here tryin ta impress no-body!"

"Rome, you's a grown-azz man. You too old ta be rockin' a do-rag in public," she pleaded.

"Man, I don't give a fuck." came the reply.

Seeing that he was dead serious, Makeba decided not to press the issue. She could only hope that he would come to his senses later. She immediately began to second-guess the whole idea of even bringing him on a cruise. *Swear, you can't take niggas nowhere,* she thought. For the rest of the trip there would be an uneasy tension between them.

When they arrived at the dining hall, Rome and Makeba were immediately impressed by the vast variety of food, so much they didn't know what to eat. Rome continued to act up in his niggerish way. Once he found out all the food was free, he began stuffing himself. All Makeba could do from being embarrassed was to simply ignore him.

Another thing Rome found even more appetizing than the food was the abundance of single women on the ship. He made a mental note of some of the finest ones, vowing to himself to get up with them later.

When Makeba and Rome finished their respective meals, they began to explore their surroundings. As they did so, Rome began to bombard her with dumb questions about the ship's itinerary.

"Rome, we gonna be at sea fa a day. When we anchor we'll be in St. Martin. From there we are sailing to Barbados, then Martinique, then to Aruba."

"We gone ta all those places in eight days, huh?" he asked.

"Yup!" she replied.

At this point Makeba desperately wanted to get away from Rome. He was just working her last nerve. Makeba would find the diversion she so desperately sought at the casino. The roulette wheel was her favorite game of chance. She knew that her chances of winning some money were the greatest there. Rome wasn't much of a gambler, so the two parted ways. Besides, he had other things on his mind, like chasing woman.

"Yo, I'm go look 'round da ship a little. See if they gotta gym on dis boat. I feel like workin' out! Afta eatin' all da fuckin' food," he explained.

"Later," she flatly replied. "I'll be right here!"

The cruise ship's casino was a pint-sized version of the other casinos Makeba had attended down in Atlantic City, New Jersey. This miniature casino consisted of several blackjack and poker tables, a few roulette tables, and tens of slot machines. Unlike the real casinos, one couldn't get lost in there. Yet there was plenty of money to be lost and made.

Meanwhile, on the upper deck, Rome sat at the bar buying drink after drink, Coke and Hennessy, waiting for lonely women to pass by. He was a shark swimming with a school of fish.

He didn't have wait long for company. Sliding up next to him was group of average-looking black women. They all seemed to be vying for his attention as they laughed, whispered, giggled, and pointed in his direction. For the most part Rome played it cool, pretending not to even notice them. He didn't want to appear pressed for some sex.

"Hey, ladies!" he greeted them.

"Hi!" they seemed to say in unison.

"Where yall from?" he asked.

"Bridgeport, Connecticut," someone replied.

"I hear dat," he replied. "Dat ain't far from da city."

Someone else said, "Nope! We stay partyin' in da city."

"Oh yeah?" Rome replied. "Whut ya'll gettin' into tanite? Where da party at on dis piece?"

One of the women replied, "They gotta lil club somewhere on dis ship. Afta we get our drink on, we on gonna see whut's good wit it."

Right then and there Rome made up his mind. He was partying with them for the night. He ordered drinks for everyone, round after round, which would all be billed to his suite. Of course, Makeba would have to pick up the tab.

After they got nice and tipsy, Rome and the women headed downstairs to the makeshift nightclub. As soon as they entered the club, they became the center of attention, the life of the party, bringing style and flavor to the dance floor with their provocative dance moves. Three women formed a circle around Rome and began grinding their bodies up against him, much to the enjoyment of the crowd.

"Go! Go!" they began to chant.

It wasn't long before a full-fledged party broke out. Everyone in the club seemed to feed off their vibe. The deejay began playing better songs and all the wallflowers began to dance. Now the party was really popping.

It wasn't long before all the originators of this excitement were swept up in the moment. Suddenly the dance floor was jam packed.

This enabled Rome to separate the woman he was dancing with from her friends. That made the task that much easier.

"Whut'z good, Shorty?" Rome whispered. "You rubbin' all up on a nigga dick and shit. I'm tryin' ta see whut da be like. Ya heard?"

The woman smiled slyly at Rome without replying. Her response wasn't exactly what he had hoped for, but Rome continued to press his luck.

"I'm sayin', Shorty, let'z take dis party back ta ya cabin or sumthin'? You fuckin' or whut?"

The woman liked Rome's thuggish, aggressive approach. Finally she relented. Grabbing Rome by the hand, she led him off the dance floor. The two made their way back to her cabin, where they engaged in some hot and heavy sex.

About an hour later Rome left the room with scent of hot, smelly sex plastered all over his private parts. The funny thing was he never did catch the young lady's name. His trip was off to a good start already.

Makeba had her own reasons to be happy. She had had the hot hand on the roulette wheel. She had won close to ten thousand dollars in a matter of hours by placing down large wagers. Her bold bets had been rewarded by lump-sum winnings.

Makeba's Caribbean romantic getaway was doomed from the start. With each designated island stop the cruise ship made, things went from bad to worse.

Coming back to their suite pissing drunk after an brief excursion to a nightclub on the island of Aruba, Makeba smelled Rome's private parts after he passed out on the bed. This was the beginning of the end. Once they returned to New York, Makeba planned to rid herself of this problem.

Back in New York, Makeba and Rome continued with their affair. But she was merely buying time until she figured out how best to get rid of him without angering him. She knew Rome wouldn't take rejection too kindly, and Makeba didn't want to be the recipient of brutal beating. She had to do this right.

Around this time, Makeba started to notice money was coming up missing. Rome was beginning to get too comfortable. He even began slacking in the bedroom. He was taking her money and taking her for granted. On top of that, he was beginning to stress her about Destiny.

"Yo, look, dat ain't cool da way you doin' Destiny," he stated. "I mean, da least you could do iz bail her out. If you don't you ain't never gonna have no luck doin' ya dirty."

Fuck you ! Fuck Destiny! And fuck good luck! Makeba thought. *Ain't no such thing as good luck. It's when preparation meets opportunity.*

Of course Makeba didn't utter a word of this. She couldn't ever let Rome know exactly how she felt about Destiny, or him, for that matter. That would make it easy for him to draw the conclusion that she had indeed set Destiny up. Makeba thought it was best to hide her hand for as long as possible.

Rome, on the other hand, had his own reasons for asking Makeba for funds for Destiny. He needed the money. Between his kids and all the new chicks he was meeting and sleeping with, his expenses were rising daily. Rome had no intention of posting bail for Destiny. He still thought that remaining in jail would convince her to have an abortion.

"How much is her bail?" Makeba inquired.

"Twenty-five hundred, with a bail bondsmen," he lied. "Or twenty-five thousand cash."

"Rome, I'll get dat dough ta you later on," Makeba stated.

"Aiight, bet! Dat way I can go get her out. She been sittin' too long. And dat ain't good fa somebody in her condition," he said.

As soon as the words left his mouth, Rome realized his mistake.

"And whut condition iz dat, Rome?" Makeba asked.

"Oh, you ain't heard? She pregnant by some nigga," he told her. "Right afta she broke up wit me, she started fuckin' wit some Harlem nigga and he knocked her up."

"Oh, yeah?" she commented.

Makeba didn't believe the lame story Rome just told her. She knew her former friend too well. Destiny may have been a lot of things, but loose she wasn't.

After weeks of pondering her situation, Makeba cooked up a fake money-making scheme. She sent Rome down South to collect a stack of company checks from a nonexistent friend. Then, like a thief in the night, Makeba had a moving company come to her house, pack her things, and move her away.

Solitary confinement had its positives and its negatives. A major positive for Destiny was just to be able to converse with Trisha. On the flip side there was a lot of downtime when there was nothing to do and nothing to say. During these times Destiny would rub her stomach incessantly in an attempt to bond with the growing fetus inside her womb. More often than not, this act helped Destiny maintain her sanity when her immediate future seemed bleak.

Most of the time solitary confinement was like a dungeon, dark and dreary. The only time the lights came on was when the corrections officers were running showers, someone was brought in, or medication was dispensed to the inmates. Other than that it was impossible to see anything but a shadow.

The sudden sounds of harsh language, heavy footsteps, and jingling turnkeys shattered the silence of solitary confinement. Immediately inmates scrambled out of their bunks, racing to their cell doors to get a look. This was excitement, a strange form of entertainment for them.

Destiny was amongst those inmates at their cell doors. Through a slight crack in her cell door Destiny peeked out and saw numerous correctional officers dragging an inmate to an empty cell. Though she put up a fight, the female was no match for their sheer numbers. As they dragged her past, Destiny got a good look at her.

Kiss my azz, Destiny mused.

She suddenly realized that she knew the chick. The girl's name was Naomi. She was from her old block on Davidson Avenue. She resisted the urge to call out her name, though. She'd holler at her later, when the correctional officers left.

Destiny couldn't believe that Naomi was on Riker's Island with her. Naomi wasn't the first person she spotted in the jail from her block, but she was the first one that she would get a chance to talk to. The street life had grabbed a whole lot of her generation and had them all meeting back up in prison. Who would have thought they'd both be in jail? Not either of them.

After female officers stripped-searched Naomi for weapons and contraband, the officers closed her cell door and left the tier.

"Yo, Na!" Destiny yelled out. "Get on da gate."

Inside her cell Naomi sat on her bunk, cooling off. She was surprised to hear her name called.

"Yo, who dat?" Naomi questioned. "Somebody called me?"

"Yeah, yo! It'z me, Destiny!" she said.

"Destiny who?" Naomi asked. "Where I know you from?"

"Where you know me from?" Destiny repeated. "Davidson!"

"Oh, shit, Destiny!" she called out. "Destiny Greene?"

"She iz I and I is she. Whut'z good?" Destiny asked.

"Damn, I ain't seen you inna minute. I heard you moved, though," she said. "They said you stopped hustlin and everything. They said you wuz fuckin' wit dat nigga Rome," she told her.

Though they hadn't seen each other, Naomi seemed to know all of her business. The streets were watching and talking. Sometime they could tell her business better than she could.

Naomi continued, "Guess whut?"

"Whut?"

"I heard ya girl Makeba fuckin' wit Rome now. He be drivin' her whips and shit. They say they livin' together now and everything," she mentioned. "Whut's up wit dat?"

"You tell me," Destiny replied flatly. "I can't call it."

She continued to listen to Naomi, acting as if she wasn't affected by the news of Makeba and Rome while hearing updates about what was happening on the streets. She may have fooled Naomi, but she couldn't hide her feelings from herself. Her heart began to sing a sad song. The pain she felt was both mental and physical. Destiny's heart sank to the pit of her stomach. She couldn't believe her ears. How could they violate her like that? She never saw this coming. This was the ultimate betrayal. She felt as if they had both spit in her face. She never thought Rome would cross her like that and began wondering what she done to deserve this. Out of all the females out there he could have got with, he chose her friend?

Suddenly she began to put two and two together. The whole time she spent in jail, Destiny wondered how Rome could have found out about Ramel. Now she knew. Makeba told him. It didn't take much to figure that out. As if being in jail and pregnant weren't enough, now Destiny had this betrayal to deal with. *When it rains it pours,* she thought.

For a moment she fell silent as she tried to digest all the bad news. Though she had accidentally found out about her friend's affair with her man, she was glad that she found out just the same. Destiny reflected on something her father was fond of saying, "What happens in the dark will one day come to light."

Trisha told her she had hit a speed bump in the road of life named Makeba and Rome. She advised her to let the incident be a learning experience—trust no one.

Destiny didn't need any more proof. A guilt verdict was already out in the streets. That night Destiny cried her eyes out and when she finished, she plotted her revenge. She promised herself that she would deal with them both when she got out.

It was Christmas Eve, and Destiny was still in jail. She tried to keep positive thoughts in her head, but it was hard at a time like this since hearing Naomi's rumor. Time and time again Destiny had changed her mind and given Rome the benefit of the doubt, thinking that he would still be a man of his word. She tried to keep faith in him as a man, but with each passing day it was waning. Yet she still clung to that flimsy hope because she didn't know anything else to do.

While Destiny fretted over getting out of jail, in the next cell Trisha tussled with her own thoughts. Here she was in her late forties, facing multiple felony counts of grand theft larceny and theft by deception. Since Trisha was a career criminal with a two-time felony, she knew she was facing a lot of time, and the mere thought of doing it made her sick to the pit of her stomach. The district attorney in her case had already offered her a plea bargain of fifteen and a half to thirty years. If that wasn't bad enough, the feds could be picking up her case any day now.

She wouldn't be seeing Christmas, Thanksgiving, or her birthday on the outside for a very long time. Trisha thanked God she didn't have any children. She couldn't bear the thought of them growing up without her.

Though she put up a brave front, often joking about the time she was facing, it was really killing her inside. She sank into a deep state of depression. When she was alone with her thoughts reality would set in. Even if she did accept the plea agreement, she'd be in her early sixties when she got released, if she was lucky enough to make parole. Trisha would be in the twilight years of her life. As far as she was concerned, her life was over.

Lying on her bunk that night, she made a bold decision to take her own life. Before she would let the State of New York take her life away by giving her a sentence that she couldn't possibly do, Trisha would commit suicide. She decided that now was the time; tonight she would leave this earth. Trisha feared if she gave her decision too much thought, she would never go through with it.

All day long she had been conversing with Destiny. It was a rare moment that they were silent. Trisha advised Destiny on how to apply for a new bail hearing. She also schooled her on the intricacies of the check game, pounding every aspect of it into her head till she was sure that Destiny fully understood it. Trisha imparted her knowledge of the game to Destiny with the full understanding that what she did with it was up to her. She had a choice. It was up to Destiny which one she exercised.

That day the two had talked well into the late evening hours, till Destiny was too tired to stand at the door.

"Yo, Trish I'm tired," she admitted. "I'ma press my bunk."

"C'mon, Destiny, hang out," Trisha insisted. "Don't be a party pooper."

It was commonplace for most inmates in solitary confinement to stay up all night and sleep their days away. Most inmates tended to think it made their days go by faster, and when one was sentenced to solitary confinement, you would do anything and everything to kill some time.

"Trish, I'm about ta fall asleep on my feet. Word!" she confessed.

"Aiight, ga'head ta sleep," Trisha said. "Good night, Destiny. Merry Christmas."

"Same ta you," she replied, falling onto her bunk.

Trisha continued, "Yo, Destiny. Say a prayer fa me."

Destiny was too tired to catch the odd request or suspect that anything was wrong with her friend.

"Yo, I ain't big on prayer. But I'll say one just fa you, if it will make you feel better," she countered. "I'm out!"

"Thanks, God bless you! Take care," Trisha declared.

The flashlight shined brightly in Trisha's face as the night shift correction officer went by, taking his count for the last time. This was the opportunity Trisha had been waiting for. She sprang out of her bed, butt naked, and began to gather the items she needed to carry out her task.

Though most inmates frowned upon suicide, thinking it was a cowardly way out, Trisha could care less what they thought about her when she was dead. They could never truly assess her situation until they walked a mile in her shoes. They could never understand why she killed herself until it was them facing all that time. Then and only then could they honestly say what they would or would not do.

There was a deathlike calm throughout the tier. Maybe this was an indication of what was to come. In the darkness of her cell Trisha took one last hard gulp of air. Then she placed the makeshift noose around her neck that she had made from torn prison bedsheets. She stood on top of the toilet and checked the firmness of the line, thus increasing her chances for success.

Without giving it a second thought, Trisha calmly stepped off the toilet into the darkness of death. She struggled and gasped for air, allowing herself to die. Her feet dangled as she lost consciousness. Within minutes she was dead. A pool of waste beneath her.

"Count time!" the corrections officer said.

Methodically he made his way down the tier, stopping at each cell and looking into each one to make sure there was a live body in it. This duty was never routine, often-times officers never knew what they would find when they looked into the next cell. Nothing would prepare this prison guard for what he was about to see.

Even before he got to Trisha's cell, he smelled the awful scent of her defecation. The odor was so strong he held his nose.

"Oh, shit!" he exclaimed. "Officer Miller, hit Cell Seventeen and call for backup."

With all the commotion being made, other inmates who had been sleeping began coming to their respective cell doors. From the tone of the correction officer's voice, Destiny sensed that something was very wrong. From her vantage point, she could see the officer standing directly in front of Trisha's cell. She wondered what had happened and hoped Trisha was alright.

"Trish!" she yelled out.

Within minutes high-ranking prison officials came running onto the tier, along with a small medical team from the infirmary. The crackling of walkie-talkies echoed throughout the tier.

Now Destiny was very worried. She sensed something bad was going on and anxiously waited along with the other inmates to see what had happened.

The prison officials huddled at Trisha's cell door, talking in hushed tones and pointing inside. Then a few correctional officers donned gloves, went inside, and cut Trisha down. Many of the officers who assisted were spooked by Trisha's eyes that seemed to be bulging out of her head, staring at them.

Before Destiny and the rest of the other inmates knew what was going on, Trisha's lifeless body was covered with a white sheet and wheeled out on a gurney. It didn't take a rocket scientist to figure out what happened. Destiny was one of many inmates who drew the same conclusion that Trisha had killed herself.

Damn! Destiny cursed to herself. *Why you go out like that?*

Later on she found out all the circumstances surrounding the apparent suicide. Destiny didn't know how she made it through the rest of the day. Her friend's death had forced her to relive some of those old feelings she felt when her father died. To Destiny it seemed like she had bad karma, because everyone she cared for died. Everywhere she looked there was death, slowly stalking her and making her life miserable. She didn't think she could handle another bout with death. In her young life it seemed to be a recurring theme.

Death made her think. Destiny began to wonder about her divine purpose on this earth. Thus far, in her own estimation, she was nothing but a common criminal. She picked up a small mirror and began to question herself repeatedly, *Is this what I am? Is this what I've become? A common fuckin' criminal? Is it my destiny to die on the streets or in jail?*

Again she told herself, *I was put here for a reason. But for what?* It was then, in a cell in solitary confinement, that Destiny was finally able to separate life from the game and put things in their proper perspective.

Trisha had always told her, "Life is a puzzle you have to figure out as you go along. It's alright if you don't have all the answers. In time they will come. With age wisdom will come."

As Destiny lay on her bed reflecting, she realized just how right Trisha was. Though they had met under peculiar circumstances, Destiny had really bonded with Trisha. She was the first person aside from her father who made her realize that her life was a work-in-progress. But by no means was it over just because she had made a few mistakes, a few bad choices. For that Destiny was eternally grateful. She would never forget her.

Destiny didn't eat a bit of food all day, mourning her friend's death. When the chow cart came by, she waved the trustee away and ignored the rumbles of her stomach.

For the first in her young life Destiny had met a street person who genuinely cared about her—Destiny the person not Destiny the hustler. Their relationship wasn't about what they could do for each other or what crimes they could commit together. It was about two people meeting and bonding under unusual circumstances. It was about two lives going in different directions, two people just spending quality time together, no matter how brief it was.

Destiny knew as sure as she lived that one day she was going to die. She hoped and prayed her life wouldn't end in a jail. She prayed it wouldn't end how Trisha had ended hers. She couldn't help but feel that Trisha was done a severe injustice, that she deserved better, that the only thing worse than taking your own life in prison was to grow old in prison. To that extent she agreed with what Trisha had done. She taken her destiny into her own hands and went out on her own terms. For that Destiny admired her bravery. But she felt it was something she could never do.

To pay homage to her fallen friend, Destiny promised herself that Trisha's death wouldn't be in vain. She would always remember her and use life lessons she had taught her, as well as the criminal lessons, to play the game of life. What didn't kill her would only make her stronger. She would use her friend's death to ultimately mold herself into a stronger person.

One day, as Destiny lay on her bunk thinking, she heard someone open her cell door. Destiny crawled out of her bed and stuck her head out the door.

"Greene?" the correctional officer hollered.

"Yeah, whut'z up?" she replied.

"Get dressed! Hurry up! You got a visit!" came the answer.

A visit? Destiny thought to herself. *Who the hell is visiting me?*

Even in loose-fitting clothes it was quite easy to see that Destiny was pregnant. Her stomach was beginning to hug the material of her sweatshirt, but her face was still pretty. Pregnancy was agreeing with her.

As Destiny was escorted by two correctional officers through the belly of the beast toward the visiting area, it never dawned on her that it wasn't a regular visiting day. She had been in solitary confinement so long, Destiny had lost track of the day and time. The absence of noise in the visiting room alerted Destiny to the fact that something was wrong. Her fears were soon confirmed. At a table nearby sat a clean-cut, middle-aged white man. He had "Fed" written all over him. Destiny's heart began to race. *What in the hell does he want with me?* she wondered. Had she graduated to the big leagues?

"Destiny Greene?" he questioned.

"Yes, dat's me," she admitted. "Who are you?"

"I'm federal agent John Turner," he said, extending his hand.

Destiny looked at his outstretched hand like it was poisonous. After all, they were natural enemies. He was a cop and she was a crook. Destiny felt no need to be so cordial, especially if the federal agent was here to advise her on an impending indictment.

The federal agent was taken aback by Destiny's cold response and quickly drew back his hand. He didn't know why most criminals responded so unfavorably toward the authorities. To him he was just doing his job.

But the flip side was that her life was at stake here. When the feds moved in criminals knew that their lives, most notably their freedom, were in jeopardy.

"Have a seat," he announced.

Destiny complied, taking the seat directly across the table. From outward appearances she looked cool, calm, and collected. But inwardly she was scared. Getting indicted was every hustler's worst nightmare.

Quickly Destiny's eyes were drawn to several manila envelopes spread out on the table. She could only imagine what was inside of them. Destiny wouldn't have to wait long to find out.

"Do you know a person named Makeba Smith?" he gently asked.

"No!" Destiny responded. "I never heard of her. Do she know me?"

The federal agent smirked at Destiny, as if to let her know he didn't believe her. He didn't know why criminals lied. There was no sense in it. Didn't they know that the feds did their homework? Didn't they know that no rock would be left unturned in an effort to bring them to justice?

In response to her answer, the federal agent opened up one envelope and produced several large, eight-by-ten color photos of Destiny and Makeba together, irrefutable evidence that she was lying.

Destiny's jaw dropped. There was nothing she could say. If a picture was truly worth a thousand words, then these were novels.

"Take a look," he suggested, handing her the photos.

Slowly Destiny filed through the pictures, getting a good look at each one. She was relieved to see that the photos contained nothing implicating her criminally. What impressed her most were the elementary school pictures they had obtained of Makeba and her together. Even she had forgotten that those photographs existed.

"Okay, so whut does dis prove?" she asked. "I'ma bad liar?"

What Destiny couldn't see was that with the pictures the feds were establishing the first links in a chain of a giant conspiracy. The conspiracy laws were so vast, yet vague, that the feds were able to try and convict hundreds of thousands of criminals. In reality the only thing they were really guilt of was association, but they could be convicted on their poor choice of friends and associates.

"You don't realize just how much trouble you could possible be in, huh?" the federal agent stated. "But you can help yourself. You're not the focus of this investigation. This is not even really about your friend Makeba. Are you two still friends?"

Destiny didn't bother to respond to his last question. She just stared blankly at him. It was obvious that he knew something about their relationship, or that he had something else up his sleeve.

Seeing her reaction, the agent proceeded to produce more damaging pictures, only this time they were of a personal nature.

"Miss Greene, would you please take a look at these," he requested.

Destiny took the manila envelope out of his hand, unsure of what she would find. She was quickly tiring of playing games and wished he would just put his cards on the table. She angrily dumped out the contents of the envelope and stared down at dozen of photos of Makeba and Rome scattered on the table. As clear as day Destiny could see the two of them sharing a tender moment, kissing in a car, holding hands while going shopping. The sight of them repulsed her. Suddenly her facial expression began to sour.

The federal agent took extreme pleasure in Destiny's sorrow. She was vulnerable at this point, so he moved in to take advantage of her momentary weakness.

"They sure make a nice couple, huh? Some friends they are. With friends like that, who needs enemies?" The federal agent continued to badger her. "Hey, aren't you pregnant by Rome?"

Destiny sat across from the federal agent, looking evilly at him. She knew it was in her own best interest to say as little as possible, because any statement she made now could come back to haunt her in a court of law. She was unable to know just how much the feds knew about her, but she was led to believe that somebody was snitching. She felt if people would just keep their mouths shut and let the police do their business, the streets would be a lot less hot.

He continued, "As I said, Destiny, you're not the focal point of this federal investigation. Your friend Makeba isn't, either, for that matter."

The federal agent went on to outline an intricate credit-card and check scheme, headed up by several Nigerians, that was defrauding America of hundreds of millions of dollars. The Americans were the low men on the totem pole, pawns in an international crime syndicate.

From another manila envelope he produced more photos, this time of people Destiny definitely didn't know. They were the Nigerians that the agent spoke of. She could tell by tribal scars that adorned some of their faces. The women wore African garments and head wraps. The entire crime ring had names Destiny couldn't even pronounce.

After the federal agent finished painting that picture, he went into another manila envelope and produced even more photos of Destiny at various banks, cashing fraudulent checks.

"So, Destiny, what I'm really asking you to do here is to help yourself. Don't go down for some foreigners you never met and don't know. And don't go down for your fake friends. After all, they didn't even have the decency to bail you out. They're out there making tens of thousands a week and you're stuck in here. This isn't about you. You got a baby to think about here. Do the right thing by your child. You're no good to your child in jail."

If the federal agent's purpose wasn't clear before, it was crystal clear now. He was trying to get Destiny to become a snitch. He wanted her to become a confidential informant for the government.

Where Destiny was from, a snitch was the lowest thing a person could be. It was right up there with being a rapist. Snitches were ostracized, exiled, and whenever possible, killed. Destiny lived by the code of the streets, something that the agent or anyone in nine-to-five societies could never understand. Her morals and principles differed from his. That was evident by the different paths in life each had chosen.

The federal agent had converted so many gangsters, thugs, and bad guys into confidential informants, he was confident he could convert Destiny into one, too. Once the feds started waving huge sentences around, he had seen even the hardest of them crack. Many criminals, when faced with substantial amounts of time, would tell on their own mother.

A smirk suddenly appeared on Destiny's face.

"So dis iz whut dis iz all about? Huh?" she said. "You want me ta snitch?"

"Destiny, I wouldn't exactly call it that," he replied. "Like I said, I'm giving you an opportunity to help yourself. You better take it before someone else does. After that I can't help you. You will be prosecuted to the fullest extent of the law."

What the federal agent neglected to tell her was that Makeba was cooperating with the local investigation. But the federal investigation was something totally different. The feds were aware of the local police actions, but the local authorities were oblivious to theirs. The federal agent wasn't worried about Destiny telling Makeba, either. There was nothing Makeba could do to avoid being indicted. She was in too deep. They had enough evidence on her to arrest Makeba right now. But instead, they were just letting her dig herself a deeper hole. The wheels of justice were slow to turn, but they did grind just the same.

"No thanks," Destiny snapped. "I'm good. Like I told you, I don't know nuttin'."

"Destiny, you're making a grave mistake here. You should take this opportunity. Save yourself," he insisted.

"Oh, really?" she remarked. "It's time fa me ta go. Thanks fa stoppin' by, though."

"Alright, fine!" the federal agent interrupted. "But at least take my card. Just in case you change your mind."

Destiny shook her head in disgust. "You just don't get it, do you? Whut part of no do you not understand? The 'n' or the 'o'?"

"Destiny, this isn't the last you'll see of me," the federal agent warned. "I promise you."

Destiny turned on her heels and walked away. She was proud of herself. She didn't take the bait. She didn't care what Rome and Makeba did to her, there was no justification for snitching.

A few days after her visit from the feds, Destiny's cell door was once again mechanically opened. This time she didn't bother to go to the door.

"Greene! Greene!" the corrections officer shouted.

"Yeah!" Destiny yelled back nastily.

"They want you in court," he told her. "Hurry up and get dressed."

Destiny's heart began to pound wildly against her chest. She thought this was it. She was going to indicted on federal charges.

Once the prison van pulled up to the Bronx Criminal Court, Destiny blew a sigh of relief. *Well, at least it ain't the feds,* she thought. Still, there was no telling just what lay in store for her in that courthouse.

Destiny's black public defender greeted her with a smile as she entered the courtroom. She stared menacingly at her. Destiny didn't see the reason why she was so happy.

"Just in case you were wondering, this is a bail-reduction hearing," she announced. "There's a good chance you'll be released today. We got the hearing in front of a different judge. She's pretty fair."

As fate would have it, the public defender was entirely right on all accounts. The judge looked at Destiny's rap sheet and found no prior criminal charges, let alone criminal convictions. Even she couldn't understand why the young woman before her had been remanded to Riker's Island. The judge actually apologized for this travesty of justice. With her judicial power, she righted the wrong and set Destiny free.

CHAPTER 20

Now that Destiny was finally freed, she didn't exactly know what to do with herself. All she knew was it was back to square one. Destiny was just glad to be out. At home she realized that her worst day on the streets didn't even compare to her best day in the prison. Destiny spent most her days getting reacquainted with her freedom. She did little things like sitting at home alone watching movies or listening to her vast collection of music on compact discs.

For the time being, she decided against seeking immediate revenge against Makeba. Destiny reserved all her energy for more positive things, like surviving. Getting her life in order was first on her list of priorities. Temporarily she pushed any thoughts of harming either Rome and Makeba out of her mind. She would wait till the opportunity presented itself. Destiny knew if she let her dislike for them drive her, then more than likely she would fail in any attempt at harming them. If she was lucky, the feds would do the dirty work for her. Though she didn't wish jail on anyone, she couldn't think of a more deserving pair than Rome and Makeba.

After a few short days of freedom Destiny came to a painful

conclusion. She decided to abort her baby. She felt as though she just didn't have enough support, family-wise or financially. Destiny thought about the old African proverb, "It takes a village to raise a child," and couldn't agree with it more. Her finances were low. She was lucky that she had decided to pay her rent a year in advance when she was hustling and making money. Otherwise, Destiny would be living in some crowded city shelter.

Growing up as a kid, when she often fantasized about having a baby, she always envisioned the child's father playing a major role in its life. She wanted her child to grow up in a two-parent household, not like she did. Based upon her current circumstances, the decision was made. She picked up the phone and dialed the number of an abortion clinic she had gotten off the Internet and scheduled an appointment. All there was left to do was be calm and wait for the day to arrive.

In her mind Destiny thought it would be as simple as one, two, three once she had made her sudden decision, but her emotions began to betray her. She would cry uncontrollably at the sight of a baby on television. Sometimes at night she would have nightmares of dying while undergoing the abortion procedure.

The day finally came for Destiny to have her abortion. Her morning seemed to drag along as if she were about to walk the plank. She glanced at the clock several times. Once it struck ten A.M. Destiny gathered her things and headed for the door. As she exited the apartment, Destiny couldn't help but think, *If Trisha knew what I was doing she would kill me.*

The abortion clinic was located inside a nondescript building in the heart of New York City. After a brief ride on the elevator, Destiny arrived at her destination. As she pulled the double doors open, her eyes were greeted by a room filled with women of all ethnic origins and their sexual partners. They all were there for various reasons, yet they were about to share the same fate, ridding themselves of unwanted fetuses.

"Hi, my name iz Destiny Greene. I have an appointment at eleven thirty," she announced meekly.

"Have a seat, ma'am. Someone will be with you in a minute," the nurse's aide replied.

Inside the clinic, it was business as usual. One after another, women were led through a series of brief formalities. Destiny Greene was lost in the shuffle, just one of many. She first had to check in at the front desk with her state-issued identification. Then she had to wait to be called. Then Destiny had to make some form of payment—cash, credit card, or insurance card. In her case it was cash. Then she was made to fill out some paperwork, a consent form, and a medical history. Next, her blood work was done. She met with a social worker to make sure an abortion was what she really wanted, and Destiny assured her it was. After that a sonogram was performed to see how far along she was. From there Destiny was sent to see the nurse and a few pills were dispensed to her—a muscle-relaxer, pain killer, and cervix softener. She had to wait about forty-five minutes for the medication to take effect.

During the entire process, Destiny's psyche began to play tricks on her. Her mind was telling her to go through with the procedure, but her body was telling her not to.

A war raged within her. Destiny became oblivious to her surroundings. Before she knew it, she was lying on her back, close to the edge, on the examination table, with both feet placed in stirrups and a machine to monitor her blood pressure attached to her arm. That was when Destiny freaked out. She had a panic attack and was overcome by a sudden sympathy for her fetus. She couldn't go through with the abortion.

She began hollering at the top of her lungs as if someone was murdering her. Destiny kicked at the approaching physician, putting the strong stirrups to the test.

After witnessing her violent reaction, the physician immediately called off the procedure. Destiny was refunded her money and quietly left the clinic.

For several days and nights afterward, Destiny cried and sulked, knowing just how close she had come to an abortion. Her indecision was killing her. Did she do the right thing?

After wrestling with her conscience, Destiny concluded that she couldn't bring herself to set foot inside another abortion clinic. She couldn't take the life of something so precious and innocent. Against all odds, Destiny decided to have her baby. She was doing this by herself and for herself. She thought, *To hell with Rome.*

Pregnancy was a new and wonderful experience for Destiny. In jail, in the early stages of her pregnancy, she couldn't fully appreciate the dramatic transformation her body was undergoing because of all the stress she was under. Her child's father played a major part in that, too. Still, she couldn't help but think how much better it would be if she had Rome around. She didn't dwell on that, but it didn't stop the thought from running across her mind from time to time. All her bitter thoughts were temporarily replaced with thoughts of joy and excitement. She was with child and it was making her a better person.

Except for the days when her morning sickness got the best of her, Destiny didn't complain at all. She just took it in stride. She was learning to make the most of each day as it came. Her good days far outnumbered the bad ones. Destiny refused to let anything get her down. She went to her prenatal classes by herself, with a chip on her shoulder that seemed to say, *I'm a single parent, so what.*

To make ends meet, Destiny committed welfare fraud. She was getting food stamps and WIC checks in several people's names. A hustle was a hustle; now she had two mouths to feed.

Eventually Destiny wanted to give up her life of crime, but she had no concrete plans for how she would realistically make a living. All she had was a burning desire to give up the game for her unborn child's sake. Destiny wanted to be the kind of mother her child could be proud of. She wanted to be admired, appreciated, respected, and above all else, loved by her child. That wasn't too much to ask for, she thought.

Destiny's due date came and went without as much as a contraction or labor pain. The doctors had warned her stay close to home and transportation as they were sure she was going to deliver any day now. During a routine prenatal check up it was discovered that Destiny was dilated to ten centimeters. She ignored her physician when he told her how close she was to going into labor and ventured out to find a bathrobe for her stay in at the hospital.

The temperature inside the Number Twelve mass transit bus was ice cold compared to the scorching heat on the city streets. Destiny sat in the back of the bus as it made its way down Fordham Road and looked out the windows at all the people sweating their behinds off. She knew as soon as she got off the bus that would be her, too. Suddenly she felt like she sitting in a pool of sweat. On second thought, she was too drenched in her private parts for it to be sweat. That was when she realized her water broke.

A gentlemen nearby had taken notice of her physical state

and notified the bus driver, who radioed an ambulance for emergency medical assistance. Before long the city bus resembled a three-ring circus with everyone rushing to the scene. Pretty soon the local news stations got wind of the breaking story and they dispatched camera crews to the scene.

Inside the bus, Destiny lay on the floor, sweating profusely. Her contractions were intense as the EMS workers coached her through the final stages of labor.

"Push! Push!" they instructed.

Destiny damn near turned red in the face from all the straining she was doing. She was in excruciating pain and wanted this baby out of her body in the worst way.

"Here it comes!" an EMS worker said. "Keep pushing!"

Destiny pushed one last time with all her might and out of her womb came a bouncing baby boy. From the bus mother and child were transported to Jacobi hospital on Pelham Parkway by ambulance, where they rested comfortably. At the hospital his measurements were finally taken. He weighed seven pounds, three ounces, and measured twenty inches long. His miraculous birth made headlines across the city.

Rome stared in horror at the *Daily News*. He was in complete shock to see a photo of Destiny and his child splashed across the front page. For one thing, he thought Destiny was still locked up. For another, he thought he had done and said enough to dissuade her not to go through with the pregnancy. "Damn!" He cursed his bad luck. All he could think about was his wife Kim finding out and all the drama that would cause in his life.

Back at the hospital, Destiny and child recuperated for a few days. Together they worked on getting to know each other, and Destiny learned some child-care skills. At this point the child was still unnamed. Destiny was unsure of exactly what to call him. For a long time she was undecided about having it, so she never really did a thorough investigation of baby names. One name was so far out of the question, it wasn't even a question, and that was Jerome Wells Jr. There was no way in the world Destiny was going to bestow such a high honor on upon some no-good, good-for-nothing, deadbeat dad. That turned out to be a blessing in disguise, because little did she know Rome already had a son named after him. Another would only cause confusion.

As if struck by a bright idea, Destiny suddenly decided to name her newborn son after her deceased father. When she saw the social worker and filled out the birth certificate application, she put down her child's name as Kenneth Greene, but she called him KK, which would be his own personal nickname, for Ken-Ken, which had been her father's.

After a few days mother and child left the hospital to no fanfare, just like Destiny had gone home with her father two decades ago. It was eerie to Destiny how her son's young life was already beginning to parallel hers. She could only hope that this was just a coincidence and not a sign of what was to come.

At home Destiny, began to settle into her role as mother. For the first few weeks of her child's existence Destiny fretted over any and everything, since she didn't know any better and she didn't have anyone around her to help her. Other than his physical well-being, Destiny worried about his immediate future. How was she going to realistically provide for her son's day-to-day care? For the time being she had more than enough clothes, food, and diapers, but her supply wouldn't last long. Destiny knew she couldn't raise her child on welfare. With all the welfare reform bills in effect the days of raising a child solely on a welfare check were a thing of the past. Welfare was something to supplement one's income. It was never meant to be a person's sole means of support. Besides, Destiny was used to more than what a measly welfare check could provide.

Circumstances dictated Destiny's reentry into the game. Like a New Year's resolution, she broke her promise to herself and God. Her period of chilling out was short-lived. In the back of her mind she knew her future was still cloudy and her troubles might only just be beginning, but there was another, even greater problem waiting in the wings. It was a federal indictment. She constantly wondered if and when that would happen.

After a few weeks of being confined to his home, KK was taken to a babysitter in his mother's old South Bronx neighborhood. This was the closest to the 'hood Destiny hoped her child would ever get. There he was left in the reliable care of a friend of the family. An elderly women named Ms. Frances charged Destiny fifty dollars a week. Destiny had to provide her own diapers and food. With her child in good hands, she was free to concentrate on criminal activities. And that she did.

Destiny's fear of indictment didn't hinder her from taking her current course of action. She told herself she would deal with the feds when the time came. For now she had to get her grind on. After a few inquiries into the who's who and what's what on the streets, Destiny came up with the name of a former acquaintance who was stealing payroll checks from her job. Immediately Destiny contacted the girl and together they formed a profitable partnership.

As the weeks went by, Destiny began to climb the slippery ladder of street success. The company her friend worked for was so huge that the accounting department hadn't yet noticed that the checks were stolen. This enabled Destiny to cash them with relative ease. Slowly but surely her stash began to grow. Destiny began to feel good about her future and that of her child's. Then one day her world came crashing down on her.

Buzzzz! Buzzzz! Buzzzz! Her cellular phone rang repeatedly.

The first few times, Destiny ignored it. Currently she was working, about to bust a check at City Bank in Yonkers, New York. While Destiny was at work she didn't let anything interrupt her. She needed to be totally focused on what she was doing. Destiny didn't disturb other people while they were on the job. She'd be damned if she let them disturb her on her job. Time and time again she fought the urge to check her phone.

Buzzz! Buzzz! Buzzzz! Her cellular phone vibrated loudly in her purse.

"Fuck it!" she cursed. "Let me answer this call for it drives me crazy!"

As Destiny retrieved her phone, she looked down at the telephone number and immediately recognized it as belonging to her babysitter, Ms. Frances. Before she even heard a word, Destiny knew something was very wrong.

"Hello?" she said.

A frantic voice on the other line greeted her. "Destiny, KK stopped breathing! The paramedics, the police, everybody is in my house trying to resituate him. Meet me at the hospital!"

Destiny began to feel woozy, sick to her stomach. She immediately bolted from the bank and caught a nearby cab. On her way to the local hospital Ms. Frances's words burned in Destiny's ears. *KK stopped breathing! KK stopped breathing!* What the hell did she mean? Destiny wondered. Perfectly healthy babies didn't just up and stop breathing. She reasoned Ms. Frances didn't know what she was talking about. Destiny pushed all ill thoughts about her son out of her mind.

When Destiny arrived at the Bronx Lebanon Hospital's emergency room entrance, there were paramedics, police officers, nurses, and social workers everywhere. This was not a good sign at all. Now she realized that something was terribly wrong. She looked around for Ms. Frances and found her sitting down looking distraught, giving a statement to the police. Destiny rushed over to her.

"Where's KK?" she interrupted. "Where is he?" Ms. Frances was under immense pressure. She was unable to take it anymore and broke down into tears.

"Where's my baby?" Destiny repeated again and again. "Where's my baby?"

Finally the police officer took pity on Ms. Frances and intervened. "Your son is dead, ma'am. Sorry."

"Whut?" Destiny shouted at the top of her lungs. "Oh my God! No! Not my baby! No!"

"Miss, I understand the situation is very hard on you, but would you please calm down," the policemen asked politely.

Destiny ignored the policemen, becoming a bit more belligerent. She asked Ms. Frances question after question but got no satisfactory answers in return. Finally a nurse pulled her to the side and went to explain her child had died of sudden infancy death syndrome, SIDS, for which there were no symptoms and no cure. She went on to explain that Ms. Frances did nothing wrong. It was just unfortunate that her child's death happened on her watch. But she insisted, it could have happened to anyone.

Once again Destiny had suffered another tragic setback in her young life. It was strange how death underscored just how precious life really was.

CHAPTER 21

Wwwwwwwaaaaannnn! Wwwwwwaaaaannn!" the baby cried.

From the kitchen Destiny could hear the faint wails of her child. "Hush, KK, I'll be right there."

Destiny continued to wash the few dishes in the sink before she headed back to the bedroom to tend to her child. She ignored his continuous cries, thinking he was becoming spoiled. It was good to let a child cry out every now and then.

When Destiny was finished she turned off the faucet. Immediately her ears were greeted by the strange sound of silence. Destiny grabbed the bottle out of its warmer and ran down the hall. Entering the bedroom, a strange sense of panic began to wash over her. As she moved cautiously toward the crib, she felt something was wrong.

"KK!" she called out. "I bought you ya ba-ba!"

She heard nothing in response. Destiny hoped the loud sound of her voice would cause the baby to move around a bit, but he lay motionless.

Destiny rushed over to the crib and reached inside, turning the baby over on his back. To her shock, her baby was blue in the face and he wasn't breathing. "KK!" she screamed. "KK!"

Destiny placed him back down inside the crib and performed CPR. She tried valiantly to resuscitate him. Just as the baby was beginning to show signs of life, she awoke.

Instead of having a funeral service for her child, a burial or cremation, Destiny decided to donate her child's remains to science. There were two reasons behind that decision. The first was she was too emotionally weak to go through with viewing her child's body at a funeral. Destiny also wondered who would attend the service. A small turnout would only plummet her deeper into depression. Surely her child's father would be absent. The other was that she didn't ever want someone else to go through what she had gone through. Destiny didn't want another mother to suffer all that pain, agony, and sadness.

Slowly Destiny opened her eyes. Fresh tears clouded her vision. It didn't take long for her to realize she had been dreaming. The scariest thing about her dream was it had been recurring. She seemed to wake up on the same part every time. That always frustrated her. In her dream, she wanted to see how it ended. Did her child survive or did he die?

In the days that followed, Destiny was still completely disoriented. Her apartment was in complete disarray, just like her life. Dishes were piled high in the sink and baby clothes were scattered everywhere. Destiny lay in her bed, wallowing in her own misery, refusing to move a muscle. She was content to do nothing at all. Her child's sudden death demoralized her.

Grieving takes on many forms. It affects each individual differently. There was no set timetable for Destiny to overcome her grief, if she could overcome it at all. The grief she was currently experiencing was unspeakable.

For about a week she curtailed all illegal activities. The initial shock of her child's sudden death never wore off. It affected Destiny deeply. She became bitter at the world. She had heard all the medical explanations and none of them made any sense to her. Her baby hadn't even begun to live and now he was gone. In her present state reasoning seemed to have eluded Destiny. For her there wasn't enough blame to go around. She pointed the finger at everyone, as if her child's death was one big conspiracy.

The coroner's report cleared Ms. Frances of any foul play. This left Destiny without anyone to blame accept God. Constantly, she questioned the existence of a superior being. Destiny stopped believing completely. *How could God let something so terrible happen to my child? How?* she wondered over and over again.

Not a day went by that Destiny didn't miss her deceased son. She missed him increasingly, so much so it was killing her. In her mind Destiny began to replay the times they spent together. She cherished these tender moments no matter how short the length of time was, but she wanted to hold her baby close again and never let go. If she could, Destiny would have turned back the hands of time and relived that fateful day. She tried hard to keep staying strong, to keep her composure. But behind closed doors she failed time and time again.

After days of reflection, Destiny took a survey of her life. The more she thought about it, the more she began to realize death played a major role in her life. And here it was again, just waiting in the wings for the right time to pounce on her. Destiny felt like she lived in death's shadow. She began thinking about what she had done to keep being punished in this way. First death claimed the life of her mother, then her father, and now her child. She wondered, Am I next? Death had taken everyone she loved or held dear in this world.

One day Jerome Wells's name suddenly popped into her head. Lately the mere thought of him made her extremely angry. The time had come to stop feeling sorry for herself and make someone else feel as miserable as she did. Makeba and Rome were about to see that hell hath no fury like a woman scorned.

Now that she no longer had her son to take care of, Destiny had more than enough cash to start over someplace else. It was time to set the wheels of revenenge in motion.

The first thing Destiny did was to break her lease. She did so by waging a campaign of complaints at the management office. For weeks she complained about rodents around the garage disposal by letter, in person, and over the phone. She became a real pain in the ass to management, so they were more than happy to break her lease and have her move out. They didn't want her kind in the building anyway. Destiny had a moving company dispose of everything in her apartment. The only thing she took with her was clothing. She then checked into a local hotel and began to pay a weekly fee to live there, knowing that once she set about on her plan of destruction that her home would be the first place anyone looked for her. It would be stupid to stay there, because there could possibly be some deadly repercussions.

In her hotel room, Destiny sat in a chair at the desk and carefully thumbed through the thick yellow phone book. She turned the pages so slowly it seemed as if she had all the time in the world. It was a part of her plan, so Destiny had to be cautious in everything she did. Failure or success depended on it.

While in jail, Destiny realized that she didn't really know Rome. No one Destiny knew really knew him, either, so she couldn't come up with background information on him by making a series of calls. No, things wouldn't be that easy. Destiny knew she would need professional help, which brought her to the phone book.

Before Destiny attacked her enemy, Rome, she needed to know everything about him—friends, family, and lovers. She needed to know what and who he cared about, who or what he loved the most, and go after it. She wanted Rome to regret the day he ever laid eyes on her.

Before Destiny knew it, a few hours had passed. Not that it mattered. She didn't care anything about time these days. In that time she had circled a dozen or so private investigators, adding their names to a list. Satisfied with the list she had complied, Destiny began calling them.

One by one she began contacting the agencies, and one by one she began scratching names off her list. Her reasons for eliminating agencies varied. Some were too expensive and others were rude. Finally, she settled on an older gentleman with over thirty years in the business. In Destiny's eyes what really made the man so attractive to hire, besides his low prices, was his skin color. She could tell by his voice that the private detective was black. That would help him to blend into the environment he would be in.

Destiny made an appointment with his secretary for tomorrow. She would have to bring with her the fee for his services and a picture of the subject. Another thing Destiny would need was a good lie.

Tomorrow couldn't come quickly enough for Destiny. She was up bright and early in preparation for her appointment. After showering and dressing she was out the door, on the subway, and headed downtown to her meeting.

There was nothing prestigious about the private investigator's downtown office. The building looked primitive surrounded by the beautiful skyscrapers and mega structures that dominated the downtown landscape. One could tell that the building had a lot of history. It had seen a lot of changes over the course of its existence. Destiny took one look at it and knew the inside had to be even worse than the outside. Her prediction was right on the money.

The building had no elevator. Destiny was forced to walk up three flights in high heels and a business suit. When she reached the third floor, she had already begun to break out into a slight sweat.

It took Destiny a little while before she found his office. There were only a few signs on a few doors that advertised the occupant's business. Finally she found it.

JOHN MATTHEWS, PRIVATE INVESTIGATOR, the sign read.

This must be the place, Destiny thought sarcastically.

After fixing herself up, Destiny began to knock on the door. The knocks were quiet at first and then they grew louder.

"Come in," a voice softly said. "The door's open."

Destiny turned the knob and entered the office, waiting not too far from the door. From her vantage point, she could see that it wasn't a real office at all. It was merely a large cubicle sectioned off, with a door. Destiny would bet her life that the man probably paid a king's ransom just for the right to say he had offices in Manhattan.

"Hello, young lady," the old black man said. "I see you made it down here in one piece."

The man extended his hand to Destiny. She shook it ever so lightly. The man's palms were sweaty. In Destiny's book that was nasty. She felt violated.

"Would you please follow me?" he stated. "Pardon our appearance, but my secretary is off today. She usually straightens up around here."

The walk to his inner office was short. Before Destiny knew it, they squeezed into a tiny room that could barely hold a desk and two chairs. Together they sat down and proceeded to conduct business.

"Young lady, what did you say your name was again?" he inquired.

"Charisa Mitchell," she lied.

"And where you say you're from?" he asked.

"I'm from Brooklyn," she said.

On the small desk the man had a piece of paper. He took notes as Destiny talked, but she didn't care as she planned on feeding him a pack of lies. The only thing she wouldn't lie about was Jerome.

"I don't know much about Brooklyn. I'm from Long Island myself," he mentioned. "I only fool around in the city when I have to, if you know what I mean. Too much traffic for me. Anyway, tell me what brings you here."

It's about time, Destiny thought.

The old man was talking her ear off about things she wasn't concerned with. She wanted to get this meeting over as soon as possible. The longer she was in this man's presence the greater the possibility he had of identifying her.

"Well, like I told your secretary my best friend is engaged to be married, and her fiancé has a bad habit of disappearing for weeks on end," Destiny explained. "He claims he's a merchant marine. I think he's cheating. I think he got him a little thing on the side. But my friend is so head over heels in love, it's making her stupid."

The old man interrupted, "So this where I come in. You want me to uncover the dirt on him."

"Yup! Pretty much," Destiny added.

"Boy, you sure are a good friend. Why are you doing all this?" he asked.

Destiny paused for a minute, looking the private detective

right in the eye. To spice up her acting, Destiny got all teary-eyed and began crying.

"Cause I love her. And I don't wanna see her hurt. We have been best friends since kindergarten," she sobbed.

"Okay! Okay! Take it easy, ma'am. Everything is going to be alright. You've come to the right place."

The man handed Destiny a box of tissues, which sat on his desk, to wipe her tears away. As she put the tissues to good use, the detective began to scribble on the paper furiously. Destiny couldn't make out what he was jotting down because his handwriting was so sloppy.

After she pulled herself together, Destiny handed over the private detective's retainer fee. Briefly they made small talk while he wrote Destiny out a receipt. Then he proceeded to ask Destiny personal questions about Rome. He wanted know his real name, his occupation, his date of birth, and his last-known address and cell phone number.

In this day and age, all the man would really need to track Rome down was his cell phone number. With technology so highly advanced, the detective would be able to pinpoint Rome's whereabouts by feeding his computer all the information she had just given him.

Destiny handed over the picture of Rome and then headed back up to the Bronx. All she was had to do next was wait for the private detective to get back to her. Then the fun part would begin. Now it was time to find Makeba. They had some unfinished business to attend to.

Destiny didn't have to search the four corners of the earth to find Makeba. After all, she was her best former friend. As the old saying goes, your best friend could be your worst enemy. She knew everything about Makeba and vice versa. The logical choice was to go directly to Makeba's mother's house. She would lead Destiny right to her. Or so she hoped.

Standing in the hallway, Destiny could see an eyeball looking out the peephole. Someone was staring at her, trying to determine her identification. Destiny stepped away from the door so that her physical features were in full view.

"Who?" the voice said softly. "What you want?"

"Mrs. Simmons?" Destiny replied. "It's me! Destiny Greene."

"Destiny, that's you?" the voice shouted. "I don't believe it."

"Yeah, it me!" Destiny smiled.

The locks were quickly undone and the apartment door swung open. The two women stood face to face, smiling and admiring each other before embracing. Then they stepped inside the apartment to finish this joyful reunion.

Destiny was honestly as happy to see Makeba's mom as she was to see her. Since Destiny began running the streets, her visits to the Simmons' home had become few and far between. Destiny was ashamed at that fact now, after Mrs. Simmons had watched Destiny grow up and on many occasions had fed her. Over the years Mrs. Simmons was the closet thing she had had to a mother. Destiny had nothing but love and respect for the woman. Her differences didn't involve Makeba's mother. She wouldn't harm a hair on her head. Her beef was strictly with Makeba. Destiny was not going to misappropriate her anger. If things went the way she planned, the right person would bleed.

"Destiny, how you been? Girl, I haven't seen you in about two years," Mrs. Simmons stated. "Where you been hiding?"

"Has it been that long?" she questioned. "It don't seem like it, though. I guess time really do fly, huh?"

"Sure does," Mrs. Simmons replied. "I remember when you and Makeba were babies. Seem just like yesterday, too. Now look at you, you're damn near a grown woman. Boy, I'm getting old."

"Speaking of Makeba, is she here?" she asked.

Mrs. Simmons looked at her strangely. Suddenly she frowned.

"Makeba don't stay here no more." Mrs. Simmons stated. "I thought you knew. She been moved out. She stays somewhere in New Jersey. I think in Teaneck or Fort Lee. I forget. Don't start me to lying."

"Oh, dat's right, she did say dat," Destiny lied. "How could I forget dat?"

"When's the last time you talked to her? Huh?" Mrs. Simmons inquired.

"Oh, it's been awhile. Not since I lost my cell phone. Makeba's number was in my old phone," Destiny explained. "I lost contact wit her when I lost her phone number."

"Oh?" Mrs. Simmons stated. "You girls need to keep in touch. Yall are like sisters."

Destiny interrupted, "Excuse me, Mrs. Simmons, can I get Makeba's home phone number?"

Destiny knew if she got her hands on that, she was in business. She would be able to drop by and pay Makeba a visit. Then she could handle her business with her in private.

"Destiny, I know you Makeba's friend and everything. But . . . ," she began. "I don't give out her number anymore. Too many people have been coming by here trying to get in contact with her. And when I give them her number, she starts fussing at me. I ain't trying to hear that child mouth. I'll call her for you and let you talk her. Let her give you the number herself."

"Okay, Mrs. Simmons, no problem. I can respect that," Destiny stated. "We both know how funny Makeba can get."

Mrs. Simmons left the room and reappeared with a cordless phone. With her ear pressed to the receiver, she listened to it ringing. On the third or fourth ring, Makeba answered the phone.

"Yeah, Ma?" Makeba said. "Whut'z up?"

"Hold on a minute. I got somebody who wants to speak with you," Mrs. Simmons announced.

"Ma, I hope you ain't openin' ya door fa everyone claimin' to be my friend. I told you 'bout dat already," Makeba exclaimed. "I don't . . ."

Makeba's mother just shook her head as she passed Destiny the phone. She had heard it all before. Suddenly her daughter had become so security conscious and she couldn't understand why.

"Hello," Destiny spoke. "Makeba?"

"Yeah! Who's dis?" she spat.

Makeba was preparing to curse out the person on the other end of the phone. She didn't like the fact that street people were showing up at her mother's door, looking for her, just because she was making money. To her this was a violation of her parents' home. She preferred that anyone looking for her catch up with her in the streets. It was times like this Makeba wished she still had Rome around to deal with these situations. He was a thug. When it came to real street matters, Rome handled his business. Makeba knew she wasn't built like that for this part of the game. Her harsh words could only go so far before it was time to back them up with violent actions.

Destiny replied, "Yo, it'z ya girl, Destiny! Whut'z up?"

Upon hearing the name, Makeba's heart sank. She thought somebody was playing a cruel joke on her, because the only Destiny she knew was in jail. She was sure of that.

"Surprise, surprise, huh?" Destiny replied. "Speak. Whut'z good? It's me, Destiny Greene, remember me?"

Destiny flashed Mrs. Simmons her most innocent of smiles. But that was a fake-out. She was feeling real nasty, like she was ready to hurt someone. Destiny was having fun tormenting Makeba over the phone. If only Mrs. Simmons really knew what was going on.

"Destiny, when you get out?" Makeba mumbled. "I mean—"

"Get out? Whoever said I was in? You must got me confused wit somebody else. Dat wuzn't me," Destiny stated. "You funny?"

Makeba's probing questions were like an admission of guilt to Destiny. She didn't need any more proof. Makeba was guilty as sin of sleeping with her boyfriend and setting her up. Destiny had convicted her with her own words.

"Yo, where you at? You comin' over or whut?" Destiny sarcastically asked. "Me and ya mother just sittin' here kickin it. We reminiscin' over old times. Wish you hurry up and get over here. I don't want ta start da party witout you."

Once again Destiny turned toward Makeba's mother and shot her a phony smile. Destiny was having a ball pretending everything was cool, but the threatening undertone of their conversation was clear to Makeba. Destiny made sure of it.

"Yo, Destiny put my mother on da phone," Makeba ordered.

"Okay, whuteva you say," Destiny insisted. "Here she go. Mrs. Simmons, Makeba wants you."

Destiny turned the phone over to Mrs. Simmons.

"Hello?" she said.

"Ma, iz everything alright over there?" Makeba questioned. "You okay?"

"Everything is alright. Me and Destiny just sitting here talking," she assured her. Destiny knew by the puzzled look on Mrs. Simmons' face that Makeba was asking her some strange questions, but she pretended not to be paying attention.

"You sure?" Makeba questioned. "You sure everything is okay?"

"I'm positive," her mother stated. "Why you say that? There's nobody here but me and Destiny. Is something suppose ta be wrong? You're not making any sense. Where are you?"

Makeba admitted, "I'm in da neighborhood. I'll be right there."

Makeba had no reason to believe that her life was in danger. Still, she felt threatened by the fact that Destiny was inside her mother's apartment, in light of all the dirt she had done to Destiny. So there was no way she was going to leave her helpless mother alone with her. She didn't know what was running through Destiny's mind. She had fucked her former friend so hard there was no telling what she might do.

Destiny had handled the loss of her child better than she had handled the loss of her friendship. But that didn't mean that she hurt any less. She had chalked the death of her baby up as an act of God. But Makeba's treason was a deliberate, premeditated, and totally inexcusable act. As tough as Destiny was, she still was human. She wasn't immune to pain.

Throughout the course of her young life, she had invested a lot of time and emotions in Makeba and Rome. Now it had seemed to her all her efforts were wasted on two good-for-nothing individuals.

There was no magic wand Destiny could wave over the situation to make things better between her and Makeba. She didn't have any special words like hocus-pocus that would repair the damage that was done to their friendship. Right now she didn't particularly care to hear any explanations, either. The only thing that would satisfy Destiny would be to inflict some pain of her own. It was the code of the street that was instilled in her.

Makeba arrived at her parents' apartment building in record time. Bypassing the elevator, she ran up the stairs, fearing the worst.

Makeba burst through the apartment door out of breath. She moved quickly through the apartment in search of her mother and Destiny, saying a silent prayer that everything was okay. She reached the living room only to find Destiny and her mother totally engrossed in a conversation.

The sudden appearance of Makeba bought their conversation to an abrupt end. Both of the women looked curiously at her. The perspiration spots on her underarms and around the neck of her blouse raised a few eyebrows.

"Why are you sweating? What you been doing?" her mother questioned.

Makeba ignored her. Whatever her mother was saying now wasn't important. Her attention was fully focused on Destiny.

"Ma, could you excuse us fa a minute," Makeba asked. "Me and Destiny need ta talk in private."

"Okay. Everything you do is so secretive these days," her mother said disgustedly. "Sometimes you make me so sick. If I didn't know any better I swear you was doing something illegal."

Having spoken her mind, Mrs. Simmons marched out the room. Makeba was so spoiled that sometimes even she forgot who was the child and who was the parent.

"Whut up, Makeba?" Destiny whispered. "Long time, no see, friend! Heard you and Rome been a lil busy while I wuz gone."

Makeba stood at a safe distance away from Destiny. She said nothing. There was no way she was going to get into an argument with her. She knew in the 'hood that arguments turn into fistfights, and a fistfight with Destiny was something Makeba knew she couldn't win. She wasn't a fighter.

It was crystal clear to Makeba that Destiny knew something,

or else she wouldn't have made that sort of statement. So she figured the best thing to do was to keep her mouth shut and hear her out. Makeba wanted to find out everything she knew and exactly what Destiny was going to do about it. As far as she was concerned, the ball was in her court.

"Yo, dat shit had me twisted when I heard ya'll wuz fuckin' around," Destiny confessed. "I ain't even gonna lie. I mean, whut wuz you fuckin thinkin'? Dat paper had you gassed like dat? Whut, you thought you wuz me? Huh? Well guess whut, ya not me! And you'll never be! Play ya position, bitch!"

Destiny sat on the couch with her hands jammed inside her jacket pockets and looked at Makeba in disgust. Unbeknownst to Makeba, Destiny was slowly running her fingers over a small .380 caliber handgun. She had every intention of using it, too.

"You know whut I promised myself, I wuz goin' bring dat shit up. Okay, I lied," Destiny said. "Can you blame me? Look, yeah I'm fuckin' mad right now. Who wouldn't be? But dis is bigger than dat. Dis iz bout our friendship. I know you did me wrong. But people make mistakes. Nobody's perfect."

The entire time Destiny talked she looked Makeba in the eye. Her vision never wavered. From across the room Makeba could feel the sincerity in her words. She began to feel comfortable. For the first time since she entered her mother's apartment, she dropped her guard.

Destiny could sense that Makeba was feeling at ease. This was all a part of her plan to gain Makeba's confidence and then extract a measure of revenge.

She continued, "Look I don't know if you know this or not, but the feds are on you. You hot! They came to see me while I wuz on Riker's Island. They had all kinds of pictures of you. And some fuckin' Africans. They talkin' bout them fuckin' checks. They talkin' bout sum international fraud ring. I'm tellin' you, you betta be careful."

All this talk of law enforcement authorities scared Makeba. Still, she figured Destiny was just trying to scare her. But there was an air of truth to what Destiny was saying. How else would she know about the ethnic origin of the people she was dealing with? Still, Makeba refused to believe it.

"If the feds came and seen you, then why they ain't come get me then?" Makeba suddenly asked. "I ain't hard ta find. You found me, didn't you?"

Destiny laughed to herself. She could see the fear registering all across Makeba face. Her tough talk was just a front. When she was finished adding some spice to the truth, Makeba would be afraid to answer the door.

Growing tired of this cat-and-mouse game, Destiny fought the strong inclination to shoot Makeba. The only reason Destiny didn't was because her mother was home. Out of respect for Mrs. Simmons she didn't pull the trigger.

Reluctantly Destiny picked herself up off the sofa and exited the apartment. She promised herself she would see Makeba another time. Whether Makeba knew it or not, she had just received a pass. Her life had been spared for the moment. According to the code of the streets, Destiny had done an honorable thing. She kept her beef in the streets. Now there wouldn't be any more passes. Destiny swore Rome wouldn't fare so well.

CHAPTER 22

A few weeks later, Destiny had finally gotten the phone call she so desperately sought. The private detective informed her she could come down and pick up the results of his investigation. On the subway Destiny clutched a large manila envelope under her arm as if her life depended on it. Her curiosity was killing her. Several times she fought the strong urge to read what was inside, then realized that the private investigator's findings weren't something she wanted to share with the general public. Surely other nosy subway riders would be reading this report right along with her. Her business wasn't everybody's business.

Back at the hotel, Destiny breathed a sigh of relief. Finally she was alone. Sitting down at the desk, Destiny pulled up a chair and carefully opened the manila envelope, mindful not to damage any of its contents, then placed its contents on the table. Much to Destiny's surprise, a half dozen photographs and two well-typed pages, a detailed report, lay before her. Destiny hesitated before gathering up the items. Although this was the moment of truth that she had been waiting for, suddenly Destiny was unsure if she really wanted to know the whole truth. She knew it could hurt.

But right now being emotionally hurt was the last thing on her mind, and she proceeded to read the report despite her apprehensions:

"Day one of the investigation: On Friday the fifteenth of March, the subject Jerome Wells was observed leaving a tenement building on Davidson Avenue in the South Bronx. This residence is believed to be that of his mother, Thelma Wells. After hailing a gypsy cab at the corner of the block, the subject was followed. From a safe distance I tailed the subject across the Bronx."

So far there was nothing startling about the report. Although Destiny was impressed by the private investigator's descriptive writing, in hindsight this was not what she paid for. So far the information was useless. Destiny began to skim through the report, digging deeper for anything out of the ordinary. Just when she seemed to be getting bored, her eyes noticed something.

"I observed the subject leaving the Tremont Avenue address with two young children, males, in tow. The subject hailed another cab and proceeded to a shopping district in the Bronx at 149th Street and Third Avenue. I temporarily lost sight of the subject as he entered a children's department store called Cookies.

"I was able to closely observe the subject purchasing items of clothing for the children. The two boys bear a close physical resemblance to the subject. I immediately assumed they were related in some sort of way. I was able to get into earshot of the subject. My suspicions were confirmed when I overhead one child repeatedly call out the word 'Daddy.' One of the young boys appears to be suffering from some kind of birth defect. His speech was slurred and the child drooled while he talked."

When Destiny read this revelation her jaw dropped. She was in for yet another surprise. The report went from bad to worse the further she read.

"Day two of the investigation: I observed the subject engaging in a heated argument outside of 1674 Macombs Road, with an African American female. From a distance of about a thousand feet it was very difficult to hear exactly what they were arguing about. But it was an expletive-laced argument. Later the female was determined to be Kim Harris-Wells."

Kim Harris-Wells? Destiny mused to herself. *Who the fuck is that?*

The name didn't register with Destiny. Nor should it have. She didn't know the individual in question. It took a while for the information to register. But when it did, it hit Destiny like a ton of bricks. This chick was married to Rome. What she read next confirmed that suspicion:

"It is believed that Harris-Wells is the estranged wife of Jerome Wells."

Immediately Destiny picked up the photos and began comparing them. There was no denying it. As far as she was concerned, the private investigator's report was 100 percent correct. The two children bore striking likeness to both their parents. The pictures didn't lie.

Destiny began to put all the pieces together. Suddenly everything seemed to make sense. This explained why, in her younger years, Rome had been taking the lion's share from the con games they played. This explained why Rome would mysteriously disappear for a few days at a time. The pictures confirmed something Destiny would have never suspected—that Rome was living a double life. Rome's infidelity and dishonesty infuriated Destiny. All this time she was messing around with a married man. It made her sick to her stomach to know that Rome could spend time with his wife's sons and not even acknowledge her own.

This report and pictures were like a declaration of war. And in every war sometimes innocent people can get hurt. Sometimes there is a thin line between stupidity and revenge, and Destiny was about to cross it.

The private investigator's report left no stone unturned. His findings were extensive and detailed. There were even addresses of other people in question written into the report, which even included Makeba's old New Jersey address. Destiny didn't know if this was standard practice, but she was glad to have that information supplied to her.

Born and raised in the Bronx, Destiny knew her borough like the back of her hand. On her own, she arrived at the Tremont Avenue address and staked it out. For days she sat in a stolen car, watching and waiting. She observed Rome's estranged family. She wanted to see what time they left the house in the morning. She wanted to know how the kids got to school. By observing the family's everyday activities Destiny accumulated a ton of information. She would need it all to carry out her plans.

Lately Kim Harris-Wells felt very guilty. She had been forced to leave her children alone at home without any adult supervision. This was due to the sporadic financial support she received from Rome. They argued until she turned blue in the face, but the results were still the same. She even tried to compromise with Rome. She asked her estranged husband to baby-sit, but Rome would have none of it. He claimed to be going out of town to take care of some business. So Kim had to do what she had to do.

Oddly, Kim Harris-Wells worked as a stenographer at the Bronx

Criminal Court. Sometimes, due to ongoing criminal trials, Kim came home a little late. Her actual schedule was unpredictable. Usually the kids weren't home alone more than an hour before she arrived. She didn't feel it was right to endanger her children in this manner, but under the circumstances what could she do? Unbeknownst to Rome, she had already filed papers with the court for child support. This was the only way she could see fit to remedy this dangerous situation.

Kim had given Anthony, her elder son, strict orders to follow until she got home. Her son was to call her as soon as they got home. She had forbidden him to cook anything to eat. He was only allowed to eat microwavable food. Anthony was to watch television with his brother until she got home.

The knock on the door brought the kids out the trance that the cartoon channel had put them in. Quickly Anthony jumped to his feet and raced for the door. He automatically assumed that the person on the other side of the door was his mother. But he was wrong. "Ma," he began, opening the door. When he saw Destiny, he asked, "Who are you?"

Destiny looked down at the innocent child without saying a word. This was too easy, she thought. All she had to do now was pull the trigger of the gun that she clutched inside her coat pocket. And just like that Rome's children would be dead. She had the power to take his sons off the face of the earth right now. But she couldn't do it. There was no way she would live with herself if she harmed innocent children. She would not be able to justify that within herself, let alone anybody else.

"Umm, I'm a friend of ya mom's. Is she home?" Destiny said as she glanced around the apartment.

"No, my mother not here right now," the kid told her.

"You know when she'll be back?" she asked.

"She at work," he admitted. "She be here soon."

"I gotta go. Just tell her I came by," Destiny said.

"Whut's ya name?" the kid replied.

"Monica," she lied. "I'm an old friend of hers. She'll know who I am."

As Destiny exited the building she breathed a sigh of relief. That was the best move she never made. She went back to the drawing board. She had to think of another way to exact revenge on Rome. All she knew was she couldn't stoop this low.

In the downtown Manhattan Federal Building, a federal grand jury had just handed down secret indictments. The foreigners were on top of the list. Makeba's name headlined the list of American defendants. Also on the list were the names of Destiny and Rome.

Once the indictments were handed down, the federal authorities scooped in and arrested Makeba at her mother's house without incident, just as they had the rest of the ring. In the middle of the night they had been roused out of their sleep and taken into custody.

The loud ringing of her cell phone awoke Destiny from her sleep. The noise was more annoying than anything else. If her cell phone had been nearby she would have probably sent the person to voicemail. Since it wasn't, she got up, walked over to the desk, and answered it.

"Who!" she barked into the receiver.

"It's me, La-La," the person replied. "You heard whut happened?"

La-La was a local crackhead that Destiny had employed as a spy to keep an eye on Makeba. Their beef was far from over. Destiny was just waiting for the right opportunity to strike.

"Nah, whut happened?" Destiny wondered.

"Turn on da news quick. It's on every channel," La-La blurted out before hanging up. "It's crazy out here right now!"

Destiny rushed over to the TV and turned it on. Changing the channel, she found the local news station, Channel Seven, Eyewitness News. She looked on in amazement, startled by what she saw.

"Federal agents have made a series of arrests in connection with an international fraud ring. Suspect Makeba Simmons was arrested for her alleged part in the ring," the news reporter announced.

Destiny stared at the TV almost in disbelief at the sight of a tearful Makeba being led away in handcuffs by two federal agents. The camera also showed federal agents carrying out computers and electronic equipment from the raid.

Reports of the raid sent shockwaves through the 'hood. It seemed like all illegal activities ceased. Even criminals who didn't have anything to do with it curtailed their activities. Everyone just played innocent bystander, waiting to see who would next be arrested and glad if it wasn't them.

"Federal authorities are also looking for several other people in connection with the alleged crime ring. Reporting live from the South Bronx, Sam Madison, Channel Seven, Eyewitness News."

The news was like a double-edged sword. Sure, Destiny was happy that Makeba was locked up, that she got hers. At the same time, she felt envious that she wasn't the one who gave it to her. On the other hand, she had a new problem. Now that Makeba was locked up, at any given moment she could be next.

Quickly Destiny gathered up a few items of clothing and fled the hotel, where she was a sitting duck. She had to stay one step ahead of the feds, if she wanted to stay free.

News of Rome's arrest spread like wildfire throughout the 'hood. Destiny felt almost certain that she was next. She couldn't bear to think of all the time she faced for the individual accounts of fraud. It would be years before she walked the streets of New York again. The only way out of this madness was to become a snitch. Destiny didn't like the idea of that, either. It wasn't in her nature. Her father was a stand-up guy. She couldn't disgrace his memory with such cowardly act. But what else could she do?

Destiny mulled her options for a few days while she managed to stay one step ahead of the feds by hiding out in city shelters. Even that way of life was taking its toll on her. She wasn't used to living in filthy, crowded, and confined quarters.

Over the course of the next few days, Destiny began to think about her purpose on this earth. She came to the conclusion that she had made nothing out of her life. Destiny realized she had squandered some good opportunities. Thus far what she had amounted to was being a common criminal, a thief. With the feds on her tail, Destiny now felt that the curtain was closing on her life. Suddenly death became the only way out.

Destiny couldn't get death out of her mind. She refused to dismiss it as a problem for another day. She knew that sooner or later we all were going to die. But for her, the time was now. The street life was draining her of her resolve to live.

The subway platform at the 176th Street station shook violently as the rapidly approaching Number Four train streaked from the Burnside Avenue station. Destiny stood dangerously close to the edge of the platform anxiously awaiting its arrival along with the other rush-hour commuters. Beads of sweat began to form on her forehead in anticipation of her act. The curtain was coming down on her life.

As the subway train roared into the station, Destiny shifted her weight with the intent of leaping to her death and felt a wave of relief wash over her. She was in a complete daze. In a matter of moments it would now be over, life as she knew it.

In horror many subway riders looked on. They knew what Destiny was about to do, but no one tried to prevent it. This was New York City; everyone here just minded their own business. If Destiny wanted to kill herself, then fine.

Destiny began to crouch as the train came closer. Suddenly her father popped into her mind. His street legacy killed all suicidal thoughts she had. Destiny fancied herself as a gangster, cut from the same cloth as her mother and father, so there was no way she was going to tarnish the family's name by killing herself. In life and death her family had a reputation to uphold.

Still, Destiny was so close to the edge of the platform that the subway train zoomed into the station and narrowly missed hitting her. Then, like the rest of the rush hour commuters, Destiny boarded the subway train and vanished in a city amongst eight million people. Game over.

EPILOGUE

The federal authorities were able to locate and apprehend all parties involved in the alleged criminal ring except Destiny Greene. Her disappearance had totally stumped them. They had no clues to her whereabouts. The case was growing colder by the day. Even the feds' confidential informants on the streets couldn't turn up a single lead pertaining to her whereabouts. Somehow she had evaded capture for now.

By cooperating with the government, Makeba received a light sentence for her role in the fraud scheme. She was sentenced to ten years in a federal facility. With good behavior she'd be released in eight. That was a light sentence compared to the ones handed down to her codefendants.

Rome, on the other hand, didn't make out too good. He received a life sentence under the strict federal sentencing guidelines. Rome was a two-time felon coming into the situation. His previous state convictions worked against him. Essentially he got convicted for association since his role was minimal at best.

As for the Africans, they all were given stiff sentences, from a maximum of sixty years to a minimum of twenty-five. They might as well have received life along with Rome. Either way one looked at it, their lives were finished. By the time they were released from federal prison they would be so old and useless that they would barely function, a burden on society in the form of welfare.

It was rumored that Destiny was somewhere in Texas. She was still playing the game to maintain her lifestyle. She had a slew of fake driver's licenses at her disposal. As time went on, she became confident that her chances of getting caught by the feds were slim to none. Wherever Destiny was, surely she was laughing at Rome's and Makeba's misfortune. Though she didn't get the chance to give it to them, in the end, they had gotten what they deserved.

SLANG GLOSSARY

Strong-arm robbery To rob someone without a weapon.

Vic An abbreviation for victim, also target or mark.

Crack whores Women or men who exchange sex for crack cocaine.

Burnt To either get ripped off or contract a sexually transmitted disease.

The game A term coined by streetwise individuals and criminals in reference to their lawless lifestyle or the kind of crimes they commit, i.e., drug dealing. ("Be true to the game and the game will be true to you.")

Seed A term used when a street person is referring to his children or child. ("I haven't seen my seeds in a minute.")

Stink-stink A parental term used in reference to a child's bowel movement. ("You made stink-stink?")

Coochie A street phrase used when one is referring to a woman's private parts. ("Did she give you some coochie yet?")

Word to mother A vow, usually used by native New Yorkers. ("Word to mother: the next person that comes to my house I ain't opening the door.")

Triflin' Dirty either in physical appearance or in deeds.

B-Boy Male participant in hip-hop culture.

B-Girl Female participant in hip-hop culture.

Scramblerz One who sells illegal drugs. ("There's a lot of scramblerz on the corner.")

Young wolves Young thugs.

Come up To get ahead, usually by illegal means. ("Yo, I need some work. I'm tryin' ta come up.")

Fiended out To place one in a choke hold until they pass out.

Extra shit Recently coined, an overdose. ("He took some extra shit.")

Man-child A boy in a man's body. Someone who is big for their age.

One-shot deal A one-time offer. ("This is a one-shot deal.")

Dickbeaters An old-school term in reference to one's fists.

SHOUT-OUTS

Cadeem Williams (my son son). I know you might think I'm helping you, but for real for real, you're helping me. I can only keep what I got by giving it away. My cousin Tonya "Naeshawn" Holmes for your input with the book. My aunt Tiscia "Barbara" Moultrie. (I know we had our differences in the past but we gone get past that. We family. I did not choose you, nor you me.) My BX Macombs Road extended family. Raymella Lowry, Gail Hunter. (Thanks for befriending me. You luv me so how can I not have luv for you?) Artasia "Tasia" Koon, Aisha Clark, Secret Martin, Sadiasha Martin, "Ms." Rosa Parker, "Ms." Dianne Lewis (you always got my back no matter what, so how can I not luv you?), Crazy George, Thelma "Lu-Lu" Walls, Kahdeja Walls, Barbara Eberhart (Yo, I apologize for what I said. Hope you forgive. My mind wasn't right. Luv is luv.). The entire 1-7-5 & Macombs.

Cousin Arlene and Henry Johnson, Cuz-o Rahseen Rergurson. (I got luv for you if you ain't gotta dime. We family, baby!) To all my extended family in the South, Atlanta, Macon, and Savannah, Georgia. Cousin Keith "DJ Breakout" Jeffery, a.k.a. Jeff to da left. (Yo, sorry it took me so long to give y'all a shout-out, but I wuz tight . . .)

To The Block, Boston Road & Fish—John "Jay" Alexander, Clarkie, His Brother Souljah, Simon, Pepe 215th St., Boston Duffy, Nelson Hayes, Ed Webber, Stan Strong (The World's Strongest DJ), Dex Adams, Ross, Black Silk, Dave Cook. (Every time I see you, I feel good. You may be proud of me, but I am real proud of you. To see who you were, then to who you are now, is a beautiful thing.) Richard "Richie T" Herbert, Leroy Salter, Jip (My Basketball Idol), Lamar "Cheese" Harris, Michael "Knot" Palmer, Gerard "Shakim" Emptage. (Hold ya head! We got bigger fish to fry.) Nigel Bailey (Dog, you can't know how good it is to see you doing good outside of the block stuff. You one of the only dudes who made it. It's luv every time I see you.) Khadija Conely Julie and Nelson Ninn, Lionel Cook, Franklin Greenaway.

My older brothers, Derrick and Bobby "Shon" Holmes. I luv y'all. Dee, I'm sorry for putting you through that, that wasn't me. (I'm still your brother, the same dude who slept in the bed with you growing up. When you peed in the bed, you blamed it on me.)

To the good people at St. Martin's Press. My editor, Monique Patterson (thanks for everything that you do for me and all the opportunities you present to me), and Kia DuPree. Thanks for everything that you have done for me. Much appreciated.

I'm not really gonna get into a long list of shout-outs. For those I got luv for, that don't change. You know who you are and you are who you be!